T0274841

DEAR HAIDER

Lili Zeng

Baraka
Books

Montréal

ISBN 978-1-77186-340-7 pbk; 978-1-77186-361-2 epub; 978-1-77186-362-9 pdf

Cover by Cover Zone
Fiction Editor: Blossom Thom
Book Design by Folio infographie
Editing and proofreading: Blossom Thom, Robin Philpot, Elizabeth West

Legal Deposit, 2nd quarter 2024
Bibliothèque et Archives nationales du Québec
Library and Archives Canada

Published by Baraka Books of Montreal

Printed and bound in Quebec

Trade Distribution & Returns
Canada – UTPdistribution.com
United States
Independent Publishers Group: IPGbook.com

We acknowledge the support from the Société de développement des entreprises culturelles (SODEC) and the Government of Quebec tax credit for book publishing administered by SODEC.

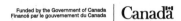

"Lili Zeng's slow-burn account of Liz's summer student internship lays the foundation for a rollercoaster ride filled with often unexpected life adventures as Liz steps into a new chapter of her life. Zeng's awe-inspiring debut novel is a fearless and courageous narrative of first love, loss, despair, and ultimately of hope and healing. Truly, a testament to the resilience and enduring faith of the human spirit!"
— Mary Anne Levasseur, caregiver
and youth mental health advocate

"A very sincere and touching story about a young girl exploring herself and love. It candidly shows the protagonist Liz, a Montreal-based Chinese immigrant's step-by-step adventures and inner doubts, conflicts and struggles in her love with a white youth and an Indian youth. Some of the real presentations and reflections on racial differences and chasm are a valuable and even most fascinating part of this story."
— Xiaodan He, filmmaker, *A Touch of Spring*

"When Liz sets off to continue her studies in Europe, her path seems clear—until unexpected love is both a distraction and a portal. But to what? A coming of age story of the struggle with one's own sense of self as it expands and contracts against the expectations of the larger world."
— Leila Marshy, author of *The Philistine*

DEAR HAIDER

To God, who watches over this wide world,
To you, Dear Haider, you know who you are,
And to my poor mother, who deserves an explanation.

Dear Haider,

I don't know where you are these days, and whether you still think of me, but I still think of you, and often. I know everything went wrong; I take the blame and I paid the price. But whatever you think of what happened between us, do not think that you loved me in vain. You showed me what life is all about, and I am who I am today because of you. Know that somewhere on this planet, someone's whole world was changed because of you. The story I am about to tell is how it all happened, as I remember it. Perhaps you will come across it one day. If you do, I hope you forgive me, inshallah, *God willing.*

Part I: Germany

1

May 15, 2011

For me, this story started the day I boarded the plane from Montreal and endured a grueling six-hour layover in London. I was exhausted when we finally took off from London towards the continent. An unrelenting throbbing was pounding at my temples. A tension headache right as the ascending plane was undergoing an intense pressure change, climbing above the hazy London skyline. I could feel my anticipation building, competing against restlessness, so sleep was out of the question. I absentmindedly flipped through the travel magazines and duty-free luxury products ads in the seat pocket in front of me. Finally, bored out of my mind, I peeked out the window. The mass of clouds below us had cleared and I saw land. The journey was coming to an end!

"Attention ladies and gentlemen," the flight attendant announced over the speakers, "As you can see, we're currently flying over Germany and are half an hour away from our destination. We will arrive in Dusseldorf Airport at 7:09 p.m. local time, as scheduled."

I tuned out as she continued in German. We were landing soon, I thought to myself. I let it sink in. What would that entail? I had an offer to work as a summer intern in a physics lab at the University of Duisburg for ten weeks. A paid job. *My first paid job.* I could feel my excitement soar

3

along with a touch of anxiety still lingering in my temples. This is fantastic, I get to live independently for a couple of months on a brand new continent, I told myself. *A new start.* I couldn't wait.

I had just completed my first year at McGill University as an undergraduate. Slain the first two semesters of the infamous Joint Honours Maths and Physics program. Some call it the most demanding program at McGill, while others deem it more difficult than comparable programs in Ivy League schools. Not without reason, in my opinion, and if I was honest with myself, I probably picked it partially out of self-hatred. But more on that later.

The seatbelt sign went on; we were in the process of landing. A surge of adrenaline rushed through me. I'd spent most of my life living in Montreal, having emigrated from China with my parents when I was a few weeks shy of seven years old. As a third culture kid, I never really felt like I belonged in Canada or in China. I was too Canadian to be accepted by the Chinese, and too Chinese to be recognized as Canadian—an outsider everywhere. Could I have hope that by spending the summer in a place that was unequivocally foreign, I'd finally be able to transcend this existential dichotomy, this tug-of-war between two cultures, to something beyond, somewhere new?

I felt the plane jolt as the wheels hit the ground. My heart soared. We were in Dusseldorf at last. For the first time in my life, I was no longer living at my parents' house, no longer a child for all intents and purposes. I was finally living my own life, on my own, like the adult that I was at barely nineteen. *Bring it on!*

It occurred to me that the PhD student I was working for, Max, was supposed to pick me up from Dusseldorf Airport and drive me to Duisburg. Dusseldorf, I knew of. But Duisburg? I'd never heard the name even mentioned in passing. I imagined a picturesque and quaint little German town with charming timber-framed houses, well-kept flower gardens, and beautiful gothic churches, surrounded by lush forests and snow-capped mountains. *Sound of Music* meets *Hansel and Gretel.*

My daydreaming was interrupted as I was propelled from my seat by other passengers into the walkway, then forced towards the exit of the plane. I hoped I'd find Max easily. I told him over email to look for an Asian girl with shoulder length black hair, thick glasses, and a black sweatshirt with *McGill Physics* written on it in red. I wore the sweatshirt on purpose: to be unmistakable as, for some reason, Asian girls often seemed to be indistinguishable to non-Asian people in my experience.

"Hey Elizabeth!" I heard as I walked out of the customs area towards the arrival hall. There was Max, a stout White guy in his late twenties sporting a disheveled beard and wearing metal-framed glasses, an old Pink Floyd T-shirt, and jeans. He looked about as informal as possible.

"Hey Max, nice to meet you!" I replied. "Call me Liz!" So physicists around the world all look alike too, just like Asian girls, I chuckled to myself.

We shook hands and walked towards the parking lot to get his car.

"Have you been to Duisburg before?" Max asked me.

"Nope, never heard of the place before." I was blunt. Tact has never exactly been my forte.

"That's why." Max laughed. "That's why you chose to come here. Dusseldorf is nice, but Duisburg, well it's a steel town, to say the least."

Fascinating. Well, I wasn't going to let this plot twist dim my enthusiasm.

He clearly picked up on my surprise followed by incredulousness.

"No, really, Duisburg's population has been steadily decreasing since World War II, and recently fell below half a million. Everyone's leaving, it's not a nice place."

What an introduction, I thought. At least he was being honest without sugar-coating the truth, like a scientist should be. I felt a mix of emotions and decided to withhold judgment until I arrived.

"But have you been on the autobahn before?" Max asked to ease the tension.

"Only briefly a few years ago."

"Well, you're going to enjoy this one at least," Max said with a grin. "Get in the car. The roads between Dusseldorf and Duisburg are some of the nicest in the country; we're going to approach 200km/h."

This. This was the kind of experience I came here for. I sat in the passenger seat with a smile from ear to ear and watched the road in front of me like I was sitting shotgun to a professional esports expert playing a car racing video game.

As we cruised at what should be illegal speeds, Max explained, "Duisburg is at the confluence of the two major rivers in Germany: the Rhein and the Ruhr, making it a highly strategic point for transportation. It produced about 50% of all the steel Germany used in the two world wars. This whole area of Germany has always been very industrial. However, since the end of the war, the demand for steel decreased and many industries and factories closed down, and now people are leaving. You will now see abandoned concrete and steel structures everywhere if you walk around the city."

"That's interesting," I lied. Not that interesting, really, but I didn't know what else to say.

"But don't worry, if you live in this place for long enough, you will learn to appreciate its charm."

The seeds of disenchantment were sown inside me, but I was determined to make the most of my stay here.

"We're nearing Duisburg," Max announced. "Let me take you on a quick tour of the city."

We got off the famous autobahn and found ourselves in the midst of nondescript buildings and vacant streets. This place thoroughly lacked soul. It barely looked like a first-world country. We passed by what Max said was the city hall, an old building slightly more ornate than the others, but which would be unremarkable in any better known city of Germany. There was the obligatory opera house, a testament to the fact that even the least cultured part of Germany was more cultured than the North America I came from. We then cruised along the port area, with concrete on top of concrete, and large unfinished public projects dotting the industrial landscape.

"I'm going to take you tonight to the new five-star restaurant they opened at the casino," Max said. "Probably the only five-star restaurant in town."

At least they *have* one. But how nice could it possibly be, considering what I've seen so far of this city? I wondered.

We got out of the car at an underground parking lot that would be colloquially called "ghetto" if it were anywhere in the Canada I knew. Dimly lit hallways and gloomy passages lead us to the backdoor entrance of the restaurant.

"It's not bad here. What do you think?" Max asked me.

"It's nice." Another lie.

The high ceilings, rugged concrete walls, outdated purple theme, and art deco luminaries all made it look rather dramatic, like an '80s movie set. It was not *bad*; it was definitely much better than what I had seen of the city so far, but I felt no soul in it. Fancy it was, but appealing, it was not.

The waiter handed each of us a menu entirely in German, and Max offered to translate everything for me. Despite the translation, I still couldn't figure out what most of the dishes were made out of. I took a blind guess and picked a main course. Soon, we were served, and I faced a plate with a piece of meat and some unknown gravy-like substance. The dish was as unmemorable as the building was extravagant. Despite the superficial decadence, the lifelessness of this city still managed to seep through the brutalist concrete walls into the dining hall.

Max and I chatted about places we'd been, and after sharing with him about my trips to Israel and Tibet, he told me about his trip last year to Chernobyl, site of the 1986 nuclear disaster.

"You won't believe it. If you think here it looks like a ghost town, you haven't seen what a real ghost town looks like. There are trees growing out of the windows of abandoned buildings. And the radiation level is incredible. We went up to the zone where the radiation is five hundred times higher than the radiation from an x-ray at the doctor's office. How cool is that?"

Physicists wouldn't mind humanity being wiped out entirely, it just occurred to me. His cold, unfeeling description of the carnage sent shivers down my spine. Could it be that he was just disillusioned, having grown up in post-war Germany? Perhaps Chernobyl felt like home to him, in a way? No. He was obviously aware that some of the most devastating weapons in history were the brainchild of physicists, people from his own chosen field. Then, as if living in a steel town wasn't enough, he had to travel to a radioactive concrete jungle to see what a post-civilization world—potentially the product of the research of his predecessors—could look like? It chilled me to the bone.

For better or for worse, though, here I was for the summer. I had no right to criticize Max. I was on my way to do exactly what he was doing: working inside an alien lab in a derelict town at the confines of human knowledge. I took a deep breath. Let's do this; it was too late to back out.

Max paid the hefty tab, for which he would probably be refunded by his department's discretionary fund. We headed out into the night. It was arranged that I stay with Xin, the daughter of a friend of my mom's, who happened to live in the nearby town of Essen, while Max figured out housing for me. Max drove me to Xin's place, helped us carry my luggage up the two flights of stairs to her second-floor apartment, and left me to unpack. It was exactly midnight, and I knew I wasn't going to get much sleep.

2

May 16, 2011

It was 7 a.m., and I was lying on Xin's couch in her living room, wide awake. Damn this jet lag! I looked around and there was no one. Of course, Xin had told me the night before that she would be starting her 24-hour shift at the hospital early in the morning. This gave *early* a whole new meaning for the lifelong night-owl that I was.

Xin had just started her medical residency training, working at the Essen Hospital, neurosurgery department. In other words, she was the poster child of the successful one-point-five generation Asian immigrants to the West that I was brought up to be. It seemed so easy from the outside. But was she truly happy doing what she was doing? I couldn't help but wonder. I knew that younger girls in the Chinese community looked up to me the same way I looked up to Xin. But all I could feel was that I was an imposter. I was not even close to who they made me out to be. Sure, I was studying math and physics, and in Germany for an internship, a prestigious paid internship. But deep down, I wondered whether I was really cut out for this. Did Xin feel the same way?

I pulled out my MacBook from my backpack. Maybe Chris was online.

Chris, my ... "ex"-boyfriend, I guess, by now?

I sighed.

I met Chris in CEGEP, a two-year bridge between high school and university unique to Quebec. I barely spoke to him back then. I was fresh out of an all-girls' Catholic high school. He had shoulder-length hair and a scruffy beard, with quite a reputation under his nickname, Jesus. To be honest, he reminded me of a caveman, with his protruding bushy unibrow and unkempt appearance. I only knew him as the famously eccentric president of the Science Club.

Then, on my first day of university, I walked into my classical mechanics class: a sea of testosterone. Relieved to have spotted a female acquaintance, I bounded towards her. I heard another voice from behind me say hello. I turned around and was puzzled to see a clean-shaven, short-haired, properly groomed White guy, with a crooked smile. I did a double-take. "Chris!" I finally recognized him. We ended up having lunch together that day, and then again almost every day for the rest of the semester.

What was it that pulled me towards him like a moth to a lamp in the dead of night? He was *smart*. Not just regular smart and witty, but the kind of astonishing genius that you only meet *once* in your lifetime. And he was incredibly interesting and attractive too, in an oddball yet charismatic way. Basically, *everything I thought I wanted in a guy*. Or perhaps even *everything I envied for myself*. He took seven courses at a time and never attended them. Instead, he asked classmates after class to summarize everything they learned for him. He'd then tell them what they had understood wrong and show them how to solve the homework problems.

Chris loved challenging people. Once in a while, he'd show up to the student lounge and write a "Problem of the Day" on the blackboard, which would spark a huge debate among friends and acquaintances alike, only for them to find out that everything they thought they knew about math and physics was wrong. The local Socrates.

A stickler for conciseness, he'd challenge himself to write out all his mathematical derivations and proofs for an assignment or a test on a single sheet of paper, in the simplest way possible. And he'd always get near perfect scores on these assignments and exams, no matter how low the class average was. *How did he do it?*

We had a particularly challenging math final exam back in December, and almost everyone stayed till the end trying to figure it out. Chris, of course, finished an hour early and left nonchalantly. When everyone walked out after the full three hours, exhausted and convinced they'd failed, Chris came back with cheesecake he'd bought for me from my favourite cafe down the street. My classmates' envy was palpable. I was over the moon. I couldn't believe that out of all of his gaggle of admirers and "apostles," he had chosen me. But had he?

I soon realized he was practically devoid of human emotions and attachments. He was all brain, and *only* brain. He was only interested in the latest math and physics problems he encountered, and the last thing he wanted to do was talk about such messy and ill-defined matters as feelings. Instead, in his spare time, he played video games competitively, and unsurprisingly, he excelled. He was a complete loner deep down and couldn't care less about most aspects of human life. He wouldn't bond with anyone except his single mother who had raised him alone by herself. I remember being invited a few times to the apartment he shared with his mom, the old, crumbling building, the damp moldy smell, the mess in his room with math-scribbled papers forming a massive mountain on the floor space, the childhood toys still scattered around, the tiny window facing a brick wall, the paint peeling off from the door and window frames, the single naked light bulb dangling from its cord from the ceiling. I felt enveloped by a deep sense of sadness that almost nauseated me. Could I love someone who lived like this? And could he love me back?

I guess we dated briefly during the winter semester, although he only begrudgingly asked me out after I invited him over for dinner at my parents' house, and practically set him up to do so. But he made sure to tell no one about it and broke it off within two months, even though we still spent all our time together and were perceived as an item by most. And true to his nature, he eschewed most displays of affection, never mind love; yet that was precisely what I craved. I didn't, and couldn't, understand the root of his aloof behaviour. Soon, seeking his elusive affection turned into seeking his overall approval of me as a person. It was a game I couldn't win because, of course, he rarely showed any feelings towards me.

Still, I was drawn to him more and more as I got to know him better. He'd find me on Skype at 12 a.m., messaging me excitedly about how he finally solved that math or physics problem he was talking about during lunch. He loved, and lived, to teach new math or physics concepts to anyone who was interested, no matter their level of background knowledge, or lack thereof. I found his intellectual passion immensely attractive and touching, almost as if it had somehow transmogrified into a romantic passion. I should have known that he only truly cared about—and loved—math and his mom. In retrospect, perhaps they were the only things he felt were truly his. He had no other relatives—being abandoned by a father who never wanted him and born to a mother who was ostracized for keeping him—only one true friend, whom he had known since kindergarten and who was an outcast due to being slightly mentally challenged, and no one else, nothing else, in his life.

Yet, torn between my unrelenting feelings towards him and the reality that he probably wasn't going to reciprocate, I kept on wanting to win him over. I couldn't help but longingly look at him when he'd tell his mom "I love you" every time she passed in front of his door when we were hanging out in his room, wishing he'd say the same to me. I wanted him to want me as much as I wanted him, and I wanted it more than I could understand why myself.

So, I stayed up into the early hours of the morning, chatting with him on the phone or on Skype, mostly about math and physics. Sometimes as late as 9 a.m. I'd stay up with him forever, as long as he was willing to talk to me. He came over too, once or twice. We did get affectionate on occasion. He could give affection when he wanted it, but *only* when he wanted it, and that was what hurt the most. We'd lay there in my room, and I'd wonder whether I'd ever be truly good enough for him, good enough to soften him into expressing *partiality* towards me at last. These hookups—I guess you could call them that—gave me the sparks of warmth I so deeply needed. Desperate for any affection I could get out of him and feeling a foreboding that our summer apart would probably mean the end of *us*, I snuck him, in the middle of the night, into my parents' house a week before I left and, surprised to find out he was a virgin too, I gave him my virginity while taking his. And now, I was in Germany, an ocean away.

I immediately regretted checking Skype.

Chris was online.

"Hi," I typed.

"Hi, how's Germany?"

I told him about shitty steel-town Duisburg and the autobahn and the absurd "five-star" restaurant.

"That's nice, seems like you're enjoying yourself. By the way, my mom says hi."

She remembered me. I felt a warm tingling in my stomach.

"She says we should talk less to each other to miss each other more."

That sucked the warmth right out of me. I remembered a few days before leaving Montreal, we were laying on the grass at a park near my house, looking at the city sky devoid of stars. "Don't worry, I'll remember you," he said. "I'll miss you too soon enough. Then you'll be back, and we'll still be friends." *Friends?* Was that all he ever saw me as? I only felt the gulf between him and me widen, even wider than the ocean that separated us. *Wide, deep, abysmal.*

"What else is new?" Chris typed, and pulled me from my trance. I could never understand how he could drop an almost mean-spirited joke on me like that and then continue on as if nothing had happened. Couldn't he understand how I'd feel? Didn't he care about how I'd feel, at all? But I went along with him without protesting, as usual.

"Max told me about his trip to Chernobyl. He seemed to have really liked the place."

"Sounds great! Would be nice to go there sometimes, instead of like Venice, as my mom is suggesting."

I laughed. Classic Chris.

"You'd go there with me?" I asked.

"I don't know when I'd be able to afford that."

Sigh. I wished I could get more from him, but knew I wouldn't. I bid him good night and closed my laptop. Time to head to the university.

I ate some toast with Nutella that I found in Xin's kitchen, packed my stuff, and headed out for the day. The U-bahn, a city tram in Essen, took me right to the Essen

Hauptbahnhof, or Main Train Station. I hopped on the regional train heading towards Duisburg and arrived twenty minutes later.

Now, Essen wasn't such a gorgeous city, but it was alright. I liked it enough, and more in the daytime than the previous night. But Duisburg ... Right when the train arrived at the station, I immediately recalled Max's grim yet candid introduction. There was grass growing everywhere between the train tracks, and graffiti on walls. I stepped onto the concrete platform and noticed the dirty glass roof absorbing most of the sunlight in its grime. This was the place I was bound to remain in for the next two and a half months. Why was I doing this? I wondered.

Walking into the Duisburg train station, I felt like I was in some prison camp. Sure, there were shops here and there, but it took the term *concrete jungle* to a whole other dimension. Everything was made out of gritty beige concrete, which made the place insufferable and completely void of character. The large main, light blue entrance hall, with its tiled grey floor and perpetually humming ceiling fans reminded me of some distant third world country hospital. Max had told me that "by the end of World War II, Duisburg was razed" and the train station was one of the first buildings they rebuilt after the war. I couldn't help but feel like only the atrocities of WWII could inspire such an austere construction. Walking out of the station and stealing a glance back at the building, with Duisburg Hauptbahnhof written in large blood-red letters above the roof, it seemed sinister, but I did feel a sense of awe towards this town that rose again like a phoenix from the ashes. A grim phoenix, but a phoenix nonetheless.

I took the tram toward the university, and as we ventured further from the city centre, the landscape became friendlier. Bordering the streets were restaurants and laundromats and all kinds of shops. I let out a sigh of relief. Normal life still carried on here, beyond that dilapidated wasteland. I got off at the Zoo station, where the university was located, a little ironically. Walking towards the campus, I felt a strange sense of familiarity. Somewhere in another life, I'd been here before. Duisburg's developing-country feeling reminded me of my home city in China, Guangzhou. About twelve years ago, before uprooting his family to pursue a new, better life in Canada, my father had been a professor of mathematics at the local university. When I was little, he used to take me to his classes, and I'd sit at the back doodling while he gave his lectures. Like father, like daughter, it seemed. Twelve years later, here I was, walking toward the Science and Engineering Department of the University of Duisburg. My dad would be proud.

I arrived at the building's main entrance and found Max waiting for me with his card to let me in. We walked up a flight of stairs and stopped in front of a locked glass door.

"This area belongs to Prof. Krugg's group," Max explained. "You will work under me and Prof. Krugg this summer."

He opened the door and we entered a main hall with small offices surrounding it. We greeted Jurgen, another PhD student, Carl, a Master's student, Hunter, the postdoc, and a few others whom I could not remember.

"Let me tour the labs with you," Max offered, after showing me his office, now our office, and assigning me to the spare desk next to his.

We walked over to the office next door where Jurgen was working.

"This machine here," Max said, showing me a large metal cylinder connected to a stack of black consoles with a mess of wires, "this machine could reach 0.1 degrees Kelvin, or -273.05 degrees Celsius. How cool is that?"

"Pretty cool," I answered, and just realized the pun. 0.1 Kelvin is just 0.1 degrees above Absolute Zero, the lowest possible temperature, where all matter is brought to a standstill. So not just "cool," but very, *very* cold. Max was a strange kind of funny.

"Over there where Carl is working, there is the gigantic 10 Tesla magnet. You better remove any metal in the room when we turn it on, else we're all dead!"

Physicists are so much like kids with their toys, I thought. I could still remember Chris playing with dry ice and liquid nitrogen during our undergraduate physics labs.

"And I have to show you my lab," Max continued with a grin.

We left the Krugg group area, passed a curved hallway, and arrived in a dark room.

"These are lasers. You know how powerful they are? This big blue one that is broken now, it was one of the most powerful commercially available lasers. This room needs to be completely dark for my photoelectric experiments, so we covered the windows with thick black rubber. Well, you see over here, half a second of exposure to the laser beam that was accidentally pointed toward this window melted through half a centimetre of this thick rubber. I'm glad it wasn't pointed towards anyone."

Yeah, me too.

"And finally, there is the chemistry lab," Max said as we walked towards the lab facing the laser room. "Here, this is hydrofluoric acid; this bottle is enough to kill half of Duisburg's population. And here is some chloroform for your use, if you meet a cute guy at a club and want to knock him out."

I smirked. And this, folks, is why people study physics. Forget beautiful and grand theories about the universe; it is the thrill of playing with danger in a way that makes even pyromania seem ordinary.

Max then showed me my work here for the summer. I was to prepare microchips with complicated layers of metals and semiconductors on them, sprinkled with silicon nanoparticles on top. The chip was then to be bonded into a circuit, and hopefully connecting the circuit would make the nanoparticles light up like LED lights. I understood nothing at all. I almost wanted to quit, but then it was lunch time, followed by the weekly meeting discussing the group's progress.

I'd had some of the blandest foods I'd ever tasted at the cafeteria, so walking into the meeting room, I was delighted to see chocolate cookies and candies being passed around. Prof. Hans Krugg introduced me to the group as the new summer student research assistant, people gave me a round of greetings, and the rest of the meeting was in German.

I sat there munching the plate of sweets that ended up in my hands after passing a few times around the table. So this was my life. Was I happy doing this? Was this what I wanted? My parents surely would be proud. My mom, like the educated, liberal parent that she was, would never admit she wanted a say in her daughter's career, but I knew this was exactly who she wanted me to be. Meanwhile, my father was openly happy that his daughter went into a STEM field like he did. But did I want this? Did I have the right to ask myself what I was really looking for?

3

May 19, 2011

I spent the next few days working in the lab. Max duly showed me every intricate detail of microchip production; I was to serve as his personal assistant in creating his experimental samples. I tried my best to stay motivated. I really did. But every day I found myself hoping for lunch time in the morning and counting the minutes until I could go home in the afternoon. How I wished to be doing something else. Anything else. But what?

One afternoon after work, Max invited all of us from the research group to go out and have doner kebab. It was basically Turkish food, German style. Everyone had a doner, which is a pita bread filled with kebab meat and salad. I wasn't that hungry so I treated myself to some stuffed grape leaves. We then went to the local bar next to the university.

At the bar, we met a bunch of grad students. Max introduced me to his friends Kurt, a tall blond guy doing his PhD in astrophysics, and Hans, a short brunet studying number theory.

"Have a beer with us," Kurt offered, motioning me to take a seat.

I obliged, knowing full well that I was risking getting drunk if I had more than half a pint, but I didn't want to ruffle feathers. The beer was seriously cheap too, one euro for one tall, heaping glass.

"Do you like it?" Max asked.

I never liked beer, to be honest. It was bitter and carbonated, two qualities I hated in a drink. I politely took a sip.

"Well, it tastes like beer to me …" I responded, trailing off. Was I supposed to say something else?

They laughed.

"This is the local brand, you know? Konig. Means 'king' in German. It's quite popular in this part of Germany," Kurt told me.

"Hey guys, wanna play a game of foosball?" Hans asked. "The table just got freed up!"

I laughed. Foosball, also known as table football (or table soccer, if you insist), must be the international sport of physicists. I can't count how many games I'd played in the student lounge during my first year of undergrad. Everyone was introduced to it, and it was said that knowing how to play foosball was a prerequisite to earning a physics PhD.

The four of us took our places around the foosball table, Max and I on the red team and the others on the blue team.

"Do you want to play defence or offence?" Max asked me.

"Defence. I'm bad at offence."

"Maybe you're secretly a pro," Kurt said as he winked, "and just want to show off by scoring using the goalie."

I went along with him. "I've actually done that once, though I'm not sure how the ball managed to penetrate through the layers of offence and defence in the middle. We call them quantum tunneling events where I'm from."

The guys laughed way harder than they should have.

We played a few games, but I was struggling to keep up with them. I felt bad for Max for being stuck with me as a teammate. Why was I always bad at everything physicists were good at? I couldn't hold my liquor, lacked reflexes and coordination on the foosball table, never played videogames growing up. I didn't know anything about Star Trek or Star Wars. How long will it take for them to see through me and realize that I don't belong here? I wondered.

After we'd finished a few rounds of the game, another group took over the foosball table, and we hung out at the quieter corner booth at the back of the bar. I noticed a beat-up upright piano against the back wall, a few feet away. I felt uneasy.

"Anyone know how to play the piano?" Kurt had noticed the piano at the exact same time.

I was quiet but felt a knot in my stomach. I didn't want to go there.

"Sure I can play," Hans said with a laugh. I breathed a sigh of relief. The can of worms remained unopened.

He gave a very rudimentary rendition of "Heart and Soul." I felt slightly better.

"You suck, Hans," Kurt quipped. "Liz here looks like she can do way better than this. Right, Liz?"

I was taken aback. How did he know? Maybe he was joking, but there was no way around it.

"Her fingers were moving the whole time you were playing, Hans," Max explained.

Oh.

"Don't be shy," Max smiled at me. "Go ahead, show us what you've got."

I sat down on the piano bench, feeling a little unsure. I played the meditative aria from the Goldberg Variations.

"Oh, she knows what she's doing," Max remarked with a nod.

"How about something harder than that?" Kurt asked. He seemed musical enough to know that this was pretty basic for me from a technical standpoint. He knew I was capable of more, my timid fingers, twitching uneasily at the thought. I didn't want to be known as Piano Girl. I wanted to start afresh as the Physics Girl.

I played Chopin's Etude Op. 10 No. 5, the Black Keys. Quite the piano equivalent of a tongue-twister, it was a two-minute-long frilly arpeggio-filled piece with the right hand playing black keys only. When I finished, our table and a few others near the back cheered and applauded. Hans interrupted the applause.

"How about Rachmaninoff's Concerto No. 3?" Hans asked. He was probably starting to be inebriated. In physics terms, it would have come across as akin to asking a random person off the street to explain string theory. "The hardest piece in the classical repertoire. I bet you can do it!"

The knot in my stomach grew so much I felt like I was going to throw up. Why did he have to bring up that piece, of all pieces? Rachmaninoff's third concerto was my first love! I felt miserable, but I obliged, knowing it was probably fate at this point. The piece being forty-five minutes long, I played the cadenza from the first movement, quickly submerging myself into the rolling, thundering, and technically demanding chords. As the music grew ever more tense, building upwards towards its climax, I couldn't help but feel, as I did every time I played this piece, the thrill of a visionary leader starting a revolution. Now triumphantly reaching the victorious march, I'd forgotten I wasn't actually commanding an army right there and then. The harder and faster the chords progressed, the more euphoric the music made me, until finally the climax eased into a dream-like resolution, bringing me back to reality.

I turned to the guys when I was done, and they were quiet and wide-eyed. The once loud and bustling bar was sheathed in silence.

"You're amazing," Hans finally broke the silence. "Why didn't you study music instead? Rachmaninoff himself would've approved of your rendition."

I started blinking rapidly to hold back tears. I felt like I was revisiting a long-lost love that I had left behind in a foreign country. As if I had chosen the rational option to end things, but deep down, I would always yearn for what I had turned away from. I was reminded of what could have been had I gone down a different path instead, a thought that always drove me down a rabbit hole of sadness and regret whenever it surfaced.

Suddenly overwhelmed by fear of being exposed, as if the entire bar was suddenly able to read my mind, I felt trapped, and was overcome by an urge to escape.

"I'm tired, I have to go," I mumbled. I snuck to the cash register towards the front of the bar, paid my tab, and slipped out into the gritty Duisburg side street before anybody could utter a word of protest.

I ran, quickly turning a corner onto the main road as the sun was setting. I was running from everything that plagued my raging thoughts, like a raging river pushing with increasing aggression against a sturdy dam. Tears streamed down my face. I did not know what I was running from, but it reminded me of those dreams where I'm being chased by something unknown, with no choice but to run for my life, jumping down staircases and scaling walls. Heaven forbid any of these guys, my friends who had suddenly turned into fearsome monsters, caught me and forced me to face what I had spent years trying to run from, this dam that I had put so much energy into building, as unbreakable and as sturdy as possible. I couldn't reveal any more of this part of my identity. It had proven to be too much.

I passed by the university buildings and continued straight. Suddenly I hit a forest. Max had told me that there was a footpath in the forest that led all the way to Dusseldorf. I saw a few stairs leading in, and I followed them.

I found myself surrounded by a lush green deciduous forest that got progressively darker, with smaller and smaller flecks of orange sunset peeking through the dense foliage. Giant beech and oak trees filled up the sky with a beautiful canopy, a roof over the younger and smaller species. In every direction I looked, it was green over green over more green. I followed the curved footpath as the ugly spartan concrete wasteland gradually gave way to pristine unspoilt wilderness, a kind of all-encompassing natural beauty that seemed almost accidental. I was starting to breathe again.

Soon I saw flowers, small, white flowers littering the ground, and large blossoms of pink rhododendron poking through the sinewing branches. While the urban landscape of Duisburg was wanting in adornments and luxury, its encroaching natural landscape had everything to offer. Life was so much more beautiful outside the lab. Why did I go into physics again? To prove to myself that I could do it, I bitterly remembered. How *ridiculous* of me, now that I think about it.

Who was I kidding though? I was not a physics and math girl, not one bit. I was a pianist. Starting to learn the instrument before I was four years old, my whole life growing up was bathed in Western classical music. My parents always dreamed that their only child would learn the piano, which to them represented the high-brow Western cultured sensibilities that they aspired to acquire for themselves, and even more for me. Unexpectedly, in the piano I found myself.

I remembered first getting acquainted with Chopin at the age of five, through a CD my dad's friend gave him, the 24 etudes played by Maurizio Pollini. Fast forward a few years, and I was learning the nocturnes, as I heard them played by Arthur Rubinstein. By the time I was twelve, I'd made a home out of Chopin's second piano concerto. Then I moved onto Rachmaninoff's infamous third piano concerto, which drove more than one young musical prodigy mad.

My inner world saw 19th-century Parisian salons organized in my living room, adorned with lavish Turkish rugs and red velvet curtains, with my imaginary friends of composers, poets and philosophers as guests. I decorated the room in such a way that these musical legends I counted among my companions every time I closed my eyes felt right at home. Wooden shelves displayed an eclectic collection of classic novels and a large repertoire of sheet music alongside curiosities like a miniature glass piano, hand-made Russian dolls, an extensive stamp collection, and a vintage metronome. A wooden beam above the door was graced with dusty yellowed postcards featuring scenes ranging from the Seine River in Paris and churches in Berlin to Tibetan monasteries and Egyptian tombs. The centrepiece was my state-of-the-art grand piano, which took up about half the room, in a way that was perhaps out of place. With its red velvet seat with golden trim and its flawless lacquered ebony finish, it looked like it belonged in a grand hall rather than the tiny living room in the modest duplex my family inhabited. I felt an overwhelming need to do it justice, to compensate for the room's shortcomings. As a result, I crammed the contents of an 18th century drawing room into a three-by-four-metre space, imitation rococo chair, miniature chandelier, and all. Atop the piano lay a finished 1000-piece puzzle that I had painstakingly pieced and laminated, containing the illustrious figures of Bach, Copernicus, Keppler, Galileo,

Handel, Newton, Vivaldi, Stradivarius, King Louis XIV, and the Greek god Dionysus. I felt more at home among them than with friends or family.

I wanted to make a career out of music by the time I was in my early teens, but my parents thought I was going too far. My love for the stories that emanated from the smooth black and white keys through my fluttering fingertips was boundless. But was love enough? Could I make a reasonable living as a performer? Music was great as a hobby, but not as a career, in my parents' eyes. Would I not subsist better if I studied something more practical like medicine or the sciences? Would I not be more *respected* if I studied medicine or the sciences?

I couldn't argue with them. My playing was soulful, but not perfect. In the intensely competitive world of classical music, it wasn't enough to win competitions or admission into prestigious music schools. After a slew of second prizes and honorable mentions at international competitions where the winner was often two years younger than me, I was convinced, or perhaps my parents convinced me, that I wasn't good enough. If I wasn't the best, why bother even trying? I graduated from high school, gave up the entire idea of music, and inaugurated my new identity in CEGEP as the physics nerd. I left music behind and didn't look back.

I passed a pond full of lilies and found myself in the middle of a clearing. In the centre was a straight stone path, with a few stairs dividing a lower terrace and a higher terrace, reminiscent of the tiered seating of a concert hall. The backdrop of the stage consisted of eight marble Corinthian columns, shimmering in and out of the shadows. In the middle was a Grecian statue, a David kissed by the waning rays of golden sun, elegantly guarding the majestic garden. Then, as night fell, I saw that both the higher and the lower terraces were dotted with tombstones peeking through the tall grass. I was in a graveyard.

I read the tombstones one by one. Most of the dead were younger than twenty, and all died between 1914 and 1919. I felt sorrowful, overcome by a concurrent sense of knowing and dread. Just shy of a hundred years ago, people my age were laying their lives on the line for their country, while I was coddled, caught up in frivolous pursuits, enveloped in needless drama. People my age were *dying*. At least I was still alive. And where there was life, there was hope, I tried to tell myself.

I had made my choice. I couldn't go back to music now, having quit practising for so long. I would never be able to catch up. If I wasn't the best then, how could I ever be better than before, when all my competitive counterparts were still practising daily while I was not? I had fallen too far behind to ever dream of going back.

The dead soldiers too were dead, buried, and left in a forgotten cemetery, consumed by the overgrowth of weeds and tall grass that served as living testimonials to the passage of time. Just as these tombstones were consumed by vegetation and mold, so too were my musical aspirations encumbered by years of idleness.

I was then hit by a flash of recognition. These decaying corpses were providing fertile ground for new plants and flowers. Sometimes death is required for rebirth to happen, I thought to myself as I was walking home in the night. Sometimes entire civilizations must collapse in order to make way for something new to grow. But between a lifeless lab, a soulless city, and a forgotten graveyard, what could grow? How could I heal at last?

A few days later, during an exploratory trek on a Saturday, I visited Landschaftpark, an abandoned steel factory that was converted into a public park right in the middle of Duisburg. I saw monstrous grotesque piping and towering steel structures amidst tall chimneys that penetrated the dull grey skies. I saw the ruins of the once bustling factory, the crumbling carts that appeared to have attempted to break free of their constricting transport rails, a mass of dirt, grime, and rust. The only signs of life came from the colourful graffiti rebelliously etched all over the dusty jumble of metal and concrete. In some places, both life and death look terrifying. I felt encased in a cocoon, waiting for spring to finally take over so that I could flutter into the sky away from my old shell. Waiting for life to come back to me, waiting to grow wings and feel free.

This region of Germany was full of post-industrial cement and steel sculptures and structures, monuments hailing the catastrophic near-end of Western civilization. From the pedestrian rollercoaster to the coal museum, I was reminded of one of those post-apocalyptic videogames Chris used to play, depicting what would be left of humanity after our demise. I showed Chris a photo of the Tetraeder, a gigantic, several-storey-high tetrahedral structure illuminated by neon lights, situated on top of a hill near Bottrop. It seemed to be the kind of thing he'd be into. "I'd like to visit it someday," he replied.

I didn't know what it was that I was looking for. Chris asked me if I liked my work. I didn't know what to tell him. I didn't entirely dislike it. I just couldn't care less about it. I felt an abhorrent indifference towards it. In contrast, Chris seemed to be enjoying his summer project in astrophysics at McGill. We chatted sometimes at night, but not often. Some days he barely came online. I wished I loved physics and math like Chris did. Math to him was like music used to be to me. It infused him with life, the lush forest to my desolate mess of rusting pipes and crumbling concrete. Sometimes I resented him for it. I wished

I could like it here. Or be like him, pursuing his passion, while I was consumed with wistfulness, sorrow, and regret. I was wishing for something I could never have. Another Sunday morning, I took the train to Köln, or Cologne. A city full of cathedrals, I spent the morning visiting seven of them, one after another. I saw domes of different sizes and stained glass windows telling different stories. All exuding the same monastic calm. I sat in the antique wooden pews of each church for some time. Waiting. What was I waiting for?

4

May 30, 2011

Two weeks later, Max finally found an apartment for me in Duisburg. The reason it took so long was that all the student residences were under renovation during the summer. So the international student services had to look for apartments elsewhere for us. Max paired me up with another girl, also a summer intern, from MIT. I was a little anxious about meeting her, but when I saw this nice Chinese American girl walking towards my office saying, "Hi" to me, I was relieved. She had a rather plain face, marked with genuineness and kindness without a hint of conceit, so I knew we'd get along. She introduced herself as Wendy. We got the keys from Max and moved in on a Wednesday afternoon. Each of us was given a large room with a bed, a table, a chair, and a cabinet, all clearly from IKEA, and we shared a kitchen.

Then I received an email from the coordinator of the RISE internship program. The RISE program is a partnership between Germany, Canada, the UK and the US, where German students get internships in English-speaking countries, and students from English-speaking countries get internships in Germany. The coordinator shared a list of the RISE interns who were in our area in Germany, Nordrhein-Westfalen, or the North Rhine-Westphalia. I looked at the names, Amina from Kansas,

Jonathan from Vancouver, Carol from Scotland, among others. Interesting. And that was when I first heard from Haider. He wrote to a few of us:

Hey everyone,

I'm Haider, from Mississauga, Ontario. I'm a student in Aerospace Engineering at the University of Toronto. I'm currently living in Essen, but I'm working at Duisburg University. Would you guys like to meet up one of these days? We can go for lunch, hang out, travel around the area, or whatever else you'd like to do together.

Cheers,

Haider Ali

Haider. Never heard of such a name before. My first thought was, was this a guy or a girl? Soon, replies came from a certain David with a Chinese last name who also lived in Essen. Then Will, presumably a White guy, who lived in Duisburg.

Who were all these people? I got curious and went online. I easily found Will and David on Facebook. Will gave me the same bad vibes that vaguely reminded me of the more antisocial side of Chris. I couldn't exactly put my finger on it, but he seemed to exude a cold, aloof, and unaffectionate demeanor. David looked like a stereotypical Chinese dude, no more, no less: scrawny, soft-spoken, and reserved. Who was this Haider? Countless Haider Ali profiles popped up when I searched for him. All men, all brown-skinned. Haider was a South Asian male name apparently. Somewhere near the bottom of this list, I saw a picture that repulsed me immediately. A blurry, dark, close-up of the face of a brown guy, looking to be at least thirty, was captured from an unflattering angle. The label below the picture was *Haider Ali, Mississauga, ON*. My gut churned a little. Why would anyone pick such a bad picture for their profile? I wondered. It was as if he was determined to make a bad first impression. What was he thinking? I couldn't help but judge him.

I was up for something new though, whatever it was. Hoping for the best, I gave these three strangers the benefit of the doubt and wrote back. We agreed to meet up the next day at the Duisburg train station.

Friday was a cloudy day, with occasional rays of sunshine penetrating the dull grey mass. I brought Wendy along with me since she seemed interested in meeting these guys too. We took the bus to the train station and arrived slightly early. We sat outside on the steps in front of the Hauptbahnhof sign and gazed contemplatively at the deserted plaza. My phone vibrated. It was a text from Haider: *We're right around the corner at the intersection of Friedrich-Wilhelm-Strasse and Mercatorstrasse, be there soon.* I stood up with Wendy and we started walking in their direction, our trepidation building with each step.

The wind was blowing from behind me, ruffling my hair and pressing my tie-dye scarf against my body. Straight ahead, three young men approached in the distance, facing the wind. The middle one, the tallest of the three, had skin of a medium brown colour that reminded me of clay, perhaps just a shade darker than the one from which I imagine Adam must have been made. He wore a loose black dress shirt over dark jeans and had black slicked-back hair. His face bore a solemn expression, and he approached with a firm gait in a way that exuded a natural sense of authority. It dawned on me that I found him actually kind of handsome. To his right was a White guy with sandy dark-blond hair, in a T-shirt and shorts that gave off a cool, casual vibe; to his left was an East

Asian guy with a rectangular face, a slightly pronounced lower lip, and thin metal-framed glasses, looking nerdy but easygoing. Haider, Will, and David. I immediately matched the people with their Facebook profiles.

Haider unfurled his brow as he spotted us, greeting us with a handshake and a smile.

"Hey guys, my name is Haider, this is David and Will. You're Liz, right?"

I nodded. "And this is Wendy, my roommate," I added, gesturing at her.

"Nice to meet you," Haider replied as he shook her hand. Oddly formal and respectful, I thought. I didn't dislike it.

We talked about our experiences in Duisburg and our internships, as we walked towards the city square. Haider was a third-year student at the University of Toronto, Will studied physics at a university in Oklahoma, and David studied biomedical engineering at a university in Ohio. Like me, they all arrived in the middle of May. Haider and David found housing in Essen while Will found a place in Duisburg.

I was relieved that all three of them turned out to be actually quite nice. We had ice cream at a small sweets shop near the city square. We had a good time and decided to visit Dusseldorf together the next day. I almost managed to shake off my first impression of Haider online. Almost, but not quite.

The next day at noon, we met again at the Duisburg Hauptbahnhof and took the regional train to Dusseldorf. Haider was quite cheerful as we sat on the train and enjoyed a lighthearted chat. Will was cool but polite. David was nice but slightly meek. None of them had been to Dusseldorf, except when they flew in from the Dusseldorf airport, which was quite far from the actual city. The train ride took us half an hour from Duisburg to Dusseldorf.

The Dusseldorf train station was nothing like the one in Duisburg. The city was lively and the people were friendly. Soon, we were surrounded by the Old City, with beautiful architecture and vibrant young people drinking pints of beer and soaking up the summer sun.

"I can't believe everyone is drinking at this hour, it's 1 p.m.!" Haider exclaimed.

"Only in Germany," I retorted. "Beer is so cheap, it's sold in plastic bottles."

"Of course," the rest replied, with sideways glances. We laughed.

We wandered around the tightly packed maze that was the Old City, with its narrow alleyways, twisting cobblestone streets, and buildings that resembled the Germany of my imagination prior to experiencing Duisburg, and soon hit the shores of the Rhein. The early afternoon sun shone in all its splendor on the glistening river, reflecting a dazzling light on the surrounding buildings. It was truly a fine day, I thought. I liked it here.

Later that day, we visited the Naval Museum, situated in an old lighthouse. We learned the history of ships and enjoyed the view of the river from the top floor. We got ice cream, cheap as always, like the beer. Germans really know how to enjoy life, I thought. We then headed towards one of the bars around the shore to have some proper German drinks and snacks.

"Guys," I began my usual speech when I was with friends, "someone will have to help me finish my beer later because I have zero alcohol tolerance." Probably because I'm an Asian girl. I rolled my eyes at the thought of being a walking stereotype.

All three guys offered to help. I felt rather cared for, for a moment, even though they probably saw it as doing them a favour. The classic symbiotic relationship, actually.

35

Soon, the beers were on the table and we were offered currywurst, a local snack made of sausage and topped with curry spice. It was delicious. In fact, it was so delicious that I almost downed the whole beer with it, to everyone's surprise, and perhaps disappointment. Fearing the consequences of further inebriation around a bunch of guys, however nice they seemed to be, I snapped out of my midday trance and promptly pushed the bottle aside. Haider picked it up to finish it.

"Let's go shopping!" I cheered. I was probably a little tipsy, but I was having a good time, so I didn't care by that point.

"Wendy, do you want to go with her?" Haider suggested. "I have to go home now to call my family, but if you girls can keep yourselves company, it would be safer for you and I'll leave with a clear conscience."

Wendy agreed to go with me, and Haider, David, and Will left. I'm not sure where we wandered, but we ended up walking along the Rhein beach until sunset, took the train home, and chatted till the next morning as the sunrise flooded through our open kitchen window. Somehow, I did most of the talking and Wendy only listened. Oddly enough, she sounded impressed by me and told me I reminded her of her good friend, a young entrepreneur who was nominated one of the top 20 under 20 by Forbes in the US. I felt quite flattered and undeserving of her judgment.

I was happy with my new friends, but internally I was crumbling. There was no Wi-Fi in my new Duisburg apartment, and I felt terribly alone without being able to talk with Chris. Almost every night, I stayed either at the Starbucks at the train station or on campus to write long emails to him. He barely replied, and when he did, it was never more than a few lines. Somewhere deep down, I was feeling like I had enough of his lukewarmness. As I went to bed one night, I thought to myself, wouldn't it be nice if I had a real boyfriend who actually cared at all? I felt ashamed of admitting my neediness, having perhaps internalized Chris's attitude that having feelings and emotional needs were a weakness.

One balmy night in early June, the International Students' Office of Duisburg University invited every summer exchange student for a barbecue at the Gruga park in Essen, a large nature preserve and botanical garden. I came with Wendy to distract myself, and we met David, Will, and Haider again, along with Patrick, who was a year younger than me, from MIT, who had also started working with the Krugg group. There were perhaps fifty or sixty people, and a good number of them engaged in small talk with me and my new friends. Someone brought a guitar, and I struggled to play something on it, relying entirely on my piano knowledge to get around my lack of experience with the instrument. Haider then took it from me—I must have been painful to listen to—and strummed a song. He was *good*, I noticed. But I had too much on my mind to delve any deeper.

I felt uneasy surrounded by all these random new people, awkwardly trying to make conversation, and left early to go back to use the campus Wi-Fi. Chris wasn't even online. I read through all the messages I had sent him about Dusseldorf, the people I met, and the work I was doing in the lab. Chris had replied to all of my detailed stories with a meager math joke. Classic. This was not how I wanted my life to be, I realized. Tomorrow, Haider, Will, David, Wendy, and I were going to spend the day in Köln. We'd be having fun, and I didn't want Chris to spoil it for me. I opened my inbox and composed a new email to Chris: *We need to talk tomorrow, be there at 9 a.m. my time zone.* I had no idea what I wanted to say, but I knew I had to say it.

5

I woke up early to a beam of cool morning sunlight on my face. I dressed silently, packed my stuff, and headed out without waking up Wendy. My stomach was in knots. My trepidation grew as I walked down the stairs, waited for the bus, and then rode the bus to the train station's Starbucks, my mind racing with conflicting thoughts and memories. I missed Chris, I genuinely did. Under his blunt coldness and distant disposition laid a kind and sensitive soul, one which I despaired of reaching. But could I move him?

I got off at the Hauptbahnhof. I rushed into the Starbucks, ordered my favourite chocolate caramel muffin, and sat on the empty couch in the corner. I was jittery without having had a drop of coffee, desperate to get it over with. My heart was pounding. Will Chris even show up?

Chris came online one minute past 9 a.m.

"Hey, what's up?" he typed.

"Hey, I need to talk to you."

"What's wrong?"

What was wrong, actually? I couldn't put my finger on it.

No, who was I kidding. I was in love with him and he didn't love me back the same way. But I couldn't possibly tell him that. I wasn't going to be vulnerable like that, *not with him.*

"Maybe it's me," I finally typed, "but I feel like I spend all this time writing to you and trying to talk to you, but you don't seem to want to do the same."

"But you don't have to write to me so often, I want you to enjoy your time in Germany."

He was right. Was my agony really just a product of my own imagination? My mind must be playing tricks on me again.

"Listen, you're always on my mind, and it drives me sick that you don't seem to want to talk to me as much as I want to talk to you. Somewhere it feels to me like you don't care about me as much as I care about you. And it hurts."

"I'm sorry, what can I do to help?"

I stared at the screen, confused at how callous this ostensibly kind statement can feel. How could he not know and understand what I wanted from him, after all this time? The Atlantic Ocean between us seemed at its widest. I looked up to the ceiling and down to my laptop. I wanted to run away, be somewhere else, anywhere.

I felt my hands fiddling with the plastic Band-Aid on my knee under the small round Starbucks table. It was from that day in the forest, while I was traipsing through the twigs and pine needles. I couldn't remember exactly when it happened, but I noticed the gash when I had reached the graveyard, after I'd stopped to breathe.

I noticed the plaster was peeling off slightly in the corner, almost beckoning me to rip it off. Yet I fumbled with it, anxiously fidgeting with that exposed corner, almost hoping that doing so would loosen its hold enough for it to come off automatically.

My emotional turmoil finally pushed me over the edge, and I could no longer hold back how I felt. Since professing my feelings for him was not a viable option, I knew there was only one other way out.

"Chris, this isn't working. If it continues, I'll have to stop talking to you at all."

"If this is what you really want, that's okay with me."

That was it. I had to do it. I ripped the Band-Aid off at once with a flourish. It hurt a lot less than I had anticipated.

"Chris, you don't understand, and I'm sorry, but this is it. I won't be contacting you anymore. See you back in school in September."

That was it. I'd said it. I thought it'd be a lot harder than that. I felt strangely calm instead.

There was a short pause.

"Alright, goodbye then, hope you feel better soon."

Time stood still as I closed the screen of my laptop. What was done was done.

I sat motionless, and slowly assessed the situation. I had just bid Chris farewell. This chapter of my life was over for better or for worse. What was next? Here I was, a girl all alone in a new land, a new continent. The future was yet to be written. I felt a quickening of emotions stirring inside me, slowly building into an uproar. Freedom, sadness, exhilaration, fear, and joy. But freedom above all. This is my life, and I can do anything now. *Anything!*

"Hey!" Haider stood in front of me, popping in out of nowhere. Of course, that trip to Köln. I'd almost forgotten.

"Hey," I replied in a quivery voice.

"Are you alright?" Haider asked.

I swallowed everything that had happened and managed a confident smile.

"I'm good. How are you?"

It was 11 a.m., we were heading to Köln for the day, and I was ready. Soon, David, Will, and Wendy showed up, and we boarded the train to our destination.

If Dusseldorf was the local big city, Köln was significant on an international level. It was majestic. The train swiftly penetrated the dense urban area on an elevated railway, and the twin bell towers of the Köln Cathedral loomed higher and higher over us. Soon we were inside the white-roofed station. We immediately felt the electricity in the air when we left the train. It was a warm day of late spring.

"Liz, you've been here before, the other week. Show us around!" Haider said as we walked out of the station.

"Here we are right at the foot of the magnificent Köln cathedral." I gestured towards the imposing gothic structure above our heads, "It's the main attraction of the city, and we have to visit it at some point, and also climb the towers, which I've never done before either."

Everyone nodded in agreement.

"However, my personal favourite place in Köln is the Chocolate Museum. We should go there first," I proposed.

Everyone, once again, nodded in approval, with enthusiastic smiles and cheers. Who could say no to a chocolate museum?

"You've got your priorities sorted out," remarked Wendy.

"Yes, let's go!" cheered Haider.

The Chocolate Museum, owned by the Lindt Company, was a boat-shaped, glass-walled building on the shores of the Rhein. We walked along the water among tourists, old couples, and punk goth teenagers doing photoshoots using the old monuments as backdrops.

"The best part of the museum is the gigantic chocolate fountain where you can dip wafers. Technically, you can have as many wafers as you want if you keep asking for them," I explained.

"That is amazing," even taciturn Will admitted.

41

"They tend to give the wafers to kids first, though," I continued. I secretly hoped there weren't going to be too many of them, and wondered whether the others were thinking the same.

"Can I pretend I'm five?" Haider asked.

We laughed in response just as we arrived at the museum entrance. We paid ten euros per person and, of course, there was neither a child nor student discount. They clearly knew exactly who the real target audience was. We were first transported to the Central American cocoa plantations on the top floor, while listening to the story of the origin of cocoa and how it was processed. After a maze in the green house, we were then introduced to the history of chocolate in the West. We were surrounded by vintage posters and old chocolate vending machines featuring dated drawings of Black youths serving hot chocolate. Another floor showed the process of making a chocolate truffle. The truffle core was covered with liquid chocolate which then rolled on a metal grid to obtain a ruffled texture. We also saw giant chocolate bunnies and eggs in the making. There were even displays of every generation of Kinder Surprise toys.

I felt like a child literally in a candy store. Few things have endured throughout my life as steadfastly as my love for chocolate. It was one of the only consolations that could make me forget just about any heartbreak. Walking down the aisles of the museum I felt light, and finally like myself. Wendy, Haider, and I laughed as we took pictures of each other pretending to eat oversized Lindors and Easter bunnies. David and Will attempted every game on the children's floor, sometimes with hilarious results.

We then all came to the main floor and there it was, the mythical chocolate fountain. Taller than the tallest of us, a silky brown liquid poured out of the tower onto varying levels, eventually feeding into a large basin at the bottom. An old lady dressed as a chef was handing out waffles which she first dipped one by one into the sweet, melted goodness. Each of us nonchalantly went twice in line to have a wafer. Three times would have been overkill, seeing all the kids surrounding us waiting to be served, but one time would not have been enough as we might not get a chance to be back on this continent any time soon. We then ended up in the chocolate store, which sold curiosities ranging from chocolate liqueurs to wasabi-flavoured candy to chocolate dentistry kits featuring chocolate teeth and dental mirrors. I bought a sea salt dark chocolate for myself while Haider got a few gifts for his sisters and mother. Each of us walked out of the museum grinning from ear to ear.

"Let's go back to the cathedral before it gets too late," I suggested.

We made our way back to the solemn building, bringing us back down to earth from the Willy-Wonka-esque extravaganza. As we approached the main entrance, we couldn't help but marvel at the intricate sculpted details covering every inch of the exterior. Angels and saints with grave faces warning us of our impending doom surrounded the entrance while gargoyles watched us from above. The stone, blackened in some areas due to an enormous fire a century ago, felt cold and impenetrable.

We walked inside. Darkness enveloped us. The quiet air contained between the stone floor and the lofty ceiling seemed to gently vibrate at the frequency of the souls that have visited the cathedral over the centuries. The afternoon sun's golden rays, filtering through colourful stained glass windows, illuminated just enough of the inside to make for a triumphant view of the altar. I felt humbled and silenced by the heaviness the church exuded.

"Let's sit down for a while," I suggested.

I sat at the sturdy, ornate wooden pew, and the gravity of existence flooded my consciousness, wave by wave. My past, my dreams, Chris, my hopes, my thoughts, all crept to the surface like waves crashing against the shore, as my eyes welled up. Chris.

This is over now.

It was hitting me with a full pang.

How am I to soldier on all alone now?

Tears rolled down my cheeks and I suppressed a sob. Wendy came over with a piece of tissue. She asked me if I finally cut ties with Chris and I told her I had done so that morning. She put her hand on my shoulder.

No, I can't break down right here right now.

I regained my composure.

Haider came over and gently whispered, with a rare level of sensitivity, "If you guys are ready, we can start getting in line to visit the cathedral towers."

I appreciated the distraction. We bought our tickets to climb the tower, and after a half-hour line, we were walking up hundreds of spiraling steps surrounded by other tourists to the bells.

"This feels like a dungeon!" Haider commented.

"Totally, this is like Harry Potter!" Wendy replied.

Light increasingly flooded the stairway as we approached the gigantic bells at the top of the tower, around three or four metres in diameter. We were propelled by the moving crowd of people onto the balcony outside. The view over Köln was incredible in the late afternoon, the sun waning over the Rhein.

"I'm so glad we came!" Haider exclaimed.

It was really beautiful. The refreshing air, a prelude to the impending nightfall, buried my sadness. The church had been cathartic. I felt cleansed. Still sad, but my sadness no longer weighed me down in a tangible way. It was something I could handle, surrounded by nice, supportive people who lifted me up. We made our way back down from the towers and laughed at the funny graffiti we saw scrawled along the spiral stairway.

"Look! 'Harry Potter was here!'" David pointed at the tiny drawing in blue on the grey marbled stone.

"These folks are nuts, drawing on a centuries-old monument," I replied.

"It's funny though," Will retorted.

"I'm not the only one who thought about Harry Potter apparently," Wendy laughed.

We arrived on the ground floor and exited the cathedral.

"Let's grab dinner," I suggested.

Wandering around the Old City, we found a small fast-food joint serving doner kebab, currywurst, and fries. We ordered all three to share and sat at a table outside, the thin legs of my black wrought iron chair wobbling against the uneven cobblestone.

"Let's play a game," Haider proposed. "I dare each of you to say something true about you that's unexpected."

"Like, love life related?" Wendy asked.

"Anything," Haider said.

There was a brief, tense silence.

"I've never had a girlfriend before," David finally interjected, with a little candid chuckle. Feeling his nervousness, we all joined him in laughing awkwardly.

"That's alright, mate, to each their own timing," Haider comforted him. "As for me, my childhood sweetheart recently got married, and I think that's when it finally hit me that things have ended for good."

I felt old. I was nineteen and Haider was twenty-one. People live at different paces around the world; it suddenly dawned on me that people my age and younger were getting married and having children. I shuddered at the thought.

"I've kissed a girl before," I jumped in impulsively, almost as if to erase the prospect of marriage from my mind.

"Did you like it?" Will interjected. I rolled my eyes at his overdone Katy Perry reference.

What's the big deal? Who *doesn't* experiment a little these days? It was the twenty-first century! We were close friends and unexpectedly developed a bit of a crush on each other. We gave it a try and both decided it wasn't for us. We never spoke about it again and had both continued to date men since.

"My best friend is a lesbian, but I'm not dating her," Wendy continued, jolting me awake from my memory I thought I'd hidden away for good.

"My ex-girlfriend asked me for a hug, and when I refused, she jumped out of a window and killed herself," Will interrupted with a flat voice.

Everyone sat motionless. That escalated quickly.

Haider finally broke the silence.

"Really?" Haider asked incredulously, his tone cautious so as not to upset anyone.

"She was kind of not okay in her mind," Will explained. "That's why I broke up with her. She asked for the hug after the break-up. I didn't feel like it, and I didn't think she'd really kill herself, but she did."

"That's really intense, I'm sorry to hear that," Haider concluded softly.

I'd have had a hard time living in Will's shoes. We finished our meal in silence and headed back to the Köln train station.

On our way to the station, a wild cohort of German girls whirled around us, many wearing pink and one wearing white with a diagonal sash from her shoulder to her waist with Bride to Be written on it in English. Clearly inebriated, they shouted to us in German and showed us various items they were selling, most of them sex toys and prank materials. One of them bandied a condom in its packet towards us. Haider stopped her and said, "No thanks, I'm single. I don't do this. I'm Muslim." I was taken aback by how sternly Haider responded. But good for him for standing up for what he believed in, I thought. I wouldn't have had the guts, if I were in his shoes.

At the station, I suddenly thought of the Tetraeder in Bottrop. Chris had wanted to go there, I thought. It would be nice to watch the sunrise there alone tomorrow morning. It'll be in his memory, in memory of our bittersweet relationship. It'll calm my soul. I made my way to one of the large regional maps and mentally calculated how to get there from Duisburg.

"What are you looking at?" Haider caught me off guard.

"Oh, just a place I want to go sometime," I fumbled.

"What are you guys talking about?" David chipped in.

Everyone turned their attention to us. I was terrible at telling lies. There was no hiding it anymore.

"There is a place called the Tetraeder in Bottrop. It's a large tetrahedral sculpture on top of a hill that lights up at night. I want to go there to see the sunrise tomorrow morning."

"Can I join you?" Haider asked.

"Can I come too?" David added.

I was silent and rather unwilling. What an ironic turn of events.

"How are you going to get there all alone at night?" Haider inquired gently.

"By night buses and trains?" I replied a little defensively.

47

"I know there are night buses in Essen, but are there in Duisburg?"

Good point. I felt deflated. We both looked at the map: there were night buses, but only until 12:30 a.m.. My spirits were failing me.

"How about you come stay with either David or me in Essen for the night, and we head there together in the early morning?" Haider proposed.

David promptly assented to the proposition.

I had to face the facts. It was the only realistic plan. I nodded.

"Who do you want to stay with?" Haider asked.

I weighed my options. The nice, familiar, perhaps a little dull, but safe Chinese guy, or the cryptic, foreign, but alluring dark-skinned dude? Seems like an obvious choice but ... I picked Haider without thinking about it. Soon I was on the train headed to Essen Hauptbahnhof with Haider and David. When we got off the train, David left, and Haider and I were alone.

6

June 12, 2011

Haider and I took the bus from the Essen train station and fifteen minutes later, we got off at his stop and found ourselves in a nondescript, mid-century residential neighbourhood. We walked to the back door of his large student dorm. Haider took out his keys to open the door. It was very dimly lit inside and the stuffy, pungent smell of old apartment buildings mixed with Chinese cuisine seeped into my pores, almost like a déjà-vu. I started seeing anything at all only when we reached the second floor. We passed by the shared washrooms, where I imagined some unholy things must have happened with so many young people living together. Promptly getting my mind out of the gutter, I followed him until we reached his apartment.

"It's a little cramped in here, but it's clean, I hope you don't mind," Haider said gently.

The door opened and I peeked inside. It was cramped indeed, with a bed, a desk and a chair, two gigantic suitcases against the far wall, a sink, and a stovetop in a corner, all tightly packed into about nine square metres. The window opened directly onto a garden overgrown into a small forest, barely letting any light through. I walked in the room and noticed how quiet it was due to the heavy carpet.

"It's nice in here," I commented. I meant it. It was quiet, cozy, organized, and clean, more than I would expect from a college guy.

Haider gestured for me to sit on his bed while he moved his guitar from his chair so he could sit down.

"This is Lisa," he answered to my inquisitive look at the instrument, an unassuming acoustic guitar.

"That's cute that she should have a name," I couldn't help but admit. "I have a piano and he's named William."

"You play the piano?" He smiled.

I nodded. Only say so much for now, I thought.

"You were quite good at the guitar the other day," I said, diverting the subject from myself.

"Thanks," Haider answered. "I've been learning new songs recently. This one I don't know very well, but I can show you the original recording. Do you want to hear it?"

I said of course.

Haider opened iTunes on his laptop. Soft guitar strumming filled the room. Soon it was joined by a male voice and then a female voice. It was a love song, I realized. There I was, spending the night with a brown guy listening to pop love songs in his room. Then seeing the sunrise at the Tetraeder the next morning? What a funny turn of events, I thought to myself.

"Do you like it?" Haider asked me after the song ended.

"It's nice; what is it called?" I asked

"It's called 'Lucky,' by Jason Mraz and Colbie Caillat."

Not that I would know, being a classical music nerd and completely ignorant of pop culture except for a brief goth phase in high school.

"Yeah, I'd love to sing it with someone special someday," Haider said, half to himself.

I silently judged him again. I understood the sentiment, but no, it was way too cheesy a thing for me to ever do with anyone. How did I find myself here?

In retrospect, perhaps Chris had rubbed off on me more than I had thought.

We listened to a couple more songs. By then it was already midnight.

"Let's rest a little before heading out," Haider suggested. "You can lie down on my bed, I'll sleep on the floor."

"Are you sure?" I asked, though the answer was predictable.

"Of course." A gentleman.

He pulled down the grey covers and revealed a wine-red pillow with a beautiful print that reminded me of sari fabric. I laid myself down under the comforter as he lowered himself onto the floor and covered himself with a navy hoodie.

"Do you mind if I switch off the lights?" he asked.

I agreed. He did so and laid down.

I lay wide awake in Haider's bed, tired but not a bit sleepy. Here I was, a single girl lying in some male stranger's bed in a strange land. What had become of me? Oddly enough, I didn't think I was doing anything wrong. I was in Haider's bed, but he was on the floor. But I had no idea what was to come. I felt some apprehension in the dead of night, my thoughts, and perhaps a little bit of justifiable paranoia as a woman alone with a man she barely knows, keeping me awake. Yet despite all this, Haider made me feel at ease for some reason. My logic and intuition wrestled between skepticism and trust, tossing and turning well into the night.

Just as I was dozing off, Haider's obnoxious phone alarm went off and we were both jolted awake. Haider turned on the lights and greeted me good morning. I laughed, it was 1:30 a.m. We had a light breakfast, splitting a Nutella sandwich between the two of us.

"I have some Indian tea, if you want," Haider proposed.

"I love chai tea!" I exclaimed, thinking about the hipster tea shop in Montreal I took my friends to, partly to impress them.

Haider laughed.

"I never understood why they called it this way, *chai* means 'tea' in Hindi. It's like you're saying *tea tea*!" he said with a chuckle, but without chiding.

That's funny, I thought. In Chinese, tea is called *cha*. I should have figured it out! I quickly reproached myself.

"There is a problem though," Haider carried on, "I have milk and I have sugar, but you can't have both in your tea, because you see, my German is bad, and so when I thought I bought regular white sugar at the store, it turned out to be strawberry-flavoured when I tasted it. If you have it with milk, its acidity will make the milk curdle. So, do you want strawberry sugar tea, or milk tea?"

I laughed out loud.

"What does strawberry sugar tea even taste like?" I asked, amused.

"I don't know, we'll see I guess?"

I agreed and Haider poured two cups of tea for us and added a spoonful of the funky pink sugar from the opaque white paper bag into each. It tasted funny but good enough. I was pleasantly surprised.

We packed our stuff, some extra food (of course more Nutella sandwiches), and headed out. It was cold, so Haider lent me a felt blanket his sister had given him, which I wore like a shawl. He wore his navy hoodie, with his backpack strapped in front and his guitar on his back because I insisted that he bring it. We could have passed for hippies.

Waiting at the bus stop, Haider told me that he was Indian by blood, but was born and raised in Kuwait, and had moved to Mississauga when he was seventeen. I made a mental note to myself to go look up on a map where Kuwait was.

"It was a crappy high school that I went to in Mississauga," Haider said quietly. "I was the only one from my year who got into the engineering program at the U of T, University of Toronto. I was also top of my class back in Kuwait, but that was a long time ago."

Everyone I met nowadays had been top of their class in high school, it seemed. Myself, Haider, Chris, and my best friend Arielle back in Montreal. It's not even something special nowadays, is it?

The bus came and we got on it.

"There were lots of contests in my high school in Kuwait," Haider continued. "I used to win most of them—I took that stuff way too seriously—but I'm most proud of winning that cooking contest once. My spaghetti bolognese was really amazing!"

Haider had a childish smile. This guy is kind of nuts. I giggled at the thought.

We arrived at the Essen train station and met a sleep-deprived but enthusiastic David. We boarded the train to Bottrop. After a half-hour ride, we arrived at our destination.

We got off the train and immediately noticed how empty the station was. We walked down the concrete platform into the tiny Bottrop Hauptbahnhof and soon were on the sidewalk. We were greeted by an eerie silence, concrete buildings, and metal fences. A billboard of a scantily clad woman posing seductively with a tube of mascara on the other side of the street seemed like an invitation to the underworld.

"There's a map over there," I said, pointing across the street. "Let's orient ourselves." I didn't exactly want to get lost in a place like this.

We crossed the street and made our way to the dusty concrete map stand.

"So, the Tetraeder is here." I pointed to the triangular shape on the map that was partially obscured by unidentifiable liquid stains and splotches of graffiti.

"And we are here at the Hauptbahnhof," Haider added, pointing to the faded star in the centre of the map.

"If we take this road straight ahead, we should arrive directly," I declared. Everyone nodded.

I took a picture of the map with my small digital camera, just to have it on hand. It came out a dirty yellow with the glare of the street lights bouncing off the map no matter what angle I used to capture it.

We made our way to the street indicated on the map, and were soon surrounded by unkempt vegetation that obscured many of the street lights, creating a dark, gloomy feel. David cautioned us to be careful, but Haider was clearly enjoying himself. Were we in our very own horror movie? We might as well have been, the three dumb college kids traipsing through a dilapidated area in a foreign country in the middle of the night, throwing away all common sense. But then again, when else would I get the chance to have these kinds of adventures without a care in the world?

We passed rundown, grim-looking apartment buildings, each illuminated by a single yellow porchlight. What sort of people lived in these places? I wondered to myself. Certainly not a group of kids like us who went to see the sunrise on top of an apocalyptic structure. What kind of life did they live? Were they happy? Was I happy?

We kept on walking and yet could not catch a glimpse of the Tetraeder. At the Tetraeder's location, as indicated on the map, was what looked like a military school surrounded by a barbed-wire fence. When we walked past it, we were in a sleepy residential area.

"Are you sure this is the right way?" Haider finally asked me.

"Maybe we should ask someone?" I tacitly admitted.

"Ask whom? Are you suggesting we go knock on doors at this hour?" Haider replied, indignant.

Of course not. We kept on walking.

The sky was turning ever-so-slightly into a deep blue colour. Some lonely birds called out to each other. I felt hopeful somewhere deep inside. A yearning for … I didn't know what.

A girl about our age walked towards us from the opposite side of the street.

"Let's go ask her for directions," I suggested.

"David, go ahead," Haider asked.

"No, my German is bad," David promptly replied. "How about you do it, Liz? You're a girl, you won't scare her."

"Haider, your German is better than mine," I nudged him. I didn't feel like speaking to a stranger.

Haider complied and went over to her, speaking some broken sentences. She stepped back cautiously, and when she finally understood what he was saying, she whispered in English, "I don't know, sorry," and quickly disappeared into the darkness.

"Man she must have thought I was a thug," Haider mused as he turned towards us.

We all laughed, but I also saw a flicker of sorrow in Haider's eyes. We kept walking.

Birds and critters were waking up all around us under the now-lavender sky. I felt my insides waking up along with the world. Something was happening in the air.

A man turned onto the street we were on. Haider asked him for directions again, and he told us to keep walking straight and that we were near.

We rushed forward as the man vanished like a vision. Suddenly, out of nowhere, a humongous structure appeared, towering over our heads; a large tetrahedral metallic construction, dark against the glorious pink sky.

"The Tetraeder!" we all exclaimed.

As I caught my breath, both Haider and David sprinted towards the small tree-covered hill on which the Tetraeder stood. We found a sandy footpath leading up the hill and followed it to the top. As we reached the end of the path, we were greeted by a strong gust of wind and found ourselves in a clearing the size of a football field.

There was the Tetraeder, in all its majesty. A ten-storey high construction, it was made out of a large metallic tetrahedral frame supported by many smaller triangles and stood on four concrete pillars. It was propped up like a rocket ready to be launched into outer space, after the entire human race has been wiped out.

Then we saw that a staircase had been installed into the Tetraeder that led to a circular observation deck on top. Haider bounded towards it, followed by David. I stood, digital camera in hand, trying to catch a picture from an interesting angle. I finally put down my camera, sprinting to catch up to them.

"Hurry up! The view is amazing up here!" Haider shouted over my head, already part-way up the staircase.

I walked up slowly and deliberately, caught in the liminal space between the earthly and the heavenly realms. The wind was whipping through my blanket shawl and messing up my hair. The sky shone an intense, blinding white. I squinted, overwhelmed by the enormity of it all.

"Come see the sun!" David cried out at me.

That was it. I let go and ran all the way up the twisting staircase to the top, where I was blasted by the blinding light and hit by the wind from every direction.

"Isn't it beautiful?" Haider exclaimed, barely audible above the howling wind.

I looked around me, into the distance. Grey houses were nestled among greyish green trees. In every direction, as far as the eye could see, large factory chimneys, fat and skinny, short and tall, blew out white smoke that billowed and twisted into the sky. The sun was shining golden between stripes of red clouds. What a strange world we lived in.

"It is wonderful," I affirmed.

Upon closer inspection, I noticed graffiti everywhere, standing out against the dull, tarnished metal of the Tetraeder deck. Hearts surrounding initials and cartoonishly scrawled drawings abounded. Who were these people who came before us? Probably some foolish young people, drunk or in love, or both. A poor choice of a place for lovers, perhaps, but they didn't have any other options if they lived in this region of the world. Then again, there I was, in memory of Chris. Was I even in a position to judge these people when I was just as foolish as they were? And over there were the two guys I came with, taking pictures of each other.

"You look like a hobo with that blanket," Haider quipped, laughing good-naturedly at me.

"You too with your hoodie," I retorted. He did, with his oversized hoodie, and his backpack and guitar strapped in front of him and behind. His skin colour also didn't help to redeem his image, I then noted to myself. I'd grown up associating brown skin with poverty, lack of hygiene, and cultural backwardness, I realized with some surprise. In China, Indians were perceived as poor slum-dwellers who were behind the Chinese when it came to progress and modernization. Darker-skinned Chinese people felt an extension of that prejudice. I remember seeing my otherwise soft-spoken father, from whom I inherited my tanned skin that was considered "dark" by Chinese standards, fume with rage when people jokingly asked whether he was from Pakistan, back when I was little, and we lived in China. These were the deeply ingrained associations with darker skin that I never really realized I had internalized.

I tried to mentally undo that connection between Haider's skin colour and looking like a hobo, but without much success. I felt guilt building up inside of me.

"I'll tell you what. You both look like hobos," David assented in an effort to diffuse the tension. It worked, as we erupted into a fit of laughter.

As was clearly tradition, we etched our initials atop one of the metal rails circling the observation deck, and climbed back down into reality. Haider produced three Nutella sandwiches from his bag and we all ate in silence at the base of the Tetraeder.

I walked towards the opposite end of the hilltop field and tried capturing the scene on my camera. The wind reverberated melancholic A minor chords as it brushed past the metal structure. Haider was on the guitar again. "Stairway to Heaven," he was playing, he told me later. I felt strange. I felt blue. Suddenly, my gloom subsided. I realized I was glad that I had come here with these two guys and that I wasn't talking with Chris anymore. Perhaps better days were ahead. Germany was full of surprises.

Sounds of church bells tolling rolled up the hill. The town of Bottrop was waking up. An elderly couple walking a yorkshire terrier passed right by me, his bark jolting me back to life. It was time to head home.

I walked back to David and Haider, and we all plodded down the hill, exhausted. Bottrop looked so much friendlier during the day. We got to the train station and soon boarded the train back to Essen. The train was as empty as the night before, and each of us claimed a row of seats to lie across, to soothe our aching backs.

"Hobo," Haider jabbed at me again, as I covered myself with his blanket to go to sleep.

"Good night, hobo," I replied, yawning.

Little did we know, we had boarded the wrong train that was going in the opposite direction and ended up in Borken. We didn't even bother getting off the train and just stayed on as it reached its terminus and pivoted back in the opposite direction. We passed again by Bottrop and finally reached Essen where we got off. I bid farewell to the guys and headed to Duisburg. I reached my apartment at 10:30 a.m. and went straight to bed.

7

June 15, 2011

Since that fateful morning at the Tetraeder, I've felt different—freer, lighter, perhaps even more cheerful. This new spring in my step took shape in spite of the fact that I wasn't any keener about the work I was doing. Max went on vacation, a road trip to the northernmost point of Europe with his brother, and left me alone laboring in the lab. Each day felt like eternity.

The reason I felt this good was our crew. We had been hanging out quite often. David and his roommate, Karen, hosted a potluck party at their place in Essen one night, and we all ended up crashing at their place after having such a blast we lost track of time. Cheap beer, sloppy homemade cocktails, engaging company, and large pots of food, what more could we ask for?

I found myself doing things I never thought I would, such as actually getting drunk for once. I quickly learned my lesson the hard way when I woke up the next day with such an awful hangover that I got sick in the lab and barely made it to the bathroom to throw up. I felt so under the weather that the mere thought of eating the bland cafeteria food made me even more nauseous, leaving me no choice but to skip lunch. I told Haider about it, and he immediately came over to my office and offered me half of the sandwich he had made for himself. He then cheered me up with some Bollywood songs on YouTube. Watching people dancing and singing on top of trains while tucking into Haider's toast with cheese and turkey breast, I felt more cared for than I had felt in years. After that day, Haider and I often had lunch together, and he was even considering moving into the kitchen of my apartment to avoid having to commute from Essen every day. The kitchen that Wendy and I shared was rather large, and she got along well with Haider. The more the merrier, right?

A long weekend was coming up. June 23 was Corpus Christi, which was a holiday in our part of Germany. It fell on a Thursday and if we took the Friday off as well, then we had four days to enjoy ourselves. We'd been talking about going to the Netherlands together among our Duisburg and Essen group. The planning somehow fell to me and Haider. We managed to book the train ticket on Thursday morning and a return ticket on Saturday afternoon, leaving Sunday open for spontaneous plans. We found a cheap hostel on the beach, with shuttle service to downtown Amsterdam, so we settled for it. I couldn't wait to get out of the cold and lonely lab and party a little in the summer sunshine.

Meanwhile, I'd been enjoying the company of Wendy. We went shopping in Dusseldorf at least twice. I was itching for something new, and decided I needed a haircut. Wendy, a self-proclaimed hair stylist, graciously offered to give me one for free. Suddenly my messy long hair was gone and I found myself with a short pixie cut. I felt very naked, looking at myself in the mirror. But it was a nice, attractive cut that suited me, I had to admit. My life was heading into unknown territory, but somehow, I liked it.

A few days later, the RISE organization invited every interning student in our area on a day trip. We were to visit the Zollverein coal mine museum and attend a concert at night. We met up at the Duisburg Hauptbahnhof, and I stood alongside Haider, David, and Will. Wendy had some important work to do with her lab group, so she couldn't make it. People were eagerly chatting away, the atmosphere a stark contrast to the awkward orientation event two weeks before. With my new sense of confidence, I introduced myself to a few girls from various parts of the US who were working in other labs across the region. I had fun getting to know them, and enjoyed the diversity.

A group of people were especially animated near the station doors. I decided to go over and have a look, and Haider, David, and Will followed me. A thin nerdy White guy wearing glasses and his tall, long haired, bearded friend were talking to the crowd, and people were laughing at all their jokes, hanging onto their every word. Wanting to see what all the hype was about, we followed along, and as the excitement cooled down a bit, I introduced myself and my friends to them. The thin guy was named Chris, and I immediately felt a knot in my stomach, hearing the familiar name. His friend was named Matt.

Soon, I realized that this Chris had nothing to do with the Chris I knew back in Montreal. He was loud, funny, silly, and extroverted. He studied medicine and was from New York. Soon we were chatting and laughing together. During the coal museum visit, perhaps against our better judgment, we climbed on empty coal wagons, one-upped each other with dangerous stunts on mining shafts, and tried every way to fuel our inner adrenaline junkies. We took pictures with weird faces mocking each other and everyone else. We probably looked like two dumb high school kids, and I relished every moment of it. I was honestly having a blast without a care in the world. Haider followed us closely from behind, watching us enviously as he cautiously stood back.

We had currywurst for dinner and our large group of students crowded the small food joint. We sat at a table, Chris, Matt, Haider, David, Will, and I. I was starting to enjoy all the male attention. Even though I was one of the few women in my math and physics program at McGill, I was generally treated as one of the guys. Here, however, doors were opened for me, food was offered to me, and compliments were showered on me. I was clearly the lady of the bunch, and it was nice.

The evening concert was in Essen. The event, which took place at the largest concert hall in the city, was surprisingly packed with easily over a thousand people who filled the mid-century tiered seating all the way up to the balconies.

The concert featured a pianist who must have been well-known given the impressive turnout. She played standard classical repertoire for the first half and improvised the second half. I felt my fingers itching wistfully, my heart pounding as I saw her sitting at the concert grand piano on stage, and I was in the audience. It felt wrong, like it should have been the other way around. Chris, the one from the RISE program, sat on my left, while Haider sat on my right. I was playing my own internal iteration of name that song by guessing the name of each piece she played from the first few notes, which both guys found quite entertaining. I knew I could have easily played most of what she played without much practice. I felt wistful, and had a fleeting thought that I might have been wasting my talents as my skills lay dormant.

After the intermission, the pianist came back and asked the audience to sing her a tune. Then she would improvise a song based on the tune she heard only once. Watching this little game she played with us brought back vivid memories of my friends daring me to play whatever random pop song they thought to sing, most of which I had never heard before given that I wasn't exactly a pop culture aficionado. It was my specialty to improvise new songs this way, and now I was watching her performing my old trick. I casually whispered that to both guys, and Chris dared me to sing a hard tune to trick her.

I debated in my mind whether I could pass up such an opportunity. Not one to normally speak out in front of so many people, my impulse was to stay silent. However, Chris continued to egg me on.

Eventually, he presented an offer I couldn't refuse. "Do it, and you can have this piece of chocolate." He winked, and showed me a piece of chocolate filled with caramel fondant, my mouth watered at the sight of it.

Imbued with the confidence of sitting between these two guys and fueled by all their attention, I raised my hand the next time she asked for volunteers to give her a melody. She picked me!

For a second, I froze. But Chris immediately nudged me.

I stood up and delivered to the best of my ability the first eight verses of "Un Bel Di Vedremo" from the opera *Madame Butterfly*. I was no singer, but my classical music training did give me an edge when it came to emulating sounds and staying on tune. The audience went quiet while I was singing, and as I finished the last few notes, everyone broke into applause. Here I was, triumphant after all, lapping up applause in a concert hall! The world felt right again.

As I sat down, Chris looked at me, mesmerized at what I'd just done. Haider had also looked at me with longing, but I didn't notice at the time. I took the chocolate from Chris's hand nonchalantly and delighted in its sweet flavours, as the chocolate melted under my tongue and the caramel dissolved not long after. I was starting to really like my life, which felt almost dreamlike. The rest of the concert passed by me as I replayed what had just happened on loop in my head. These kinds of things don't happen to people like me, or do they?

That night, Haider insisted on going far out of his way to escort me all the way back to the Duisburg Hauptbahnhof before heading back by himself all the way to Essen.

The next day, during lunch, Haider told me he wasn't feeling well. I asked him what was up, and he confided in me that a close friend of his had decided to stop talking to him. He was quite upset.

"Her name is Jane," he said. "She's a Korean girl, your age, living with her single mom. She's one of my only friends over the past two or three years. I know it might be hard for you to believe, but I don't get close to people easily, but I guess I've been rather fond of her. Her mom however, from what I gather, has been hurt by men more than once in the past, and I feel sorry for her. Unfortunately, she saw me as no different from these men and told Jane to cut contact with me."

I wondered if it had anything to do with him being brown skinned. This kind of thing wasn't unheard of. It was just one of those things you think but never talk about. Strangeness is an unspoken enemy for most, and his South Asian brownness might have been too much for their lighter-skinned East Asian heritage, a culture with its prejudices similar to mine. It might not be malicious, but subconscious, so pervasive that I even saw some of this reticence in myself. The exact reason for this instinctive distancing wasn't apparent at first, but it dawned on me when he brought up what happened with Jane.

"I'm sorry to hear that," I responded. I genuinely was sorry. Not just for what happened with Jane, but for the unfair, dismissive way I had found myself treating him. I vowed to do better from now on.

"I hope it is for the best."

I hoped so too. I told him that I also recently cut contact with someone. I told him about Chris, our failed relationship, about how he didn't want me the same way I wanted him, so I needed him out of my life, and how I was still hurting somewhere deep inside.

"People in your life will leave," Haider said, "this is how this world works. But new people also enter your life to make it richer and fuller."

He was right. *Was he one such new person?* I stood there, surprised at where my mind had taken me, but this surprise left me with an unusual tingling of warmth and comfort.

Despite everything, I was feeling alright, better than before. I was looking forward to something new. I was looking forward to our trip to Amsterdam.

8

Today is the day was my first thought when I woke up. My phone indicated 6 a.m. I was early even for the early morning train, which was unusual. I had been looking forward to this trip for days.

A few moments later, Wendy was up and had put herself together. We whipped up an unusually elaborate breakfast that consisted of milk, eggs, and good old Nutella toast. The beaming sun was shining high and bright near the peak of the summer solstice. After showering and packing up, I put on my new shorts I had made the week before from cutting up my old pair of jeans that had ripped when I skinned my knee in the Duisburg forest. I used to feel that shorts were too daring and revealing for me, but more and more I had been venturing out of my comfort zone lately, and so far, I loved it, so to hell with self-made rules. Feeling the waft of crisp cool morning air through our kitchen window however, I topped off my outfit with my favourite white sweater, with a Pegasus spreading its wings printed on it, and a bright yellow scarf. I combed my short pixie-cut hair so that it was all sticking in the right direction, and we headed out.

We met up with Haider, David, and Will at the Duisburg Hauptbahnhof to embark on the long-distance ICE train to Amsterdam. It was truly a beautiful day, without a cloud in sight, and our spirits were high. The international train was substantially more comfortable than the regional trains, with two groups of three seats facing each other separated by a table in the middle. We stuffed our luggage into the overhead compartments and sat in our seats, cheerfully awaiting the whistle of the conductor that signaled the train's impending departure. Soon we were cruising at the speed of the autobahn.

After a three-hour ride, we arrived, half asleep from the train's gentle rocking, but nevertheless enthusiastic. The weather, though, was playing a trick on us and it started pouring rain. I was the only one with an umbrella, and after trial and error, we established that one umbrella wasn't enough to cover five people. We ran to the nearest tourist information booth and shop. Haider got an umbrella, the only kind available, in the city's iconic neon orange hue.

"No car's ever going to hit you with a flashy umbrella like that," Wendy teased him.

"You can't look more like a tourist," David joined in.

Haider laughed along but seemed a little annoyed. I offered to exchange my sky-blue umbrella from China with his, and we both felt happier for it.

"Alright, let's find out what we can do in this city," Haider declared.

We settled on taking a free walking tour of the city, followed by a boat tour through the canals in the early evening to soak up every extra hour of daylight. We each bought a three-day pass that gave us access to most museums and tours. The rain slowly subsided as we arrived at the intersection where the walking tour was to depart from.

"Hello everybody! My name is Andreas, and I will be your guide this afternoon!" A young man with shoulder length curly blond hair announced over a speaker. "How's everyone doing? Louder? Did I hear you people say 'good'? Great, welcome to Amsterdam! You will soon notice that we Dutch people can be a little bit quirky and have a weird sense of humor. Don't fret, deep down we're nice people even though we don't seem so when we're riding our bikes and yelling at pedestrians and cars!"

And thus began our introduction to Amsterdam. I felt rejuvenated by the young and cheerful crowd. Amsterdam's canals, bridges, and old buildings spoke to my inner European. I felt like I'd been here, in another life, as cliché as it sounds. I'd have worn a camel-coloured trench coat over a vintage knee-length dress, with a black umbrella over my head, which was adorned with tight ringlets. I imagined myself having come back from the market, with fresh produce and bread, on my way home to a cute but narrow house facing a canal. How strange and surreal. I marvelled at all the little shops, the beautiful boats full of flowers, the overflow of bicycles, the sharp triangular roofs of the houses bordering the water. What a world of difference from plain, grey, industrial Duisburg.

"Don't be fooled by the prettiness of the canals," Andreas suddenly warned us. "Do you see that boat with a mechanical arm right there? Do you know what it's doing? Fishing for bicycles that people dump in the canals instead of properly disposing of them. Do you know how many they fish out per year? Fifteen thousand. I'll let you guys digest this for a bit."

I suppose every place has its quirks. The chic slender windows of the tall, narrow townhouses surrounding us kept me wondering. What does it feel like to live inside a fairytale?

"I think you've all noticed how narrow and tall the buildings in Amsterdam are," interrupted Andreas. "This is because the land tax is determined by how wide the facade of a building is. Here is the skinniest building in town, it's 2.2 metres wide. That would be the only building I could afford to live in, I think." Andreas chuckled to himself.

What an odd world we live in, but it isn't without its charm. The guided tour gently eased to its end.

"All I ever hear about this city is the Red Light District and the cannabis," Haider commented. "I didn't realize it was so beautiful."

I agreed. It was beautiful as long as we chose to see beauty in it. We grabbed some stroopwafels around the corner and headed to the port for the boat tour. Food in hand, all of us were exuberant. We sat in the boat, and soon were off into the bay. We took pictures in every direction and then took pictures of each other.

"Liz, look into the camera," Haider called out.

"No, look into *my* camera," David teased.

"Hey, over here!" Will mocked.

"Guys, I can't!" I laughed until my cheeks started feeling warm and tingling. So much attention on me. This was starting to be a trend, especially over these past few weeks. I wrapped the yellow scarf I had in my hand around my head over my face. "No more pictures," I pleaded. Everybody laughed. They probably knew I was secretly enjoying it.

The boat was now roaming through the canals, and people strolling across bridges and walking along the shores were cheering at us. They were waving their hands, shouting hellos, and singing. I had never experienced anything quite like this before. The atmosphere was exhilarating.

"What a party we're in," Haider shouted into my ears.

"I'm really enjoying it too," I replied.

Haider smiled and asked me to take a picture of him standing against the clear blue sky.

"Here, you like it?" I showed him the picture.

"Yes! Don't I look happy?" Haider remarked, grinning.

After the boat tour, it was time to head back to the train station. We barely made it on time to catch the 8 p.m. shuttle to the hostel that was located a half hour outside the city, near the beach. The five of us squeezed into a seven-passenger van that already had three people besides the driver.

"Everybody ready to party some more?" the hippie-looking tattoo-covered driver shouted as the old car started moving and squeaking.

We cheered to dance songs by MGMT as we watched the iconic Dutch windmills whirl by us on the side of the road.

"Have you been to the Flying Pig Hostel before?" The driver asked us, a joint casually dangling from his mouth.

"First time in the Netherlands!" all five of us replied in unison.

"You guys are going to like it so much there," the driver said, smiling at us. "We're all just like a family up there, and we're such a diverse group that you'll all fit right in!"

We arrived at a beat-up little house, half falling apart, painted in cheerful colours both inside and out. Walking in, we faced a giant mural featuring a pink pig with wings. We checked in and left our luggage inside our rooms, the boys in a shared six-person room, and Wendy and I in a four-person room facing theirs. It was already 9 p.m. by the time we got there, but it was still light out. We decided to hit the beach.

Haider carried his guitar out, looking more laid back than usual in his black flip flops, followed by David and Will in their usual T-shirts and khakis. I came out with

Wendy a couple minutes later, having swapped out our light sweaters and comfy sneakers with tank tops and flip-flops. The beach was a mere five-minute walk away, right around the corner after a few luxury hotels. The weather was too cold for a swim, but not chilly either. Soon we all sat on the bare sand and enjoyed the light sea breeze.

"It's been a while since I've been able to run on a beach," Haider said. "You guys watch my hoodie and stuff. I'll be back soon."

He left barefoot and was soon lost in the distance. Wendy was sitting beside me, and David and Will were across from us. I looked at them. Then I looked at Haider's silhouette disappearing in the distance. I felt a strange longing, so I stood up and started moving in his direction.

The sun was glaring golden in the middle of the North Sea to my left, making the water glitter like a handful of scattered diamonds. The sky stretched from yellow to pink to purple. The fancy hotels on my right, facing the ocean, were basking in the waning day's warm hues. I saw Haider slowing his run to a steady-paced walk in the distance.

"Haider!" I shouted.

He heard and turned around to face me. I waved my hand at him, and he reciprocated.

"Hey!" he called out. "I'm glad you came!"

I was glad too, I told him. I was enjoying the sunset and the sea. Soon, I was walking alongside him. Haider's skin was glowing red in the setting sun.

"I spent last summer in Singapore for an internship at the NUS, the National University of Singapore," he told me. "It was a rather dark period of my life. I was severely overweight and barely sleeping at night. When I got to Singapore, I thought to myself, here I am far from home, it is time I piece my life back together. And so I started getting up at 4 a.m. every day to run. The air was humid over there, and breathing was hard. The first day, I ran a hundred metres and was exhausted for days. But then I started running two hundred, five hundred, one kilometre, five kilometres. I lost 30 kilos by the end of the summer. I haven't been able to run since that time because I developed runner's knees."

A gentle breeze from the ocean blew our way as a rare seagull flew past us, gliding gently above the water.

"I missed those running days," Haider continued, "and I missed the sea, which I haven't seen since Singapore last year. I grew up by the sea in Kuwait, and it was such a familiar sight."

He paused a little, and then continued, "You know, it is nice to live at home. I love my mom, and my dad too. I love my two sisters dearly and will defend them with my life. But the solitude of travelling brings something else. It makes you crave something new, something foreign, something extraordinary."

Haider stopped in his tracks and turned his whole torso towards me. "I've been observing you for the past few weeks. How you talk, how you walk, how you interact with others. And I've been wondering about you. Are you happy? What will make you happy?"

Could that have come off as creepy? Perhaps to other girls, but in that moment, I knew he was genuine. I stood still and held my breath.

"Liz, can I make you happy?"

Haider extended his hand out for me to hold. I stood between Haider and the sea. As time came to a standstill, something in the atmosphere changed imperceptibly, as if we were crossing the thin threshold between one world and the next. I looked at Haider, his hand in mid air and his face pleading. I glanced back at the sea, deep and impenetrable. There was only one thing to do at this moment that made sense. I hesitated, and went for it, oblivious to consequences and repercussions.

I reached out my hand to his, and his large palm grasped my slim fingers in a firm and warm grip. In an instant, my whole life tumbled and turned onto its head irreversibly. How we got from the edge of the world back to the beach, where the five of us hung out earlier, was a blur. By the time we got there, the sun had set, and we found our sandals half buried in the sand, without any trace of our bags or his guitar. Probably the three others took everything back with them.

We made our way to the Flying Pig Hostel in semi-darkness and found the lobby full of young people sitting around and laughing, doing what drunk young people do.

"Hey guys!" Wendy shouted as she saw us from the window. "Apparently Will has won the bet!"

"What bet?" Haider and I asked in unison as we entered the front door. We exchanged quizzical glances.

"He said that you guys were going to come back holding hands. Honestly, we all thought so too."

Haider let out a hearty laugh. I giggled nervously. How did everyone see it coming before I did? Was I this blind to human affairs? Was I really a clueless, heartless physics nerd?

Haider and I sat for a while side by side on the couch, tired from the long day, surrounded by Wendy, David and Will. We made a little bit of small talk. Haider had his arm loosely around my back, resting on the backrest of the couch. It suddenly dawned on me that nobody, not even my own father, had ever gestured toward me like this before, protective of me. I smiled to myself as the chatter wound down, and we all headed upstairs to our rooms.

"I'll be running again tomorrow morning at 7 a.m.," Haider whispered to me before I entered my room. "Good night, Liz! Sleep well!"

Was that an invitation? I wondered.

I spent the night tossing and turning in bed. Should I wake up for the 7 a.m. run? Of course I was going to be there. That wasn't even a question. But where were we heading like this, the two of us? What would become of me? What was the meaning of life and the meaning of what happened tonight? Why did he ask me if he could make me happy? Could he make me happy? Could anyone make me happy? What was the meaning of happiness anyway? Was I happy? Were things getting out of hand? What would tomorrow be like?

9

June 24, 2011

The next morning, I woke up naturally at 7 a.m. sharp, awakened by the thought, "Is Haider out yet?" I dressed quickly and quietly, wearing a sandy wool poncho over a light blue T-shirt and jean shorts. Peeking my head out into the hallway, I saw the door to Haider's room was ajar. Haider was out already. I took a bag of assorted cookies I had brought from Duisburg Hauptbahnhof and headed out of the Flying Pig Hostel.

The day was bright but cloudy, and I was hit by the sudden chill of an ocean wind. When I arrived at the beach, there was no one, only Haider's sandals. I walked in the direction he had taken the night before. Whereas last night the sea water was warm, this morning it felt cold to the touch. I held my poncho tightly against me and walked at a steady pace. Where would I find Haider? Where would I find comfort?

"Liz, you came!" Haider's eyes brightened as he suddenly appeared beside me. "How was your night?"

"It was a long one," I answered him earnestly. "How was yours?"

"I barely slept either. But running on the beach this morning made me feel better. Come, run with me."

And so we slowly jogged along the shore at a steady pace, feeling our feet pounding against the soft sand, hearing the waves crashing with that gentle sound. As the tide came in, the sea lapped against our feet with increased frequency, beckoning us. I jogged in silence, the sound of his and my breathing pulsating rhythmically with the predictable sound of the waves.

After an indeterminate amount of time, Haider spoke up. "I have known you for but a few weeks," he said. "And yet my heart has set itself upon you and will not have anything else. The heart has its own reason, they say. I've never understood the statement until now."

Haider paused a little.

"You're so quiet, Liz. Are you alright?"

I'd been in Germany for barely a month and in the Netherlands for barely a day. I had officially broken up with Chris less than two weeks ago, and last night, I held hands with a near-stranger. This was all happening way too fast.

"Haider, I don't know where things are going. Here I am, alone in Europe with a bunch of people I've known only for a couple weeks," *and yet, somehow we feel like family,* I thought. Nevertheless, I couldn't help but ask, "What will become of all this?"

"Liz, are you happy with how things have turned out so far?"

"I don't know, to be very honest. It's been happening too fast."

"Is that your mind or your heart talking? Listen to your heart; let it tell you what it wants."

I felt perplexed. What did that even mean? Out of nowhere Haider came into my life. What was I to do with it? Perhaps he was ready for love, for a serious relationship. Perhaps he had prepared his entire life for this moment, as per his culture. But not me. I was still trying to figure every-thing out. I was frozen in silence. Could he understand that?

"You know, there is a famous Bollywood movie. It's about two young Indians living in England who met on a trip to Europe. They fell in love, but the girl was already engaged to someone back in India and was about to get married. The guy whom she met in Europe chased her down to India and convinced her whole family to let her marry him instead."

"And what happened in the end?"

"They ended up together. It's a happy movie."

"That's sweet."

"Life is not always a smooth path, but if you follow your heart, *dil*, as we say in Hindi, it will lead you to the right place."

I nodded. But deep inside, I felt a quiet uneasiness. What did I want exactly? I'd not asked myself that question in a long time now, because I didn't think I could have a say anymore. *Not since I'd given up my music dream.* But I didn't want to think about that, so I tried to push the thought away.

At my anxious face, Haider smiled and proceeded to hum a Bollywood tune to distract me. He was a good singer, I had to concede.

"What song is that?" I asked him, curious.

"It's the theme song of that movie."

"I want to learn a Hindu song," I said.

Haider laughed and rolled his eyes.

"Sweetie, a Hindu is a believer in Hinduism. You mean Hindi, the language."

"A Hindi song," I corrected myself, laughing, but continued, "I have a goal, which is to learn songs in as many languages as possible. So far I know songs in eight languages."

"Which ones?"

"Chinese, English, French, Spanish, Russian, Latin, Hebrew, and Italian," I said, regaining my confidence.

Haider looked impressed.

"I'll teach you a Hindi song, the one from that movie."

"Deal!"

And so he began singing, verse by verse, while I repeated after him. He stopped abruptly.

"I see what you've got here …." Haider, smirking, was staring straight at the pack of cookies I had hidden under my poncho until now. "Why didn't you tell me?"

He snatched them right out of my hands with a grin.

"Hey, they're mine!" I protested.

I jumped towards him, and he started running. I ran as fast as I could on the slippery sand, caught his shirt, and pulled the cookies towards me.

"Ha! Got them!"

Haider laughed, crying out, "No, give me!" as he ran towards me.

I slowed down and we shared the cookies while laughing about what had just happened. Haider and I sat down on the cool morning sand, and he put his arm over my shoulder.

"Thanks for bringing the cookies, Liz. You're so sweet." Haider smiled at me.

I smiled back at him. I was feeling better than earlier. We were about to sit back and enjoy the moment a little when the overcast skies opened wide and poured down upon us. A big storm was brewing over the once-gentle sea.

"Let's go!" we both exclaimed. We needed to find shelter.

We found our flip-flops and ran towards the nearest hotel along the shore. One of the fancier hotel buildings, it had a canopy that extended over the sidewalk and we stood underneath it. My poncho was covered in large raindrops, their dark splotches interspersed between dry patches. So was Haider's T-shirt.

"What a day." Haider laughed. "But thoroughly worth it!"

"This hotel looks really fancy," I remarked.

Through the glass door of the hotel, we saw a beautiful marble hall with lush red carpet, a dazzling crystal chandelier, and many smartly dressed valets walking about.

"Next time, when we come back here," Haider said, winking at me, "we'll stay in a place like this."

"That would be so sweet." I couldn't help but smile.

The rain was slowing down.

"Come, let's head back to the hostel and join the others. It's getting late," Haider said. He held out his hand again for me to hold.

I took his hand, and we walked back hand in hand to the Flying Pig Hostel.

We joined Wendy, David, and Will for breakfast, and all of us spent the day touring museums, starting with Anne Frank's house, the exact building where she hid for two years from the Nazis during the Holocaust. The house was packed with tourists.

"Who is Anne Frank?" Haider asked me, unexpectedly.

"How could you not know who she was?" I asked incredulously. I was rather shocked. Wasn't this supposed to be taught in every school's curriculum?

"Sorry, I come from a different part of the world," Haider replied quietly.

He was right. I should've been more considerate. I told him about Anne's diary while we were touring her hidden apartment. I spoke about her legacy to the world. Haider listened to me intently and grew steadily in his appreciation of the exhibition.

"I can't imagine how hard it must've been for her," Haider told me as we were heading out of the museum. "I survived the Gulf War in Kuwait when I was a toddler, and we had to flee back to India for safety. I don't remember much from it, but it left a mark on everyone in my family."

What was it like for anyone to survive a war? I wondered to myself. How far-fetched it was from my own reality. I realized that as much as I was inspired by Anne Frank's diary, Haider had a better understanding of her situation than I did, even though he hadn't heard of her before.

We headed to the Van Gogh Museum next.

"He's the one who painted the sunflowers, right?" Haider asked.

"Yes!" I was happy he knew him at least.

The exhibit went over the whole life of the painter, from his childhood to being a missionary to his days in the asylum and possible suicide.

"Who knows how much darkness can hide in his soul when looking at how beautiful his art is?" Haider commented.

I could relate to Van Gogh though, having spent most of my years since childhood fighting unknown demons and trying to escape reality, to an imaginary world. I grew quiet and left the exhibit in a pensive mood.

"Any plans for the evening?" Wendy asked.

"We're in Amsterdam, we gotta at least check out the Red Light District a little bit," I proposed. "What do the guys think of this?" I asked with a wink.

"Sure, you girls go ahead," Haider answered firmly. "It's not my thing."

"Yeah it's overrated," Will continued.

"Let's go back to the beach hostel," David concluded.

Did all three guys just turn down an opportunity for free eye candy? I couldn't believe it. Was I really more foul-minded than three college-age guys? I thought back to the stereotype about people from Quebec, that we are more, shall we say, sex positive than the rest of the West? I always felt like I was extremely conservative and backward sexually compared to my friends in Montreal, but here I was the experienced daredevil. For once in my life, I was the cool person who was showing everyone else the ropes. It felt kind of empowering.

"Let's ditch the guys and head to the Red Light District on our own," Wendy said, smiling at me. I was pleasantly surprised to be hearing that from her, as I had always thought she was rather innocent and cautious.

"Alright, sounds like a plan!" My curiosity had gotten the best of me.

We spent the evening walking through dimly lit streets packed with men and, surprisingly, many women stopping every so often to catch a glimpse of window after window of scantily clad women posing under neon lights. "Don't even think of taking their pictures," tour guide Andreas had warned us the day before. "They will jump out the window and smash your camera into the canals." I was surprised to see how diverse the women were: there were the tall, blonde, young Dutch women I had expected to see, but also older women, women of colour, and women of all shapes and sizes. I was impressed.

We kept an eye out for blue lights inside windows; these workers, according to Andreas, did kinky stuff. We saw some leather corsets and a few whips. We walked past sex shops and erotic shows. Having been exposed to what felt like a lifetime's supply of X-rated content, Wendy and I came back to the downtown Amsterdam branch of the Flying Pig Hostel only slightly past midnight. We had decided to save ourselves the trouble and not go all the way back to the beach hostel that night. Instead, we found two beds in a cramped eight-person room.

I made a pack of instant noodles using the hostel's dishes and hot water. Sipping the artificial chicken-flavoured soup, I felt happy and free, wishing for more days like this.

The next day, Wendy and I met up with the guys who came from the beach hostel on the shuttle van around mid-morning.

"Our train is in the afternoon," Haider said. "Do you guys want to go visit that cheese factory we passed on the walking tour on Thursday?"

"I was going to suggest the same!" I answered. We were in sync, it seemed.

The cheese factory was offering a one-hour cheese tasting session. We happily signed up and we were presented with different cheeses: nutty flavoured, stinky, mild, soft, hard and everything in between. In between each tasting, wine was served to cleanse the palate.

"Boy I'll be drunk by the end of this session," I whispered to Haider sitting next to me.

"I'll serve you smaller sips then," he answered. "That's more for me!"

Haider was a mess of contradictions, which I loved because I knew that I was as well. He was too conservative for the Red Light District, but totally on board with alcohol. *I thought Muslims didn't drink.*

After the cheese tasting, we chatted with the men working at the gift shop. One of them even offered to sing us a Dutch song using Haider's guitar. I loved how open and warm the Dutch people were. Haider happily lent Lisa, his prized instrument, and a jamming session ensued. Haider also played a few songs, to my delight. I always had a thing for musicians, and he was actually good.

"Let's head to the train station before it's too late," I reminded everyone.

We headed to the station and passed by a church on the way. Both Haider and I wanted to take a look, so we went in. We faced an eight-person choir preparing for a recital. We were on the early side for our train, so we had plenty of time. We sat down and let the music sink in.

"This is so beautiful," Haider whispered to me. "What a beautiful ending to our trip here. Did you have fun?"

"I think I did." I smiled back.

Soon after, we were boarding the ICE train back to Duisburg and most of us fell asleep in our seats. It was late afternoon by the time we arrived. I looked at Haider as we got off the train. Was this it? Was he going to bid me farewell?

"Liz, do you want to hang out at the Starbucks for a bit?" he finally asked me.

I did. We headed to the Starbucks, but David followed us.

"This trip was so much fun!" David exclaimed.

"It was." Haider smiled, and I nodded.

"What are you guys up to now?" David continued.

"Just chilling," Haider was kind enough to answer him.

"Sorry, am I disrupting you guys?" David finally realized.

We both laughed.

"It's okay man." Haider smiled at him. "I have to go anyway. I have to pack my stuff, I'm moving to Liz and Wendy's kitchen tomorrow!"

"Aw man, good for you," David smiled back.

"Let's go to Essen together," Haider suggested as he stood up. "Liz, I'll see you tomorrow at 9! Take care!"

He kissed me on the forehead and left with David. I stood in the middle of the Starbucks, all alone. What on earth had come over me on this whirlwind trip to the Netherlands? I stood disoriented. Was this how a love story was supposed to start?

10

June 26, 2011

The next morning was a Sunday, and we were all off work, so Haider came with his suitcases and a small mattress that his supervisor kindly gave him and delivered at our door by car. He was grateful to be closer to where he was working at the University in Duisburg. The long commutes from Essen by train were a drag. Wendy and I both suspected that he just wanted to be closer to me, but that's just speculation.

Wendy and I were happy to have Haider join us. Our neighbourhood already had seven foreign students including Wendy and me. They had gradually trickled in after we moved in. First, there was Siddhartha, a Nepali-British guy studying aerospace engineering like Haider, who was sharing a flat in the next building with Kimchung, an American guy, originally from Hong Kong, studying physics, whom Siddartha called "Ching Chang Chung" to tease him. Then, Patrick from MIT moved into his own flat around the block. Finally, two new girls moved into a flat right downstairs from our place: Camilla, a White American girl studying physics, and Lilian, a Vietnamese American girl studying chemical engineering. Having so many students in our vicinity made living here a lot more fun and exciting. I felt a lot less like a foreigner since we were all foreigners, so … none of us were?

Wendy and I spent the morning helping Haider settle down. We moved the kitchen table to the side and put his mattress under the window. The kitchen was so large that it didn't appear crammed at all. Haider was very grateful to be there and thanked Wendy and me profusely.

I watched Haider unpack his stuff. I was the queen of light packers, and my friends were often shocked at sleepovers when I would come with just my cloth hippie purse I had bought off a street vendor in New York City. Meanwhile, Haider looked like he had double the amount of stuff I had brought to Germany. *I thought guys were supposed to be lighter packers than girls.*

"What can I say, my mom won't let me go without having everything 'just in case,'" Haider explained with a shrug. "Mother's love, there's nothing you can do about it."

My mom didn't even look over my luggage once, I thought to myself. *What did it feel like to live in such a close-knit, warm, and caring family?* I wondered. Why were people in my family so distant and reserved in comparison? On the other hand, I appreciated my independence and couldn't imagine being watched over like that well into my twenties.

"What are these?" I asked Haider about a collection of old pill bottles Haider had arranged in a neat line on the wooden square-shaped kitchen table. I was a little concerned, and, of course, Haider read it on my always-transparent face.

"Spices." Haider laughed. "In case I cook, my mom wanted to make sure I have what I need."

"Is she expecting you to cook fancy meals here, all alone by yourself?" I asked, incredulous.

"Am I supposed to waste money by eating out every day or have only ramen for three months?"

Well, that was a good point, I guess.

"Liz, how do you ask a girl on a date?" Haider suddenly asked me.

I giggled shyly.

"Why are you asking me this?" I replied.

"Liz, I've never done this before," Haider said in a serious tone. "I come from a conservative country. The furthest I've been before was shaking hands with a girl I like. That was the girl who's now married to another man."

I silently pondered the ocean of difference between our relationship experiences, thinking back to when I gave Chris my virginity in the middle of the night after our last final a month before. I was the last one in my friend group to cross that threshold. Now I was the experienced one?

"In movies, the guy asks the girl out," Haider said, "and if she says yes, he drives to her house to pick her up, and then he takes her to a restaurant. I want to do things the right way. But what do I do now since we're already living in the same apartment?"

"Do what you think is best?" I mused. I wasn't one to talk about conventional relationships. "Be creative."

"I have been cooking lately in fact, and I think my skills are improving," Haider said. "Let me cook a meal for you and let's date in our own way at home."

"What are you making me?" I winked at him, actually trying to be flirty with a guy for the first time, I just realized.

Haider flirted right back.

"What kind of food do you like?"

"I like Italian food." I said in a dreamy voice, "When I was little, one of our neighbours was an elderly Italian lady, and I've come to call her my Italian grandma. My mom would come home late from work, and I'd stay at her place, and she cooked the best Italian dishes. She used to work at an Italian restaurant."

"Well hold on a bit," Haider replied. "My cooking is hardly restaurant quality. For that I'll have to invite you to my mom's house. But I did make risotto the other day and it was rather good. Do you like risotto?"

"I've never had it before, but if it's Italian food, I'll give it a try." I smiled.

And so that evening, Haider took over our kitchen and took possession of all our utensils, which my mom's friend's daughter, Xin, had lent to me. They had never been used by Wendy or me. He mixed chicken stock with water in a pot, and sautéed the rice with mushrooms in a saucepan. I was impressed by his setup—more than one thing on the stove at a time? Unheard of. A little sage and thyme here, a little butter there. He looked like a pro to me.

"I'll have to skip the white wine though, that's not within the budget," Haider explained.

"It's way fancy enough for me as it is," I answered.

"We'll also have to skip the romantic candlelight part I'm afraid, perks of dating a sketchy brown guy," Haider continued, "but you can have me, all of me."

I chuckled. "This is getting corny," I said. Secretly I loved it.

We both laughed. Dinner was ready, and I was treated to a rich mushroom risotto with garlic bread and salad on the side. Homely, if not downright fancy in my opinion, even with the spartan kitchen, the wobbly wooden table, and the mismatched chairs. It was really delicious, I had to admit. We enjoyed the meal in silence—it was a pleasure in its own right—until we were both done, and Haider and I locked eyes.

"Can I kiss you?" Haider asked.

"Come closer," I answered him.

Haider moved his head closer to mine over the table. It was small enough that if we stood up and arched our backs, we could meet in the middle. I looked at his silky brown skin, his high arched nose, his fierce angled brows, his thin brown lips just a touch darker than his skin. I couldn't help but wonder how I ended up with such an ... exotic-looking guy? He was completely different from what I was used to. But I closed my eyes, held my breath, leaned in, and kissed him on the lips.

"I love you, Liz," Haider said as we both opened our eyes.

I felt a flicker of fear inside me. That was way too fast. What did this mean? What did his love entail? What did he want from me? I still barely knew him at all!

"Liz, let's go into your room, let me hug you."

We both walked into my room, closed the door and sat on my cheap IKEA twin bed that looked fit for a child. Was I ready for this? What was I getting myself into? Naturally, he could see the apprehension on my face.

"Are you alright, Liz?"

I felt empty inside. This talk of love frightened me. Chris flashed into my mind. How desperately I wanted him to love me, and yet as Haider loved me so fiercely, so freely, after such a short time, here I was, recoiling and unwilling to accept it? What did I really want?

I was enthralled by him, of course I was, but I'd also just come down from a barrage of milestones, with changes hitting me at once from every side. Finishing my first year of college, losing my virginity, moving out of my parents' house for the first time .... It was all so overwhelming; it was all happening so fast. I was torn between wanting to slow down to catch my breath and wanting to give everything a try since I knew I only had one summer here with him. But it wasn't just that.

It then dawned on me that giving up my childhood music dream, which had meant the world to me, followed by resigning myself unhappily to math and physics, had turned me into what felt almost like an empty carcass. An empty carcass who was lost and only trying to find its way home. But how did I tell him?

I wanted to seize this love, this kindness he was offering me. I recognized the preciousness of having someone genuinely care about you, of being allowed to open up, to be heard, and to be understood. And I needed that, I realized. I took a few seconds to gather my thoughts, but they never truly settled.

"I ... I guess I ..." I could sense the concern on his face, which gave me the confidence to finally speak, "I've been hurting inside for years," I began. I trailed off, not knowing where to go from there. "Pain, from how my parents never understood me, from how the world is indifferent to what I want and how I feel, from Chris who rejected me. I put on a happy face in front of people, but that's not the truth ...."

My thoughts drifted back to my old life, back in Montreal. Since my teenage years, I'd become the dark, cynical one in my friend group, who wore all black and had long hair with long, thick emo bangs that obscured my eyebrows. It was almost as if I was hiding from the world, and perhaps from myself as well. I'd been using this trip so far as an opportunity to try on a different life like I would a new outfit at a store. An outfit that was not my usual style, but spoke to me somehow. I now found myself at a crossroads. This new bubbly persona I'd been taking on lately had become so embedded that I was now confused as to who I really was. Was this who I wanted to become permanently? What would make me happy?

"You have to be kind to yourself," Haider said, as if he were reading my mind.

"But how? The only thing I know how to do is hurt myself further to distract myself from the pain I already

feel. I'm a stranger to the kind of love you talk about."
Maybe I had been so enamored with Chris because he
gave me the only type of love that I thought I deserved?
A love so cold and distant and conditional that it didn't
really feel like love.

Haider looked concerned. He looked at me, hesitated,
then finally spoke.

"I've seen marks on your legs, were these done by you?"

My heart sank. He hadn't even seen the scar on my
chest above my breasts, or along my upper arms, or just
below my ribs.

Haider picked up on the fear in my eyes. The feeling
of exposure. Here I was, in my bedroom, naked, but fig-
uratively, not literally.

My thoughts had scattered like shards of glass amidst
grains of sand. By this point, I felt like a small animal
about to get trapped, blinded suddenly by the light of the
hunter's flashlight. The tension within me started to build
with each second I remained silent.

"Liz, I want to help. Feel free to tell me anything and
everything. I'm here for you."

I could tell he was genuinely concerned, which was
unlike anything I'd ever seen before. I was so overwhelmed
by the novelty of it, I didn't know what to do with it. So,
scrambling for words, I told the truth.

"Yeah, I used to hurt myself whenever I felt like
I wasn't good enough," I admitted.

"Liz, Elizabeth ..." Haider's brow furrowed with
worry. "That's not okay. It's never okay to hurt yourself."

I might have scoffed at such a comment normally.
Who did he think he was, just telling me to stop hurting
myself as if he had any idea of the kind of pain I felt, pain
that made no sense logically, so I subconsciously had to
make it real. These scars were the physical manifestation

of mental tumult and pain. How could he possibly know anything about that?

But somehow, I felt comfortable around him. I felt compelled to tell him the truth, because I knew on a deep level that he truly cared, that he was safe. Did this mean I loved him? Was it possible to love someone this quickly? I owed him an explanation, at the very least. He had earned his access to that part of me.

"The largest scar is here, above my left breast," I finally uttered, revealing my raw self. My words were so loaded that it was almost as if I had to handle them with care to avoid bursting.

I showed it to him, the discoloured burn mark in the shape of a cross about 4 cm wide and 8 cm long. I did it by sticking a scissor blade into a candle flame, then burning myself with it. I'd just turned fourteen and had failed to win a first prize at my first international piano competition despite months of intense practice. I had worked so hard, yet it just wasn't enough. On one hand, I felt that my efforts should have translated into results, but on the other hand, I was ashamed that I had cared so much about winning, that I had even thought I was good enough to deserve to win. Who did I even think I was? How dare I be this entitled? The only natural response was to punish myself for my undeserved pride.

I saw my disappointment at something that should have been a huge triumph, my best placement to date, as a sign that I had veered into sin, as I had been taught by my Catholic high school, which, having failed to make me a believer in God, had still made me internalize Christian morality. What's more, not only had I been proud enough to believe I deserved to win, but I had been greedy in wanting the victory and envious of the person who won it. I only had hatred for myself.

Haider's look of concern stood in stark contrast with Chris, who had actually thought the scar looked *cool*. I did not want to think about what Chris thought. *Especially not now.* I tried to push the thought away, as far from me as possible. Why was I caring about someone like Chris when I had someone like Haider?

"Oh dear God Liz!" Haider whispered, not just shocked, but flinching in a way, as if he was feeling my pain. "I've known you for such a short amount of time, but you already mean the world to me. Seeing you hurt makes me hurt so much. You know, I have something for you."

He stood up, went back to his luggage, and came into my room holding a small wooden angel painted in white in his hand.

"This was a gift from my sister. It's an angel that watches over you every time you are hurting. She gave it to protect me, but now it is yours, because you need the protection more than I do. Please, when you are hurting and want to injure yourself, think about the angel who still watches over you, think of me also hurting for you."

He handed me the angel and gave me a full frontal hug. I stood awkwardly as he held me in his arms, still overcome by the rawness of our exchange. I felt the angel in my hand. It reminded me of the dull, lifeless plaster angel statues inside my high school's chapel. His hug brought me little comfort.

"Has no one ever given you a hug before?" Haider finally laughed as he let me go. "You stood rigid as a log. We have to work on this. I have to teach you how to hug someone."

"I'm sorry, I'm a stranger to all of this," I said meekly.

"No, don't be sorry, sweetheart, you will learn how to hug, care, love, and be kind to yourself and others, I know you will," he comforted me.

Sweetheart. Nobody had ever called me that before. I couldn't help but feel warm and fuzzy hearing it. A feeling that was foreign to me: wanted, needed, treasured. It almost didn't feel real.

The following few days, I was slowly getting used to Haider's presence in my life.

"He's a really good guy," Wendy commented. "Be nice to him."

But I still resisted the idea of him. How on earth did he come into my life and what was I supposed to do with him? *Accept him, let it be,* Wendy would say. But was he even what I was looking for? What exactly *was* I looking for? Haider's ways confused me. What could he possibly want from me? I wondered.

We spent most of our days together, and everyone was happy that Haider was around. We hosted a potluck dinner party at our place the following Wednesday, and Haider wowed all of us with a casserole dish made from everything leftover in our fridge. We had a great time with the cheap beer that Kimchung brought and some burnt food, which Patrick had tried to cook up at our place. I showed them a new song I'd written using Haider's guitar, which I was starting to get the hang of. It was about our Netherlands trip.

Later, the boys all sat on my bed to play video games, and the poor little cheap IKEA bed collapsed under their collective weight. "Five boys sat on my bed and broke it," I chuckled to myself. "That sounded way dirtier than what happened in reality."

I was slowly warming up to Haider, and we spent much time cuddling on each other's beds. Then the next day, Haider asked me if he could just move into my room with me.

"Liz, I really want you in my life," he said. "Let us live together."

"Sure," I said. I was apprehensive—what could go wrong, right? But I decided to go with my gut and give it a try. I wanted it, wanted it a lot actually. Who was this person who agreed to share her room with a guy? I remembered how I was so adamant at the beginning of the summer to have a female roommate. What happened?

We reorganized the room entirely and removed the broken bed frame. It was clearly too frail to sustain both of us sleeping on it. The bare mattress was placed on the ground by the wall next to the bedside table. We decided—perhaps illogically—that one twin mattress was enough for both of us. It made things cozier. The desk and chair were placed at the other end of the room.

"This is our first place together," Haider declared exuberantly, as if it were a milestone we needed to document for posterity. "Decorate it at your will!"

I already had the map of Germany I had brought with me from Canada stuck on the wall above the bed. I added to it the map of Europe I had got at the Hauptbahnhof. I took out my collection of random colourful ads for concerts and events I had picked up at bars and cafes, and pinned them haphazardly on the bare white walls. Then I added to it my collection of postcards I had bought in Köln, Amsterdam, and Dusseldorf. Finally, I added a touch of music by hanging some sheet music, which I always have on hand anywhere I go. It wasn't that I was actually intending to play the music when I was out and about, but I always felt comforted somehow by its proximity to me.

On the other wall by the desk, Haider printed out several of his poems in pretty calligraphy-inspired fonts and pinned them in a row. The plain white walls of my room suddenly looked cheerful and inspired.

Digging through the pile of ads and random papers on my desk, Haider found a tourist ad with I ♥ Duisburg printed in large letters.

"Liz, let's hang it, this is perfect!" Haider exclaimed.

"Do you love Duisburg?" I retorted. "I don't. It's a small industrial steel town with nothing to do."

"You will miss it once you're back in Canada, trust me. It will be our Duisburg, the place where we had our first home together."

Our Duisburg. *Our* first home together. I had to let it sink in. Yes, I really just moved in with a guy for the first time in my life, a guy I didn't know existed a month ago. It felt surreal, like a whirlwind marriage. I was happy, yes, I was exuberant actually. I liked my new life. I liked this place that suddenly felt homey for the first time. This grey decrepit little town had somehow wormed its way into my heart after all. I was also shocked at how fast it all happened.

"Do you believe this is real?" I asked Haider. I still felt like I was living a life that was meant for someone else, like I had to pinch myself to make sure it was real, and that it was actually me that it was happening to. "Are we living in a dream?"

I just couldn't believe this was happening to me of all people. I felt this burst of happiness and optimism in me, of a kind I had never felt before. It was as if, for the entirety of my life, I was on autopilot, and now I finally was living, breathing, thriving. When I called my best friend Arielle back in Montreal, she told me matter-of-factly, "It's love, Liz, that's what love feels like."

I was loved. It was mind-blowing.

Haider looked back at me with the same intensity I looked at him.

"This is as real as the fact that you and I are standing together in this home of ours. Let me kiss you here, in our new home."

Haider literally swept me off my feet and held me in his arms. I grabbed his neck and we shared a breathtaking kiss that I thought only happened in movies. I felt my spirit soar despite myself, despite my anxiety, despite my misgivings, despite my disbelief at the way our lives had merged.

11

It had been a few days since we'd been living together, and the infatuation had only gotten more intense. We felt like our own little island in the middle of a barren world, and all we wanted to do was be together as time ran away from us. Haider and I barely came into the university to do work anymore and we spent all our free time together. Luckily for us, our supervisors didn't seem to care either, which goes to show how much undergraduates actually contributed. We didn't care about the consequences anyway, as we were all that mattered. Everything off our island was trivial. Was it love, I did not know. But when I saw Haider naked for the first time, I was repulsed.

Dressed, Haider was rather handsome. Tall, dark, put-together, and clean shaven. But with his shirt off, layers and layers of loose skin and stretch marks from his years struggling with weight issues were revealed. Luckily for me, I'd lived my whole life with the privilege of having a body that conformed to cultural norms, being slender and fairly light-skinned. I couldn't help but feel jarred when confronted with his reality. His nipples and genitals were charcoal grey, and having never seen a dark-skinned person naked, my first reaction was one of visceral disgust. I couldn't help but remember my mother who, after seeing a South Asian person's hands for the first time, commented that brown-skinned people looked like Chinese people who don't wash themselves. I tried my best to swallow my feelings down my throat, to flush them away.

"You don't like how I look," Haider clearly noticed my reaction; as much as I tried to hide it, I was, as usual, incapable of hiding my feelings. I felt awful. I knew how much his weight was a touchy subject for him, and I was ashamed at my intrinsic reaction to his colour. Dejected, he stammered apologetically, "I'm sorry I undressed too early. I'm sorry about my baggage. I'll wear clothes again."

"No, *I'm* sorry," I forcefully replied, feeling flooded by guilt. I was desperate to make up for this blow that I had inadvertently dealt him. "I never meant to make you feel bad, please forgive me. Come let me give you a blow job."

"You don't have to prove to me that you're fine with how I look. I know how you really feel." His response was biting.

I felt a mild panic at the turn of events. Did I blow everything? Did my disgusting, learned reaction just ruin the best thing that had ever happened to me?

"I'll have sex with you, really," I tried to turn things around. I pleaded with him, even convinced myself that having sex with him would somehow wash away these prickly feelings.

"Do you think I'm merely looking for sex?"

"Are you not?" I was surprised. "What guy isn't looking for sex?"

"Liz, Elizabeth sweetheart, you've disappointed me." Haider looked me in the eye. "Since the first day, I've told you that I wanted your happiness. I love you. I want you in my life. You, all of you, every facet, the good and the bad. And you still think I just want to sleep with you. How am I going to make you understand?"

I felt tears well up in my eyes, and I blinked fiercely to hold them back. Could I truly believe him? *Was he for real?*

Wasn't I told growing up that all guys were only after that one thing? Was I lucky enough to have met a unicorn?

I definitely felt like a monster for having judged him so harshly over something so superficial and immaterial, over *looks*. I thought I was better than the prejudice I was imbibed with, I thought I had risen above it. Was I doomed to repeat what I came from, to perpetuate the cycle? I suddenly felt trapped in a vortex I wasn't sure I could escape from.

"Here, sweetheart, don't cry," Haider put his arm around my waist and let my head rest on his shoulder. "Everything will be okay, I'm not angry at you. It's not your fault. Let's spend the evening watching some movies, shall we?"

I was so wowed by his empathy, the depth of his character that he had just exhibited, his ability to see past his own insecurities and understand where I was coming from with such clarity. He had given me the benefit of the doubt when I had done something so insulting, so unforgivable, that anyone else would have cut their losses to avoid any further damage. He was *committed*. That gave me a new-found appreciation of not only his heart, but even the body that sustained it. I had to see beyond it. I couldn't possibly let a man like this go.

We spent the evening watching *The Notebook*, *Amélie*, and *Breakfast at Tiffany's*. Happy endings had a way of getting to me. I cried my eyes out the whole time. I hadn't been able to cry like this for years; instead I'd been cutting myself using a knife to let blood out for temporary relief, resisting crying as a sign of weakness until, eventually, I grew numb to that intrinsic human urge. In my world, people didn't love each other. If they did, they didn't admit it. In my world, people didn't chase after pipe dreams, or when they did, they came back empty-handed. Could it be that true love still existed in our millennial generation, who spent more time inhabiting the digital world than in real life?

That night, we went to bed late. Haider held me in his arms as we lay facing each other, and I felt the warmth of his breath on my lips. We started cuddling gently, then tightly, and then passionately. We kissed as if hungry to swallow each other's faces. I felt his hands explore along my back, on my sides, on my thighs, as if he wanted to survey every inch of my body. Our legs twisted and interlaced, and our tender spots almost collided. As we grew closer and closer to each other, my heart was beating, then pounding, and I was panting. What was I getting myself into? I asked myself in between his caresses. This must be it. Having tasted this, I no longer was and could never be a child again. Here, in the dead of the night, I had grown, I had lived, I had learned, and I had changed. And I would never be the same. I felt both alive, and lonely at the same time. *You, who are holding me so tight right now, do I really know you? And do you really know me? Are we but strangers in an embrace facing the brink of adulthood together and everything that it brings? Where has my fate led me?*

I tried to hold on to Haider. But I had dissociated from him. I no longer knew who he was. I no longer knew who I was. I no longer knew what I stood for and felt like a stranger in a strange land once again. As if startled awake from a dream, I removed myself from Haider's fierce embrace, and sat up on the side of the mattress, still panting.

"What's the matter?" Haider asked. "Are you alright?"

I felt hot tears rolling down my cheeks.

"Haider, I don't know. I feel like I'm losing myself. It's easy for you, you've chosen me. But for me, I have to weigh the pros and cons of staying or running away. I'm scared. I don't know who I am. I don't know what I want. And I'm longing for home. For something to call my own."

Something didn't click, but I couldn't put my finger on what. Maybe it was just too good to be true and my subconscious was desperately trying to find the catch? Or maybe I wanted none of this, and, now that it was freely given to me, I didn't know what to do with it?

"Liz, we can create a home together. Trust me. We can do this together. Do you trust that I'm being truthful?"

"Yes I trust you." I did. Genuineness radiated from every inch of him. I knew, at my core, that he was for real. Was he just entranced? Perhaps. But I knew that right here, right now, he believed everything he said with complete conviction.

"Liz, sweetie, come, let's go to the Tetraeder again tomorrow morning. Let's put a padlock with our initials engraved on it. To prove to the world that we're going to be together for good. And let's even go to that other place you mentioned, the Stairway to Heaven, that stone sculpture on top of a hill at the end of an infinite flight of stairs."

The next night we packed a guitar, blankets, food and the padlock Haider bought at the hardware store at the corner of our street. We headed out hand in hand, stopping at every street corner to kiss. We walked by the Starbucks that was open till late, catching the faint wind of the chorus of Rihanna's "We Found Love in a Hopeless Place" edging toward us. That song seemed to be playing everywhere this summer, and I never noticed its relevance until that moment.

We took the last bus before they shut down for the night. The streets of Duisburg no longer looked hostile, and when we got to the Hauptbahnhof, it stood aglow, like it was gloriously celebrating us. We sat on the same old platform where grass was growing, under its filthy roof.

"Liz, take out your camera, I want to immortalize this moment for us to remember when we are old and senile."

"Alright, look at the camera," I called out. We got closer and I took a selfie of us.

"One more, and another one. And one more."

"Sure."

I angled my camera differently each time to capture the full breadth of the experience.

"Alright, let's look at the pictures," Haider said. "That's sweet. I like this one where I'm kissing you. And look at your cute face kissing me! You have such a baby face! But my favourite is the last one. It's just a selfie with both of us looking at the camera, but we look so happy together, our eyes are shining. Who would have thought that this place could look so beautiful as a backdrop to our pictures?"

"It's still pretty dirty and all," I retorted in my usual sardonic tone, "but the lighting does give nice colours."

We boarded the regional train and arrived at Bottrop in what felt like a blink.

"This place," Haider began, "it's like we've been here only yesterday. And yet how different it feels! There's you and there's me, and there's love."

Yes, I suppose.

"I have a song for you," Haider continued. He sang: *Suddenly I'm famous, And people know my name …*

"What are you talking about?"

Haider went on about how his heart was captured by a funny little smile, despite thousands of girls being after him. I rolled my eyes.

"Oh come on Haider, what song is that? Did you make it up yourself?"

He playfully ignored me and continued on how people called him stupid for treating me like a queen, but he couldn't care less because I seemed to be glad around him.

"This is really cheesy, Haider, stop."

He smiled, knowing I was secretly enjoying it. He really knew how to read me, I realized. Unlike anyone else. The chorus was about how neither of us knew where things were going, but he still hoped for more. And about how surprising it was that I treated him like a boy while he treated me like a girl.

"It's so cutesy. What is this?"

But I couldn't help but smile.

"The song is called 'Funny Little World' by Alexander Rybak," Haider finally answered. "Look it up, my sister showed it to me and dared me to sing it to someone I liked."

"You devil, I really thought you made it up just now. I wouldn't have been surprised."

"You think I'm always this corny and cheesy and cutesy?"

"Yes, you are. Let's call this CCC and if I ever say CCC in public, then you'll know you have to stop," I mused.

"Alright," Haider conceded, laughing.

We were approaching the Tetraeder, and the sun was already on the horizon.

"Look at the Tetraeder!" Haider exclaimed. "How majestic! And here are bunnies running around us, and the birds are chirping. What a happy world!"

We ran up the hill and climbed up to the observation deck. The sun was shining golden, and the chimneys were blowing white smoke as always. But how balanced the world looked, as if everything made sense at last. I felt like I was looking at a completely different structure than the one I had visited previously. The colours were brighter, the sounds of the birds chirping and the wind rustling in the trees grew more vivid. Had I accidentally slipped LSD into my breakfast? It definitely seemed like it.

"Here, take the padlock," Haider said, handing it to me. "I used my pocketknife to inscribe *H+E* on it. Attach it where you wish. Then throw the key as far as you can."

I attached the padlock to the handrail surrounding the upper deck of the Tetraeder. Then I took a deep breath. I threw the key with all of my might.

Haider looked at me, gently wiped my hair from my face, and kissed me with a deep, passionate kiss.

"There, there, we're together now. I love you, and now the world knows it," Haider whispered in my ear.

I smiled back at him, and we headed to the Stairway to Heaven, which was in Gelsenkirchen, the next town over. The Stairway to Heaven was not just a Led Zeppelin song. It was a stone pillar at the top of a barren hill, with a road that circled the hill, climbing up gradually. The last part of the climb was a flight of stairs several storeys high. By the time we reached the bottom of the hill, the sky was overcast and it was a little past noon.

Walking along the circular road as it gently meandered up the hill had a meditative effect. The factories, houses, trees, everything around us were slowly dwarfed as we climbed higher and higher. If the climb to heaven felt like this, heaven must be a lonely place, I thought. The barren hill was but a mount of stone, with rare sprigs of thin grass growing between sandy cracks.

"Haider, why must we be in such a desolate area of the world?"

"Desolate, you say. But I see it is full of life. Imagine, if such a beautiful love can be found in a desolate place like this, how much better it will flourish in a richer and finer location! If shitty Duisburg is our starting point, how much room do we have to grow!"

I nodded.

"The sky is grey, and the hill is barren, but how far we can see as we reach the top!" Haider continued. "Here, climb first on this last flight of stairs, I'm following you from behind. Climb and feel your wings expand into the sky."

I climbed faithfully, step by step. The stone structure on top of the hill was filled with graffiti. I fixated on it and indeed felt like I was taking flight as we reached the top.

"Look!" Haider called out. "In the distance, that is the Tetraeder! See how far we've come already!"

"It looks so small and fragile from this far," I answered.

"Our love might start small, but it will grow."

"We found love in a hopeless place" was playing on loop in my head the entire time. Part of me was enjoying it as it really captured the mood, but part of me just wanted Rihanna to shut up.

We took pictures of us standing tall above the world. Later, when we were climbing down, Haider said, "My childhood sweetheart, her name is Zahra, you know about her. She gave me a bracelet made out of a string, as a good luck charm. I had decided it was time to part ways with it. On top of the barren hill, I threw it into the distance. I feel so free, so light."

I was touched but overwhelmed. Had he really thrown away such a deep, long-term crush for *me*? I was worried I would let him down. The last thing I wanted to do was hurt this sweet guy; his pure soul did not deserve the darkness I might bring. He was too on top of the world to notice that my presence was mired with uncertainty, with constant second-guessing of my own emotions.

By the time we walked back to Gelsenkirchen, it was already late afternoon. We decided to find something to eat.

"Here's a Lebanese restaurant!" Haider exclaimed. "Oh how I miss Middle Eastern food after moving away from that region of the world! I'll get to introduce you to the food of my childhood!" He was so excited, he sounded like a child himself.

I looked doubtfully at the dive he was gesturing towards. It was small and modest, if not slightly sketchy looking. The neon sign was half dead, and the tables and chairs were rusty. But Haider was insistent, so I went with him.

We had kebabs and they turned out to be really delicious. They even gave us a plate of stuffed vine leaves, to my delight, and a plate of olives.

"These are authentic Middle Eastern olives," Haider explained. "If you're not used to them, they might taste strong and bitter. But I love them."

I tried a bite. It was strong and bitter indeed. I didn't really know whether I liked the taste or not. I looked at Haider in wonder. How close we were to each other, and how far we had travelled in order to come together. He was like a whole world that was opening up to me. Some of it I embraced. But some of it was harder to take in. I stood at the threshold between my world and his. I hesitated about taking the plunge, knowing I would never emerge the same.

12

July 13, 2011

I think at this point, my lab mates had started resenting me. I spent my days at work in daydreams, spent my lunch hours with Haider, and ran home as early as possible. I had no idea what I was doing in physics because I was kind of on another planet, and to be honest, I didn't really give a damn.

One night, after slipping out of the lab early to meet up with Haider, we decided to head out to Dusseldorf. There was a temporary fairground set up like a carnival along the shores of the Rhein, and we decided to check it out. It was a bright day as we headed towards the Duisburg Hauptbahnhof.

"See this station, with its plain walls and all?" Haider asked as we waited for the train to come. "You will come to miss it so much after you've left. Do you believe me?"

"Haider, don't make me fear the future more than I do already."

"Fear? What is there to fear?"

"I fear an unforeseen day where we have to part ways."

"Nonsense, my darling. You will have me as long as I live."

We sounded like a 19th-century romance novel. I couldn't help but giggle at the thought. But the nostalgic in me delighted in us talking this way.

We arrived in Dusseldorf and took the local subway to the carnival. At the entrance, we paid 5 euros each for a day pass. What a fun world we entered! From cute food joints selling cotton candy and popcorn, to games where you can win giant stuffed animals, to carousels, to the gigantic ferris wheel, it was an idyllic place where children and young people came to celebrate life, or perhaps escape it. The contrast between the vibrant carnival teeming with exuberance, and the desolate rest of this part of Germany, was like day and night.

"Sweetheart," Haider began, "I want you to enjoy as much as possible. What do you want to do? I'm all ears."

"Let's go to the games! I want to win a stuffed animal!"

It was a childhood dream of mine to win a giant plushie, something I've never managed to accomplish.

"Alright, let's do this!" Haider cheered.

And off we went. We tried throwing darts to pop balloons and were both equally bad at it. We tried fishing coins inside bowls floating on water. We tried shooting BB guns and throwing basketballs into a hoop. All we ever got were two plastic roses as consolation prizes.

"Haider, it's okay if we can't do it," I reminded him, matter-of-factly. "We don't have to keep losing money like this."

"No, you deserve to have every dream come true, so we'll try again." Haider was adamant about it.

I looked at the easygoing and cheerful crowd. In a sea of white people enjoying the day, Haider's tensed expression and posture looked out of place. There was a glimpse of anger in his eyes, and I was taken aback.

"Haider, it's okay!" I was worried, unsure of what was going on.

He looked into my eyes. "Liz, I'm sorry. I want to be good enough for you. I don't want there to be a single reason for which you could leave me. You look so uncertain now. I have displeased you. What's the matter?"

I looked away. He had seen through me yet again.

I felt guilty thinking this, but his heavy presence—not literally, but emotionally—seemed to put a damper on the lighthearted, fun mood I was trying to soak up. What was it about him that felt so … incongruous in this happy carnival?

"It's not you, it's me," I tried to assure him. "Something about us feels off, but it has nothing to do with what you did. I never even asked you to win me anything, I was going to do it myself."

"Liz, please give me—give us—a chance! I don't know if I can live without you …"

I felt the familiar flicker of fear again. The more he made this kind of declarations, the more my uncertainty grew. The way he held on to me made me shudder; was I ever going to be able to leave the relationship if I had to?

However, I only saw earnestness in Haider's eyes as he looked at me. I felt a knot deep in my stomach. I was worried, for the first time not for me but for him. If for any reason I changed my mind about us, I could cope, but could he? Could I always be there for him the way he needed me to?

Chris was the opposite extreme, never needing me a bit. I felt guilty. Didn't I want someone who wanted and needed me? Wasn't this why I didn't want to stay with Chris? And here he was, the man I always thought I wanted, and I didn't know what to do with him.

I wondered if, maybe, a bit of a role reversal could make me feel like this was more balanced. Maybe if I see myself as someone who could reciprocate the way he deserved, I would be able to envision a future with him?

"Haider, let me do it," I tried to reassure him. "Let's switch roles. I'll win a stuffed animal for you, alright?"

"You're so sweet, Liz." Haider looked relieved. "Here's 3 euros. Let's play this throwing hoops on bottles game."

The guy staffing that game's booth gave us three rubber hoops to throw on a row of glass bottles with little stuffed dogs inside of them.

"If you throw three hoops on the same bottle and the bottle has an animal in it, you win the animal," he explained.

I threw one. Got it! Two, and then three! I won!

Haider was cheering for me, and I received a little black and white Bull Terrier wearing a pirate hat with *Captain* stitched on it.

"My darling, I'm so proud of you!" Haider exclaimed. "How adorable he is! He looks naughty just like me!"

"What do we name him?"

"Name him Captain Ali, after my nickname. Whenever you miss me, hug him, it's as if I'm there."

We decided to end the day with a ride on the Ferris wheel.

"Liz," Haider said as we were waiting in line, "all my life, I've been a winner. I got the highest marks of my class, no, the highest marks of my grade, every single year from elementary to high school. The Indian school system I was in had two international standard examinations at Grade 10 and Grade 12. I sat the Grade 10 exam before I left for Canada. I got the second-highest grade in the whole Middle East region, where around one million students took the test. If I had gotten the top grade, I'd have met India's prime minister."

I looked at him, incredulous.

"It's true." He continued, "I've never told anyone outside my family before. And now, for my first three years at college, I was in the top five percent of my classes in the Engineering Science program, the hardest engineering program in the country. And my classmates all voted for me to be the representative of our Aerospace Engineering class next year."

I looked at Haider in awe. I had never realized that this guy standing in front of me could be anything other than a lovestruck romantic.

"In fact," Haider carried on, "I've never really lost at anything I've put my hands on. The victory never really mattered to me. But since I laid eyes on you on the day we met, I realized that one victory will matter more than every possible victory combined. It's the victory where you are my reward."

Wow. I was astonished and couldn't find words to respond to him. I was swooning over his adoration, too awestruck and too young to ever read it as patronizing.

We boarded the Ferris wheel, and Haider and I sat alone in one carriage.

"Let me kiss you, my darling", Haider pressed me against him. I was enthralled by the feeling of living in a 19th-century romance novel. Who doesn't want a Mr. Rochester?

I kissed him, and we took selfies of us soaring above the sunset by the shores of the Rhein. I looked at Haider again and I felt so small against him. I felt privileged. I felt wonderstruck. What a big world we live in.

We spent the evening enjoying cotton candy and eating hotdogs. As we left the carnival and walked back to the Dusseldorf Hauptbahnhof, there was a crowd around two musicians in the plaza by the station. It was a man with long wavy black hair playing the guitar and a woman, in a hippie-style flowy dress, singing. After their song, Haider walked forward and asked them if he could use their guitar to sing a song. They happily let him.

"This is for my sweetheart, Elizabeth," Haider announced, as they handed their guitar to him. I rolled my eyes at how corny this was while secretly enjoying the song, which went on and on about how the smile on my face, the look in my eyes, and touch of my hand all told him about how much I loved him. The chorus concluded with: *You say it best when you say nothing at all.*

I felt my cheeks turning a bright shade of red. What a cheesy piece, once again. Once CCC, always CCC, clearly. I playfully nagged him about it, and he laughed.

"I'll never stop singing you cheesy songs; this is one thing you can expect from me," Haider said. I guess he knew I secretly liked them. After all, if anyone was able to read me this well, it was him. "I have another one for you."

He began singing in Hindi as we walked towards the train station.

"What is this one about?" I asked him, curious.

"It is from a Bollywood movie called *Jab We Met*, or *When We Met*. The song is called 'Tum se hi,' meaning 'Because of You.' It's a guy who loves a girl, but she loves someone else, so they each went their separate ways. But as he lives alone and does his work, everything reminds him of her, and he feels as if she is around and inspiring him."

The train finally arrived at ten to midnight. We danced our way onto the train and collapsed on the seats.

Haider sang into my ear:

Na hai yeh paanaa,
Naa khonaa hi hai.
Tera na hona jaane,
Kyun honaa hi hai,

"What does it mean?"

It isn't a gain,
But it isn't a loss either.
You are not here,
But I still feel that you are here.

Haider's singing and the train's movement peacefully rocked me to sleep as I lay my head in his lap. What a beautiful day we had.

As we got to Duisburg Hauptbahnhof, we realized that it was past 12:30 a.m. and there wasn't going to be a night bus for us.

"Let's walk home then!" Haider exclaimed "We're crazy enough for this!"

I laughed gleefully at his burst of confidence. He looked triumphant in the dead of night. He seemed so happy, I thought. Could I really inspire so much happiness in someone else? I couldn't possibly think of taking it away from him, could I? I was amazed at him, and at myself.

We walked past a building and saw a man in a suit shouting, "I love you" on the sidewalk towards an open window above him. A woman, in a white dress, poked her head out of the window and shouted, "I love you too" back at him. I couldn't believe that actually happened. How apropos.

"We're not the only crazies out there," Haider said, reading my mind. We both laughed.

We passed by sleepy neighbourhoods and bridges over dark rivers. Our place on Volkstrasse was seven kilometres away. We hugged, we kissed, we sang, and we laughed. We had no idea where we were going, but it didn't matter. It didn't matter at all. We were here, we were together, and there was nothing more to ask for. We were oblivious to darkness, wind, and thunder.

And wind and thunder it did. Soon, rain was pouring down on us. We danced instead of looking for shelter. Our hair and clothes were soaked, soaked with water and happiness.

"Liz, let me pick you up like in that scene from *Jab We Met*," Haider said in my ear.

He grasped my waist, and lifted me up into the sky, twirling me around under the rain, lit by the glow of the street lights.

"What a beautiful night!" I cried out, oblivious to the time, and those around us who might be sleeping.

"And how beautiful you are, my darling," Haider answered me.

He put me down on the ground, him panting and me dizzy. I leaned myself against him and we kissed again and again.

"That's it, I'm never carrying an umbrella in my life again," Haider said. "The rain is a blessing. Let us enjoy our blessing fully!"

It was past 5 a.m. when we stumbled upon a bus station, nowhere near where we lived. We sat on the bench to rest a little when, surprisingly, the bus came. We asked the driver if it would take us to our neighbourhood and he said yes and smiled at us, lost youth as we were. We boarded the bus and got back to our apartment after 6 a.m.

"Guys, where did you go all night?" Wendy asked us as we opened the front door. "And oh dear! How wet you guys are! Did it rain last night? I was so worried about you both!"

Haider and I laughed.

"We had a little too much fun," I explained, "and yes there was a thunderstorm last night and we missed the last bus. But here we are, so all is well!"

"Wendy, can you tell both our supervisors that we're sick and not coming in to work today?" Haider asked.

"Of course," Wendy said with an understanding nod. "Have a nice day, guys!"

She left the apartment. Haider and I slowly undressed each other, and we took a shower together, massaging each other's aching muscles from the long walk. We then laid on our bed, sleepy-eyed.

"Oh my dear Liz," Haider whispered as we were falling asleep, "I had not truly lived before I knew you!"

13

July 16, 2011

It was one of our last Saturdays before the end of my internship. There was a festival of light in Köln, so we decided to spend the day there. As the train approached, the Köln cathedral looked more majestic than ever. We got off the train and walked towards it.

"It was here that everything started for me," Haider began.

We sat on one of the stone benches bordering the cathedral.

"That day when we came here, I saw you cry in the cathedral, and my heart hurt. It was then that I made a wish. I wished for your happiness."

"You saw me cry?" I didn't realize he had.

"I did, but I didn't want to infringe on your privacy, so I asked Wendy to console you."

I was touched but taken aback. I didn't expect him to be so subtly considerate.

"We're here again at the cathedral, and I think I want you to make me a promise. Can I ask you for three things?"

My heart was beating loudly. What did he want from me? I hope it wasn't a promise I couldn't keep.

"You are such a great girl, but I realize you're very insecure. I have no idea what made you this way, but it hurts me to see you like this. Especially, you don't seem to think I'm truthful with you and you seem to believe I'm too good to be true. Is that correct?"

I nodded. I never understood how someone could be so gentle with me and read me so well. It was something alien to my world.

"Well," Haider continued, "First, I want you to promise me that you'll never say 'thank you' to me again. Everything I give you is yours. I am giving it willingly and you don't have to thank me for it. Rather, thanking me feels cold, as if I'm making you owe me something."

That was easy, I supposed. I was relieved that he didn't expect anything from me that I couldn't find it within myself to provide.

"I promise," I answered.

"Then, the next thing, it might be harder. I want you to never say you're sorry unless you've truly hurt me, which you haven't until now. You say sorry for every little thing, and doing so undermines your own value. You don't have to apologize for your existence."

"I promise." I wondered about what the third thing was.

"And finally. This one is a selfish one, I admit. It is for me. Can I ask it from you? I want you to never disappear from my life without warning, for any length of time. We can always talk things through. I respect your space, and if you want some silence, tell me for how long, and I'll grant it to you. But if you just disappear, I will be hurting, you don't know how much."

Haider paused and looked at his feet.

"Can you do it for me?" he asked again.

I felt anxiety rise inside of me. This one is asking a lot from me. Disappearing was my only weapon against anyone who asked too much of me. Was I now bound to face Haider forever, no matter what? What was I getting myself into? Unknowingly, I'd been led by Haider further and further into another world. Was it too late to turn back? Did I want to turn back? I wanted that security of being able to turn back, which I was worried would be taken away from me if I accepted this last request. It didn't matter whether or not I wanted to turn back. I just wanted to have that option.

But I looked at Haider's face, and all I felt was compassion. I saw myself in his eyes. I understood his pain. I recognized the way he felt towards me as the way I felt towards Chris. I couldn't hurt him the way I was hurt. So, I nodded and promised him in earnest.

Haider's eyes grew bright and watery. He hugged me gently, and we quietly rocked back and forth, as a unit locked in an embrace, at the edge of the cathedral.

"You're such a blessing, Liz," Haider finally whispered "*Alhamdulillah.*"

"What does that mean?"

"It's an Arabic phrase meaning 'All praises to God.' You're a blessing from God."

"How do you know?"

"My heart knows. My heart knows that God sent you to me."

I pondered the meaning of what he said. How can a human heart know the will of God?

We spent the rest of the day in the streets of Köln. We walked by the shores of the Rhein and came across a small outdoor market. They were selling all sorts of candies, and I was in heaven just looking at them.

"Buy candies to your heart's content!" Haider said, "You're my princess and I'm your Aladdin."

I laughed.

"You can't ever stop being corny, can you?"

"It's my trademark," he winked. "Do you know what Aladdin actually means?"

"I don't."

"Aladdin is an Anglicization of Ala ad-din, meaning nobility of faith."

Wow. Now that was something worth aspiring to in his culture.

I ended up buying 10 euros' worth of candy of all sorts, mostly gummies and lollipops.

"Watching you enjoy yourself really brings out the kid in me," Haider told me later as we were settling ourselves near the banks of the Rhein to await the illuminated boats that mark the start of the Festival of Lights. "I never really got a chance to be a kid much. I missed out on a childhood."

I was wide-eyed. "How come?"

It was near sunset and the waning golden rays hit the side of Haider's face, producing a gleaming aura.

"It's a long story. But one you ought to know," he began. "My parents married according to the wish of my father's father, who was also my mother's uncle. He passed away early, and the rest of their families opposed the marriage. But my parents loved each other, so they went for it anyway. They relocated to Kuwait to be away from the family drama back in India. But the family put a lot of pressure on my father, even from afar. My mother had two daughters, my elder sisters, but she didn't have a son. My father's family taunted her for it and made her life really difficult."

I looked at Haider's face in the reddening sun. It appeared a deep scarlet.

"My mother made a trip to the local mosque. At the mosque was a *sheikh*, a learned man, who was a friend of our family. He was gifted with the ability to know things unknowable to ordinary people. People would inquire about something, and he would say a prayer, open the Quran at a page at random, put his finger on a verse, an *ayat*, and the verse would indicate an answer."

How different are the ways of people on Earth, I thought to myself.

"My mother went to the sheikh and asked him if she would have a son. The sheikh answered: 'It is not in your destiny to have a son. Your destiny only has two daughters.' My mother asked, 'Then how am I to ever face my in-laws? My husband and I are being scorned for not having a son!' The sheikh said: 'There is a way out, my lady. If you pray very earnestly to Sayyidina Ali, the Prophet Muhammad's son-in-law, he might intercede for you, and you will be granted a son. You shall therefore name your son after one of the names of Ali.' My mother was relieved. The sheikh continued however: 'Your son shall be a gift, and he will be an extraordinary man. There are two possibilities. Either, he will be a great man, accomplish wonderful things and be a blessing to the world. Or he will be a tyrant, a mean and despicable person who will bring dishonour to not only your family, but all of mankind. It is in your hands to educate him into whichever destiny you choose.'"

The sun had just set, and Haider's face was dark, with only his eyes shining. I felt a shiver in my spine as a cold breeze blew from behind.

"My mother went on *hajj*, a pilgrimage to Mecca, from their home in Kuwait. She prayed sincerely, and a few months later, I was born. My mother named me Haider, which is one of Ali's titles. It means 'lion' in Arabic. A few months after I was born, the Gulf War started, where Iraq invaded Kuwait. Our family drove away from our home all the way to India as refugees. The trip was extremely dangerous, and many roads had been bombed. We travelled through famine- and disease-stricken areas. My mom would starve all day and barely had any milk for me. Many doctors told her that I would not survive, but I did against all odds, and I grew up healthy. We drove through a desert once, desperate to flee, and the road had been bombed and was broken. When a day later, we emerged from the other side of the desert, people were looking at us incredulously. They asked, 'Your family just drove through a minefield and you were not hurt?' My mom has always believed that all these miracles were on account of me."

It was completely dark by then, and Haider's silhouette cast a dark shadow against the street lamps.

"I grew up, and my mom was twice as hard on me as she was on my sisters. She always insisted that I was the best. And I managed to be because I thrived under the pressure. I won contest after contest and broke records in school grades. The schoolteachers all hated me because I didn't attend their evening tutorials. They were greedy and didn't teach all the material in class, forcing students to pay them for the evening tutorials in order to learn everything. But I learnt everything on my own. My mom ordered textbooks from India for me, my eldest sister helped prepare mock exams, and I learnt everything. I was like a machine, waking up at 6 a.m. every morning, and my days were planned like in the army. Do you know how exhausting it can be to live according to a mission like this? To come close to living up to these types of expectations?"

I looked at Haider, silent. I didn't know what to say. It sounded like one of those stories you hear from long ago, with genies who granted wishes, and oracles who predicted the future. The kind of stories that were too far-fetched to ever occur in real life. But I couldn't help but believe Haider. He was not a liar, I knew it deep down.

"I feel old and ageless sometimes. And I'm afraid of the future. I have carried on my life's prophecy since the day I was born. Can I live up to the world's expectations of me?"

"You're doing great, Haider," I tried to reassure him. But I feared as much as he did.

"But I've been feeling light for the first time in my life since this summer. I felt like, for once, I've been able to enjoy my life instead of fighting against everything to succeed at all costs. Because you came into my life and gave it meaning."

Haider looked me directly in the eye.

"I'm not one of those people who want to change the world. No, and I never will be. They say, if you change the life of one person, you've changed the whole world. If I could change someone's life through how much I love them, that is enough for me. Liz, I want the world to remember me for how much I loved you."

I felt my head spinning. Thoughts and feelings jumbled up inside of me. I tried looking at Haider, but I couldn't focus my eyes on him. How on earth was I supposed to go on after having heard this story?

"Liz, you look worried. It's okay, you can forget everything I said. I'm sorry I burdened you with too much at once. Look, the boats are coming towards us."

Boats sumptuously decorated with strings of light of all colours started parading along the Rhein, with the bridge right by us shining with lights as well. Then, fireworks started.

"Liz, cheer up. It's the festival of light! I feel like it's Diwali, and it makes me happy! I'm glad I'm here with you. We can forget the past! It doesn't have to affect our future!"

I looked at him smiling and I looked at the parade of boats. I was somewhat relieved, but I remained deep in thought. If Haider wanted to be remembered for how much he loved me, how could I live up to his love? How could I ever honor Haider's life, his sacrifice, enough? His story wouldn't leave me be, reverberating in my head.

On our way back to Duisburg on the train, Haider said, "I want to tell my mom about us. Not my dad, he will not accept me bringing home a girl who is not Muslim or even

Indian. But my mom might understand. She might want to speak with you, but don't worry, she's kind."

I nodded. I thought perhaps I could do the same, although I had no idea how my parents would react at all.

We got to the Duisburg Hauptbahnhof and Haider decided to call his mom from a bench outside the Starbucks. He spoke to her in his mother tongue, Gujarati, he said, the language of the province of Gujarat. They spoke for a good fifteen minutes, then Haider handed the phone to me.

"Hi," I said tentatively.

"Liz, that's your name?" she asked in a heavy Indian accent.

"Yes"

"Liz, I trust the choice of my son, and therefore you're like family to us. I only have one son and I love him so much, you can understand. And his poor mother is growing old. Liz, please take good care of my son. I want you guys to be happy together."

I reassured her to the best of my ability, and handed the phone back to Haider.

"She asked me a lot of questions," he told me after the phone conversation, "about where you were from. She was worried that you are from an atheist family. But I told her you were a little Buddhist, and she felt better. It's not going to be easy for you to win my family over, but it's doable, and I will always be on your side."

Haider tried to be reassuring, but I only saw a growing problem. I decided to call my mom too. She answered, and when I said I had a new boyfriend, she said, "okay," and left it there.

How anticlimactic.

Didn't she want to know more about him? I wondered to myself. But she had already said she respected my choice and didn't want to interfere with my life, then hung up.

"Is it really respect? Or is it a covert disapproval?" Haider asked me later, unsure of what to garner from this terse conversation.

I didn't know whether things were better off in my family or his. But sooner or later, we would have to face both families. It was inevitable, if we were to last beyond just a summer fling. We went to bed apprehensive that night.

14

July 20, 2011

My ten-week internship in Duisburg had come to a close. It would officially end at the end of this week, but for the next few days, all RISE interns were invited to beautiful Heidelberg for a conference and industry visits. I had planned to travel around Europe after Heidelberg for another three weeks, and then fly back to Montreal on August 10.

Haider and I both took the day off to pack up. We woke up that morning to birds chirping in the trees outside our window. Despite the so-called sketchiness of our area—which was full of immigrants, most of them Turkish—this place made me feel at home like nowhere else in the world. There was a light drizzle outside, and I decided to lay in bed for a little longer. Haider kissed me good morning and got out of bed, heading for the kitchen.

I lay in bed, thinking about where our future lay. This was it, I was leaving Duisburg for good, and leaving this place behind. I felt an indescribable sadness inside my throat. What will become of us?

"Liz, bunny, hop hop come for breakfast!" Haider cheerfully returned into the room.

I got out of bed, and went to kiss him.

"Come on, get some clothes on, don't be indecent!" Haider chided gently.

I put on a pair of underwear and Haider's black shirt to tease him. It fit me like a baggy dress. There was nobody home anyway.

We went into the kitchen. Haider had heated up the last piece of naan made by his mother that he had brought frozen to Germany. He had boiled several packets of black tea in the pot with milk and sugar. He then put the piece of naan on a plate and poured the tea inside a bowl.

"This is the closest to an Indian breakfast we can get in Germany," Haider had explained. "Back home, we drink tea inside saucer-like shallow bowls."

Haider sat in the last remaining chair by the kitchen table and gestured to me to sit in his lap. We shared the same piece of naan and the same bowl of tea.

"This is how we roll," Haider exclaimed, "two people, one table, one chair, one plate of naan, one bowl of tea, one single twin mattress to sleep on. We're two hearts but one soul."

I gazed at him as he poured more tea from the pot into the bowl. How elegant he looked. I had not noticed that before. His eyebrows looked like the wings of an eagle soaring in the sky. His highly arched nose granted him a look of nobility. His high cheekbones and long face gave him a solemn air and a certain dignity. His thin-framed glasses gave him the appearance of a deep thinker, an intellectual. I wondered if such would have been the look of Gandhi in his youth.

"Please honey," Haider protested, "you have no idea what you're talking about. Gandhi's great, but don't compare my looks to this frail little man."

I laughed at the contrasting images of him and a frail old man, but then chided myself a little. We finished our breakfast, and Haider moved the chair against the wall. He sat on the chair and asked me to sit on his lap and face him.

"Liz, put your face right in front of mine. I want you to look deep into my eyes. Then tell me what you see."

I sat on Haider's lap and turned my head to face him, my nose almost touching his. We breathed in synchronized rhythms. Haider's eyes were a light brown that would turn golden under the sun. Just like mine, in fact.

"We have the same exact shade of eye colour," I noticed. Until now I'd seen Haider as this otherworldly stranger, yet here we were.

"Indeed we do. The eyes are the windows to the soul. We have the same soul. Now look even deeper than my irises into my pupils."

What did he mean by that? I thought to myself. I just realized I'd never really looked at anyone in the eye before. In fact I tend to shy away from looking people in the eye. I was afraid of what I would see. I sat still and stared into the abyss of his pupils. I could feel my heart beating along with his. And I looked and looked. I saw the desert, and I saw the sea. I saw faraway countries and cities. I saw sky, clouds, and stars. I saw the Netherlands beach where we held hands for the first time.

"Haider, I saw the beach where we held hands for the first time. But I only saw myself in your eyes, I didn't see you. What does it mean?"

"What do you think it means?"

"I'm afraid of the future. Maybe I will have to walk alone, without you, do you think that is it?"

"I don't see it that way. I am the frame through which you were looking. I am holding the empty frame inside of which you paint your life. Through me, your soul will grow and expand and fill the universe. And you will never be alone. Do you think this is a better scenario?"

I nodded. But I was worried. A summer fling is one thing. But how were we to survive the future, living in different cities?

"Liz, I know you worry about us. There is something my mother always says, 'Let go and let God.' We try to plan things, but God plans better. Let Him plan for us a beautiful future. Let's trust Him, Who is The Most Kind and Merciful. If we're right for each other, God will keep us together. I promise."

I looked at Haider. His eyes were earnest. How beautiful was his faith, I thought to myself. Haider's word was good, I tried to reassure myself. I had no choice but to trust him, at this point. But the fact that he relied on God brought me some comfort.

But today was bittersweet. As my internship ended, my apartment lease ended too. Haider had to move out as well and arranged to go live with Siddartha for the rest of his internship, which was five weeks longer than mine.

"Our time in this beautiful first home of ours has come to an end," Haider said solemnly. "I've come to love Duisburg despite everything. I really have. It will be a sad day when I return to Toronto."

I looked at the I ♥ Duisburg sign on our wall. I took it off the wall, and placed it on the table. So many emotions were inside of me. I started unpinning every item on the wall, folding it, and inserting it into my suitcase. Haider helped me, and we laughed and cried over every memory we had made in this part of the world, reflected in these souvenirs.

"Look at this tiny Ganesha you drew on the paper that I pinned on the wall," I said. "Can I keep it? It is so adorable."

"Sweetie, keep everything. It is all yours."

On our bedside table, we found the angel, our Bull Terrier Captain Ali, the plastic roses, the aftershave that Haider's father had given him, seashells from the beach in the Netherlands, and assorted beer bottle caps, two of which happened to have our initials printed on them.

"Take a picture, Liz, this represents our entire summer."

I looked at our clothes, his and mine side by side in the closet. Our shoes, his and mine alternatingly placed in a row. How intertwined our lives had become. I sighed. I suddenly was apprehensive about leaving. I wanted to freeze this moment in time so that it could last forever.

Haider, who had by then rested his arm on my shoulder, hugged me gently. He knew.

"Sweetheart, I know the future is uncertain and it won't be easy. I know. But as Anne Frank once said, where there is life, there is hope. Cheer up, long-distance relationships are common nowadays with the technologies we have. It's going to be okay, really going to be okay! Alright?"

Haider cooked spaghetti for lunch, *Brown style*, as he called it. "You can take a man out of India, but you can't take India out of a man."

"First we sauté minced garlic and diced onions," he patiently explained to me, "then we add spices. Chilli powder is obvious, then dhanya jeera powder, or coriander seeds. And even some cumin. Then we add chopped tomatoes and tomato paste. You have to fry the tomato paste a little to make sure it's cooked. Otherwise it doesn't taste good."

The dish turned out really delicious. We ate, sitting on one chair, with one plate and one fork. Without even realizing it, we have truly merged into one being. I remembered that Greek legend I had learned about in English class in CEGEP. According to the legend, people were created with two heads, four arms and four legs, but were split in half as a punishment for their pride. People were then doomed to look for their other half for the rest of their lives.

We spent the rest of the day packing slowly and lazing away. I felt a knot deep in my throat. I remembered the first day and my initial dislike of Haider. I remembered feeling afraid of him. I remembered being amazed by him. And now I wondered how I could ever live without him.

"Liz, it's been years since I've prayed, but today, I feel like praying," Haider said in the late afternoon. "Do you mind?"

"No." I was curious and asked, "How do you pray?"

"I'll show you. First you have to wash up. It's called the wudhu. You wash your hands three times, then rinse your mouth three times, then rinse your nose three times, then wash your face three times, then wash your arms up till the elbows three times, then pass wet hands over your hair and wash your ears, and then wash each foot three times. You are then fit to converse with God."

Haider went to the washroom and washed himself. He then rummaged through his luggage and took out a prayer mat.

"This was a gift from my grandfather. Upon it is a depiction of Mecca."

He looked at the sun and figured out the angle at which to prostrate.

"Mecca should be in the southeast direction in Germany."

"The prayer consists of multiple rakats. During one rakat, you recite standing up the first surah, or chapter, of the Quran, which has 7 verses. You then recite another surah of your choice if it's the first and second rakat of the prayer. Then you bow at ninety degrees, stand up again, then you prostrate, sit up, and prostrate another time, and then sit up another time. The afternoon prayer, or asr, has four rakats, so you repeat these positions four times."

Haider unfolded his prayer mat onto the ground, laid a small piece of paper at the position where his head was to touch the ground, a *turba*, and started reciting the prayer quietly. The afternoon sun shone through the window, illuminating the gold and black prayer mat. Haider's silhouette appeared dark against the golden light, like a shadow. I held my breath and looked at him from behind, completely amazed at how he bowed and prostrated onto the ground.

Having grown up in an atheist household in a secular country, the way of religious people fascinated me to my core. How powerful a force faith could be if it could make a grown man touch his head to the ground. "Islam means submission to God," I remember Haider saying. "If you submit yourself to God, you won't be a slave to anyone else on earth." I looked at Haider, now kneeling on the ground. I felt a strange power greater than us at work.

"You didn't mind me, did you?" Haider asked me after praying.

"No, I thought it was beautiful."

"Prayer is beautiful, indeed. And now I feel better. I feel at peace."

Haider's features looked softened indeed.

"I'm not a religious Muslim," Haider said. "I used to pray as a child, but I gradually gave up, like my sisters. Now in our house, only my mother prays five times a day. I don't fast during Ramadan either anymore. But I remember my grandfather, who used to take me to mosques on his shoulders when I was little. My grandfather was not a religious man. But he was pious and he was kind to everyone. He barely made any money as a street sweeper, but he lent generously to anyone who asked. He had faith in God and his religion was kindness. And he taught me that. He died on the Laylat-ul-qadr, the holiest night of the year where the gates of heavens are open. Anyone who dies on that night enters heaven directly."

Haider's words stayed in my mind for the duration of the afternoon. If his religion was kindness, what was my religion? Slowly, I realized that this talk of God made me feel strangely safe. I was glad I was loving someone who believed in God.

Camilla and Lilian held a potluck downstairs in the evening to celebrate the end of my internship and our trip to Heidelberg. We spent the evening with food, beer, and tequila. Haider made tequila sunrises for everyone. It was a jubilant evening.

When we came back to our apartment, Haider said, "Tomorrow we will head to Heidelberg, and then we will go to Baden Baden by the Black Forest for the weekend as we had decided. After that, I want you to travel on your own as you had planned. I will never hold you back from what will make you happy and help you grow. Fly free, my darling. Then come back to me, I will receive you with open arms."

That evening, we laughed and we cried. And as Haider gently held me in his embrace one last time in our home in Duisburg, I thanked my lucky stars for my fate and I made a wish for a beautiful future.

15

July 21, 2011

Haider and I woke up at 7 a.m. to a gloomy day. Our bags had already been stowed at Siddartha's place. We lay on the mattress and looked around us. How empty it felt. These were the plain white walls that I had encountered when I first moved into this place, almost two months ago. This place, which had grown to feel like home, now stripped from our presence, felt so raw, so foreign. A light rain was pouring from the sky outside. I felt sorrowful.

"Liz, look ahead." Haider comforted me, "Our time here is over, but don't mourn because better things are in front of us! We're going to beautiful Heidelberg, and after hearing you talk about it, I really want to go there! Then we have time for us in Baden Baden by the mythical Black Forest. And then you will be travelling all over Europe! How exciting! Come sweetie, cheer up!"

I tried to feign a smile. Haider was right. I should not be so pessimistic.

That day, we took the train southward and passed by Köln with its eternal cathedral. We then arrived at Koblenz to switch trains. In Koblenz, we met several other RISE students, all Heidelberg-bound. We met up with David, and his roommate, Karen, along with Roger, a physics student working in Essen, who had been dating Karen since Haider and I got together. We met many others from different parts of Germany, and we were a lively and friendly crowd who had clearly gotten to know each other over the last couple months.

We arrived in Heidelberg late that evening, and were accommodated in a large youth hostel. During dinner, I talked to many people and even met a few people from my home province, Quebec. We spoke French, and everyone else seemed super impressed. When I said I was from Montreal, several guys mentioned that Montreal girls were the most beautiful. I was somewhat flattered, but then wondered if I could really be considered a Montreal girl, if I wasn't born there? If I wasn't White? Some questions didn't have answers.

I shared a big room with five other girls I didn't know, whereas Haider was accommodated with the guys. Before going to bed the first night, Haider passed by my room and kissed me good night. The other girls teased us, but Haider said it was because they were envious. Perhaps he was right.

The next day, RISE students were invited to visit local industries. Germany was hoping that a few of us would come back and work there. Haider was part of the group that visited an automobile factory in Frankfurt. I was part of another group visiting a glass company that made touch screens and organic materials in Mannheim.

A long-distance bus took around thirty RISE students in the morning and we got to Mannheim half an hour later. On the bus I got to meet Emily, from London, who promised me that if ever I wanted to visit London, I would be welcome in her house. I tried my best to be friendly and enthusiastic, but I missed Haider every minute.

At the glass factory, we were shown to the exhibit room. We saw beautiful plasma screens and transparent glass that became opaque once you applied an electric current to it, all sorts of LED lights, and other curiosities. I tried my best to be interested, but I was only half there. We were then invited to a presentation by the head of the company, and I was bored to tears. I couldn't wait to get back to the hostel and see Haider.

That evening when Haider and I were reunited at the hostel, we didn't leave each other for a second. We attended the conference where RISE alumni presented the options for pursuing graduate studies in Germany, but it was all a blur. We only had eyes for each other. When we got back to the hostel, Haider brought me to his room and introduced me to his roommates.

"Are you guys cool if she spends the night with me here?" He asked them.

"Yeah sure, you guys are cute together," they replied.

And so I stayed with Haider that night, sharing the lower bunk of a bunkbed. When the staff announced the curfew and checked that everybody was in their rooms, I hid under Haider's blanket and they didn't notice. Lying next to Haider, I felt secure again, and confident that we were not to part ways. I needed him more than ever. We woke up the next morning feeling refreshed despite being crammed in such a small bed.

Today was a free day, where all of us could explore Heidelberg at will. I had been to Heidelberg before, on my last trip to Europe with my family. I was eager to show Haider around.

"We have to visit the ancient castle ruins," I said. "It is so beautiful and surreal."

"Let's go then, darling."

We bought an entrance ticket and wandered in. We were surrounded by broken walls and still standing arches, everything built with red brick. As we walked, each facet of the castle started revealing itself.

"I think this pigeon has been following us," Haider pointed at the bird.

"What do you mean?"

"Since I was in Essen, I keep seeing a grey pigeon around me. And now I see, it is as if it's the same bird."

We were facing a wall full of Roman windows, but the rest of the building had been destroyed, so the windows opened up to the blue sky behind them. The pigeon sat on one of the windowsills.

"Little pigeon, where is your other half?" Haider called out.

"There it is," I answered.

A white dove came and sat on the window next to the pigeon.

"That's you and that's me," Haider said and smiled. "And wherever I go, I know you are around. Remember? *Na hai yeh paanaa, naa khonaa hi hai. Tera na hona jaane, kyun honaa hi hai.*"

"It isn't a gain, but it isn't a loss either. You are not here, but I still feel that you are here."

"That's right! Come let's take pictures around this beautiful place!"

We walked around and saw stairways leading to nowhere, arches opening into gardens, and we wandered inside the remaining part of the castle that was still standing. It was dark inside, but the windows opened up to a view of the Rhein Valley, and we could see the old town of Heidelberg below. Every house had a red brick roof and looked lovely from the height of the castle on the mountaintop.

"You know, life is like a trip," Haider said. "You were so sad that we left Duisburg, this place that you used to despise, that you've grown to love. But see how beautiful a place we've come to now. Do not regret the past; it is already gone. And don't you worry about the future; worrying is futile. Just enjoy what the present moment brings. Let go and let God."

I nodded. Perhaps yes, perhaps there was some hope.

We descended from the castle and went wandering in the old town of Heidelberg. We saw beautiful little shops and quaint little streets. It was truly lovely. We wandered into a clock factory, making traditional pendulum cuckoo clocks out of oak. Each clock was different, with different animals and designs on them. How I wished I could bring one home, but they were far too big and delicate to fit in my suitcase. We passed by artisanal ice cream and candy shops and we stopped in front of a scarf shop.

"Let me buy you a new scarf," Haider said. "I stole your yellow scarf that you wore that day at the Netherland beach."

"You devil, I wondered where it went!"

"I'm sorry, but I need your reassurance when you aren't around. I need to smell your smell to bring myself to sleep at night."

"Alright, take that yellow scarf as a gift then, to remember me by." I smiled. "And please buy me a new one, I'm a scarf collector."

I picked a square linen scarf with a forest green paisley pattern and bright orange detailing, and Haider paid for it.

"Look at you looking so fashionable!" Haider exclaimed. "How lucky I am to have a girl like you!"

We spent much of the day wandering around until it was time to board the train again. We took the train to Karlsruhe and had some hotdogs at the train station for dinner.

"This will be our last time together before you head out to travel on your own," Haider said, "then God knows when we could be together again. Let's enjoy our time to the fullest."

I looked at Haider sitting across from me at the table. No, I wasn't ready to face the future. I went to his side and hugged him tight against me.

"We're not parting ways yet," Haider gently reminded me. "Here's the train to Baden Baden. Let's go and enjoy ourselves."

We boarded the train right as the sun was setting.

16

July 23, 2011

When we got off the train at Baden Baden, it was completely dark out. We walked out of the station and realized it was raining. Our hostel was a twenty-minute walk away, so we started in that direction.

Trees were glistening under the ornate and antique looking street lamps. The leaves reflected the white street lights every time the wind would rustle them. The eerie quiet was broken only by the pitter patter of the rain and the leaves tossing against each other. Haider and I walked along a pedestrian path surrounded by wet grass shining in the dark.

"What a place we're in," I whispered.

"We're walking inside a fairytale," Haider answered. "Don't break the spell!"

At midnight, we finally arrived at the hostel, a typical old German timber-framed country house. An old man was sitting at the reception desk.

"We booked a room for two," Haider told him.

"For tonight?" the old man inquired.

"Yes."

"Nice weather to stay out late like this." The old man smiled at us, his eyes beaming with a nostalgic recognition.

We were shown to our room, a tiny place with a bunk-bed and a small window opening into the dark courtyard.

"Sleep well, kids," the old man said as he closed the door.

That night, we held each other close on the tiny mattress on the bottom bunk. Indeed, we were in a fairytale. We did our best to hold on to the spell, to not let it escape our grasp.

In the morning, the room was flooded with sunlight from the lone window. The bare little hostel room felt like a luxurious farmhouse in the countryside. I opened the window.

"What a lovely garden!" I exclaimed as I looked outside.

The backyard of the hostel was full of flowers of every colour, lushly growing in bushes. At the end of the garden was a tiled area, where black and white tiles formed a giant chess board. Human sized pawns, bishops, kings and queens in black and white were sitting amiss on the tiles.

"What a beautiful place we're in!" Haider commented as he looked outside as well.

Haider raised me up and made me sit on the windowsill. He held my legs as I leaned my torso outside and faced the sky. There was not a cloud in sight and the morning sun was glaring in my eyes like never before. I felt like I was flying in this otherworldly garden, soaring high into lands of beauty and luxury, away from shitty Duisburg into new worlds!

"How beautiful you look, my darling," Haider cried out to me.

He grabbed my torso, lifted me up from the windowsill where I was sitting, and passionately pressed me onto the bed. I could feel his weight on me. His heart was beating against mine, and in that moment, I wanted him like nothing else in the world. As he bared down, I felt his body against mine, and I reached my hands all over him, feeling his every nook, exploring him, and every touch felt like fire. We kissed as we undressed each other, and Haider lowered himself, kissing me all over my neck, my bosom, my navel, and lower. Bliss was the only thing I felt, and my heart was beating along with his.

Without warning, the door opened and the janitor was here.

"No! Not now!" Haider shouted as he reached for the blanket to cover us.

"Sorry!" the janitor shouted as he realized what was going on. "I will come back later."

He promptly closed the door.

Haider and I started laughing. Normally, this would have killed the mood, but not in our case.

"What a naughty pair we are," Haider quipped.

"Being walked in on by the janitor!" I replied. "Yeah we're getting indecent."

"You say that like it's a bad thing!" Haider coyly retorted. "What do you expect from two young people passionately in love? I say it's beautiful! Love is beautiful! No one should be ashamed of it. And I can't wait for the day when we will make love for the first time!"

These declarations had become the norm for him, but I was no longer skeptical, I knew he was completely genuine. With time, I allowed myself to let go and let him in.

He looked into my eyes. And in that gaze, I felt my insides roar and call to him. Yes, I wanted him, all of him.

"But let's wait," Haider put his hand on my shoulder. "Let us wait until the right time. For now, we have Baden Baden to explore."

We had breakfast downstairs. I had cereal with milk and Haider had a piece of toast. We couldn't decide on which kind of tea to pick, so we went with a cup with both a mint and a raspberry teabag. It was so delicious that we poured another cup with orange blossom, blueberry, and green tea teabags. People looked at us strangely but we laughed. We were truly enjoying ourselves and did not need external validation.

We walked outside into the courtyard. I looked at all the flowers whereas Haider went straight to the giant chess pieces.

"Come, let's play chess!" he cheered. I loved his childish enthusiasm, how he encouraged me to try new things. "You know how to play chess, right?"

"I know the basic rules, but that's about it."

"I used to play chess in high school and played in a chess championship in India back in the day."

This guy never ceases to amaze me, I thought. What *can't* he do?

Haider picked black and I went for white so that I could move first. At every step, Haider duly explained every potential risk and benefit of the next move ... and the potential moves and outcomes that would result in each case. I was amazed at how he was able to think so many steps ahead. After half an hour, it was a clear victory for Haider and a blatant defeat for me. Normally secretly competitive, I had no expectations of winning against a chess champion, so I just smiled meekly.

"You've got potential though," Haider reassured me. "You're actually quite good at this."

I rolled my eyes. I knew better than that, but I was flattered.

We wandered out onto the streets of Baden Baden. The trees that lined the streets were lush and green, and every house, embodying the classic German pastoral "cottage-core" style, was more beautiful than the next.

"This must be heaven on earth," Haider said in admiration of his surroundings.

I felt the same. We stopped by a little fairytale coffee shop. The porch was ornate, decked out with pink roses. As we entered, we noticed that every little wrought iron, white-painted table and chair was covered with white lace. The attention to detail was stunningly immersive, making me feel lost in a dream.

"Guten Morgen!" A little old lady greeted us good morning in German as we walked in.

We sat at a table and looked at the menu. Cakes and pastries abounded, one more intricate and luxurious than the next. I was in total delight.

"Oh look, they have Black Forest cake!" I cried out. "It's my favourite type of cake and what better place to order it than on the verge of the Black Forest?"

Haider ordered a small cup of coffee, which was served to us along with my gigantic slice of cake.

I indulged in a large spoonful and suddenly realized that this was the *real* deal. I didn't know that the original version of the Black Forest cake contained cherry liqueur.

"Lord is it delicious, but I'm going to be tipsy all day!" I laughed whimsically, letting myself absorb the happiness and roll with it. If I was going to get tipsy, I might as well enjoy it.

"Alcoholic I see? Those Germans! Fun!" Haider replied playfully.

We shared the piece of cake and walked outside into the sunshine. We wandered into the Lichtentaler Allee, a lavish, well-kept park along the Oos River. The beautiful landscape was as lush as the surroundings of Duisburg were desolate.

Haider began to sing:

Hey Jude, don't make it bad.
Take a sad song and make it better.

"What song is that?" I asked. Haider ignored me teasingly, as if I were kidding, and continued. It must be a really popular song for him to take it for granted that I knew it. He knew how clueless I was about pop culture.

As Haider carried on about Jude, whomever that was, I couldn't help but marvel at all the music that existed out there, but that I'd never heard of.

"It's 'Hey Jude' by the Beatles," Haider finally answered me, after singing another verse and the chorus.

"I only know 'Yellow Submarine' and 'Across the Universe' by the Beatles." I must have grown up under a rock.

"I like the Beatles. When I was in Kuwait, I always wanted to learn to play music. My mom taught me Hindustani music, but I wanted to learn Western music as well. Finally, I was given a guitar by a family friend, and I started learning English songs. My mom thought they were inspired by the devil. But my musical horizons expanded and I never regretted it. I bet I know more English pop songs than you."

"You're probably right," I conceded. Everyone knew more English pop songs than I did.

We sat down on a bench in a quiet corner that was isolated from the rest of the park.

"I want to teach you 'Let it Be.'" Haider began singing.

I listened to Haider sing. I really liked the song. I didn't realize the Beatles had such depth, since I always associated them with popular music, which I assumed was frivolous by design.

"Remember, my darling," Haider said after the song, "when times get hard, and they will get hard when we get back to Canada, remember this: 'There will be an answer, let it be.'"

I nodded.

"In a couple hours, we will part ways," Haider continued, "Let's immortalize this last day when we are together. Let's take a picture on this bench. Let us kiss but hide our faces with the umbrella."

We asked a passerby to take the picture for us.

"This shall be our picture," Haider said. "When we write songs and poems, this will be the picture the world will know us by."

I looked at the picture. We could see Haider's feet on the ground, and my legs over Haider's. My sky blue umbrella hid most of our bodies. It was so romantic and so cheesy at the same time. But it was very undeniably us.

We spent the rest of the afternoon in silence, just taking each other in, soaking up those last moments together. I thought about my plans over the next few days. I was to spend a day in Ulm visiting a friend from McGill who was interning there. Then, I was to visit Italy with my old friend Arielle from Montreal. Then, all of us Duisburg people, including Haider, decided to meet in Munich for a weekend. And then I will travel onward to Austria and Eastern Europe hopefully. I took a deep breath and put a brave face towards the future.

"Remember sweetheart," Haider said, "we're parting ways for a week, not a lifetime. I'll see you in Munich and we will kiss and we will miss each other and you will tell me everything you've seen on your trip, and we will be happy together again. Alright?"

I nodded, but inside I was sad. I didn't realize how much I needed him until the prospect of his absence was on the horizon.

Around 6 p.m., Haider and I walked back to the Baden Baden Hauptbahnhof. I could feel tears well up inside of me.

"This is farewell." Haider was solemn. "A chapter in our life has closed. Now go catch your train. You have a beautiful future ahead of you! Fly high, my darling, and don't you cry!"

I looked back at Haider and climbed on the train, waving back at him. As the train departed, I looked at Haider's hand waving at me until he was gone from my sight. I sat alone with only a backpack and let reality sink in. Yes indeed, my 10-week internship was over and so was my life together with Haider. What future awaited me?

I opened my laptop and I saw that, on the desktop, Haider had saved a video of himself singing with his guitar! I plugged in my earphones and watched it as my eyes welled up with tears.

"Hey sweetie," Haider began in the video, "this song is for when you are away and miss hearing my voice."

I was balling my eyes out by the end of that first sentence alone.

"Just close your eyes and hear me out:

> *I hate to see you cry,*
> *Laying there in that position ...*

As the song bid me to dry my tears and went on about how to look at the bright side of things, despite the pain that was intertwined with life itself, I was sobbing hard. Yes, it had just sunk in that Haider was no longer by my side. I was going to miss him terribly.

17

July 24, 2011

The evening I departed from Baden Baden, I arrived in Ulm in the southwest of Germany. Marie, a girl from my program at McGill was staying there for her RISE internship, so I crashed at her place. The next day, I wandered around Ulm, touring the narrow winding streets with the same timber-framed houses typical of Southern Germany. Ulm was the birthplace of Albert Einstein, and I went to check out the Einstein memorial and house. The exhibit was closed that day, but I took a picture with a sculpture of Einstein outside. Obligatory nerd fangirl moment for anyone claiming to be a physics student.

Then that night, I took the night train from Germany through Switzerland to Florence in Italy. My friend Arielle, whom I've known since CEGEP, spent every summer in Italy with her family. Her father was a wealthy jewelry merchant. They invited me to stay with them at their five-star hotel.

That night, I slept in the train in a tiny compartment along with five other people, but I managed to sleep so soundly that I woke up after eight in the morning while the train was supposed to arrive in Florence at seven. I panicked, thinking I missed my stop and was on my way to Venice. The man next to me reassured me that the train was at least three hours late. Right, we were dealing with romantic Italians, not punctual Germans. I breathed a sigh of relief and opened the curtains to look outside. The morning sun was shining on the lush hills and beautiful houses of Tuscany, what a treat to the eyes! I was baffled by the beauty of what I saw and only wished Haider was here to bask in it with me.

We arrived in Florence at nine o'clock. It took me a whole hour to find the hidden entrance of the luxury five-star hotel where Arielle's family was staying. When I finally found the place, I walked in with my messy hair, wool poncho and backpack. The front desk officer almost called Security when, all at once, Arielle's father emerged and greeted me with a loud "Good morning!" I was promptly shown to their suite. Two suites in fact, one for the parents and the other for Arielle and her siblings.

That day, Arielle's father hired a private tour guide and we visited all the main attractions of the city plus the Florence synagogue, the largest synagogue of the region, an obligatory visit for any Jewish family on holiday. We had authentic Italian pizza for lunch and wandered around the high-end shops the rest of the day.

Arielle and I were glad to see each other. We talked about our love lives, and it felt like a reversal of fortune for both of us. She was falling out of love with her amazing boyfriend of one year while I ditched Chris to end up with Haider. Arielle was upset at the turn of events, and I tried my best to comfort her. But deep down I was afraid that fate would do the same to me.

The next day, Arielle's family went on a day trip to the Tuscan countryside, while I chose to stay in Florence to explore it on my own. I visited the Galleria d'Uffizi, the must-visit art museum of Florence. I saw Michaelangelo's *David* and other marble works of art. It was beautiful, but to be honest, I was bored. When I left the museum, it was late afternoon, and I wandered around the Arno River. It had just rained, and now in the sunshine, everything was glistening brightly. The heavy metal chains bordering the water were full of padlocks of every size and shape. I noticed initials engraved on each padlock. I remembered the padlock Haider and I left on the Tetrader. How far have we come since!

I looked at the Arno, at the surrounding hills straight out of Renaissance paintings in the late afternoon sun. There was nobody, and the city was quiet with only sounds of church bells in the distance and my own footsteps. I wondered if this was what happiness felt like. I thought of Haider. I thought of my whirlwind stay in Duisburg. I thought of my luxurious time in Florence. Was this happiness? Or had I left happiness behind?

The next day, Arielle and her family left Florence for the seaside town of Capri, and I was left alone in Florence. I spent the morning at a coffee shop, with a small espresso and a plate of cookies. It was raining, and as I sat there with the treats and my laptop, I felt rejuvenated and adventurous. I decided to visit Pisa, which was nearby, so I booked a hostel bed in Pisa for the night and set out to the train station.

I took the train in the afternoon and arrived in Pisa around eight in the evening. Right from the train station, I saw the leaning tower, white marble against a colourful sunset. How surreal! I walked straight towards the tower, oblivious to everything around me. I walked through small streets bordered by colourful buildings with windows and blinds wide open. Pink and white curtains blew out from the windows. It was a cozy afternoon with folks coming home after work. I saw a couple holding hands and stopping in the middle of the street to kiss. The man was wearing a white shirt and the woman wore a red dress.

It appeared to me, to my surprise, that Italy was just as romantic as described, if not more so. It made me wish Haider was there with me.

The leaning tower loomed larger and larger over my head, until I stood a few feet away from it. How majestic and surreal, like the carcass of a ship at the bottom of the ocean. I held my breath and observed it in its splendour. I noticed there was a small restaurant right by the tower and decided to have dinner right then and there, enjoying the spontaneity. For once in my life, I had complete control over where I went, what I did, and how I went about my day. I ordered penne arrabiata and installed myself alone at the table. Captain Ali, the stuffed dog we got in Dusseldorf, sat beside me and I took out *Mandala* by Pearl S. Buck, the only book I had brought with me to Europe. It was, uncannily enough, a love story between an Indian prince and an American pianist. My friend Elanna had lent it to me before I left for Germany. How spot on!

I had the best pasta I'd ever tasted in my life. By the time I was done enjoying this leisurely solitude, I had read a chapter of the book and noticed it was completely dark outside. The problem then dawned on me: I had the leaning tower to guide me when I came here, but how would I find my way back to the hostel I booked for the night? I did not have a map of the city, silly me. I decided to walk back and retrace my steps. I tried to recall which streets I took. I walked and walked, and ended up in a desolate area by the highway. I did not recall ever seeing a highway on my way there.

I was starting to get worried and decided to ask a few locals who were smoking outside their house. The man barely spoke any English, but enlisted his friend to help, and then his neighbour, and then there were three men arguing loudly in Italian about which way was best to return to the train station, which was right next to my hostel. With no consensus in sight, I thanked them and wandered off on my own. I saw a bus station and decided to wait for the bus. Perhaps the driver could tell me if the bus went back to the train station?

I sat at the bus stop, and a while later, a young man wearing a white embroidered tunic came to the station.

"You are Japanese?" he asked me.

"No."

"Vietnamese? Korean?"

"No, I'm Chinese."

"Ah. Hi, my name is Karim. What is your name?"

"Elizabeth."

I told Karim about getting lost and he laughed.

"What a tourist you are. Lucky you, the next bus does take you back to the train station. I'll escort you back to your hostel."

I thanked him profusely, and as the bus came, we started chatting. Karim was 25, from Tunisia. He had spent some time studying science in France, but he didn't like it, so he moved to Italy to study Italian literature in Pisa for three years. He knew Pisa like the back of his hand. He then found a job as a sailor, working on boats crossing the Mediterranean.

"It pays well!" Karim recounted, "and I get to visit lots of places."

The bus arrived at the train station and we got off.

"It's barely 11 p.m.," Karim said. "Do you want to take a walk with me? I'll show you around Pisa."

I knew he was a strange man in a strange country at this hour, but I was in a spontaneous mood, so I thought why not, and agreed. It was always nice to tour cities with locals. Karim showed me around his university campus, the parks, the port around the Arno River. We ended up back at the leaning tower and the Duomo cathedral around midnight. There was an eerie silence, and the moon was reflected on the marble floor. Karim and I chatted about our childhoods and the pains of being a third culture kid.

"I used to hurt myself too," Karim said. He showed me his arms with several burns from cigarettes. "Us Arabs have different values than Europeans. My mom thinks I'm up to no good and that I'm 'whitewashed.'"

Karim paused and looked at me.

"You look beautiful under the moonlight," he said.

I was taken aback. I didn't expect the compliment.

"I like you and only wish you were single," he sighed.

"I should get back to the hostel," I said.

He nodded and we stood up and started walking slowly towards the hostel.

"Do you know Charles Aznavour?" Karim asked me.

"The French singer?"

"Let me sing you a song from him," Karim said.

Wow, he was very forward! It reminded me of Haider, and I wondered if Haider's over the top displays of love were a cultural trait. Arielle had told me that Haider's approach reminded her of the Israeli guys on her Birthright trip. She said they fell in love hard and fast, moved quickly, and then fell out of love just as quickly and just as abruptly. I hoped that wasn't true about Haider. Yet here was this guy who also had a similar cultural background, being so forward and demonstrative when he barely knew me.

We crossed a bridge over the Arno, and Karim was serenading me with a love song in French in Pisa, only a few days after I had left Haider's embrace. Oh how unpredictable life is!

We arrived at my hostel and Karim stood in front of me, not wanting to leave.

"Please give me a kiss before bidding me goodbye."

I said no, I was taken.

"Please, just on the cheeks!"

I said no meant no. Karim tried to force a kiss on my lips, and I pushed him aside as much as I could.

"Please give me your Skype or Facebook name then. Add me."

I refused.

"You're the most stubborn girl I've ever met," he said. "But do you know if you'll still be with that guy in five years? Who will you be in five years? Where will you be living? Do you know?"

I felt the edge of fear growing inside. How did Karim get under my skin? I felt like just listening to him made me disloyal to Haider.

"I don't know," I said earnestly.

"That's right, you don't. So don't forget me and tonight."

Karim left, and I was all alone at the door of the hostel. I stood, stupefied. What had just happened, I wondered. Karim had caught me offguard in a vulnerable moment. I was suddenly second-guessing myself, afraid of the future. What would become of Haider and me in five years? Five years was a long time. I'd be twenty-four by then and Haider would be twenty-six. Would we still be together? So many questions but no answers. I spent the night tossing and turning.

The next morning, I used the hostel Wi-Fi to write an email to Haider.

"I'm ashamed of myself," I wrote. "I met a guy who was hitting on me, and I feel dirty for enjoying his company. And then he tried to kiss me. And then he frightened me by asking if I knew I'd still be with you in five years when I declined."

Haider wrote back a couple minutes later. "My darling, that guy can go screw himself for doing this to you.

Hold on sweetheart. We're meeting in Munich tomorrow. Let me hug you tight then. You will forget all of this, I promise."

I held on to his hope. I ran to the train station and booked trains all the way back to Munich, regardless of the price. As I sat on the train, my thoughts were all about Haider. Had his love for me cooled down in my absence? What would our reunion be like? How I longed for his embrace!

18

July 30, 2011

I spent the night on the train and arrived in Munich in the morning. As the train was pulling into the station, my heart was pounding. Would Haider be there to greet me? How would it be, meeting him again after a week's absence? It was a week that felt like a year. I made my way to the exit early, hoping to get off first.

I climbed out of the wagon, and looked around the platform. Haider was standing right near the head of the train. I ran to him and he received me with open arms.

"Oh my bunny," Haider whispered, "how I've missed you!"

"I missed you too," I answered.

Haider's embrace was so warm against the cool morning air. Indeed I had missed him. More than I even realized myself.

"Come, we're together again," Haider said. "Don't you worry. Let's have breakfast. I've been waiting for you since my train arrived this morning at six. I was at that Starbucks over there. Let's head there."

At the Starbucks, Haider ordered a London Fog for me. I got my favourite chocolate muffin with melted caramel inside. Haider and I sat down side by side on the bar stools, and we chatted and chatted about everything we had seen and done over the past week.

"I'm so glad you enjoyed Florence," Haider said. "And please forget about that sketchy dude in Pisa. Don't let him affect us."

I nodded.

We joined the rest of the crew, David, Karen, Roger, Will, and Wendy, at the entrance of the station around ten. We wandered around Munich, visiting the Cathedral and the Town Hall. For lunch, we went to a local pub and had *weiss wurst*, or white sausage. It was so delicious and we had so many of them. I almost finished one whole pint of beer, and ended up lying on Haider's lap for a while. Haider stroked my hair and caressed my face. I felt cherished, so cherished.

Later that day, we visited Nymphenburg Palace, the baroque summer residence of the former rulers of Bavaria. It was beautiful and we even got to witness a wedding. I looked at the bride's extraordinarily long white dress and the photographer capturing her in the garden, the beautiful sports car that drove her there, and the groom admiring her. I felt an itch in my stomach. For the first time in my life, weddings did not leave me feeling indifferent anymore. I looked with hope at Haider. I looked away, I knew it was too early to think about this.

While the others were still photographing the palace, Haider and I wandered into the woods near the palace gardens. We held hands and walked in silence. We desperately needed to be together after so long.

"Liz," Haider finally broke our silence, "as I lived alone in Duisburg this week, I kept thinking about you, and I missed you so much. But doubts were mounting in my mind. I was afraid, I admit. What if during this time, you'd forgotten about me? What if things would be different when we meet again?" Haider paused. Then he picked me up in his arms.

"I was so relieved," Haider said, "when you ran straight into my arms this morning. Oh my darling, I've only had eyes for you. I'm so glad that we love each other more than ever. I'm so grateful!"

We kissed, and in Haider's arms, I felt like I was floating on a cloud. The forest surrounding us felt so serene, so peaceful. Indeed, any time we had together was a gift to be cherished.

That night, we had to sleep in separate rooms because our friends booked a room for the guys and a room for the girls. Everybody went to parties outside, and Haider and I sat alone in the common room downstairs. We talked about anything and everything and went to bed very late.

The next day, we visited the Deutsche Museum, a science and technology museum. Corny as it sounds, Haider and I did not pay much attention to the cool tech artifacts. We had eyes only for each other. We were torn at the thought that we would have to be apart again as Haider had to return to Duisburg, and I was to carry on my travels.

After dinner, I accompanied everyone to the train station. My stomach was in knots. I didn't know how to carry on alone and dreaded it. As we arrived at the station, Haider sat with me on a bench and we were silent.

"How I wish I wasn't going away," Haider whispered.

"Do you have to go?" I asked, my eyes pleading.

Haider looked at me. I saw sorrow in his eyes. Then I saw hope.

"No, I don't have to go," he exclaimed. "You're right. We are free beings. Let me stay one more night with you. Let me call in sick!"

And so Haider and I bid everyone else goodbye and ran out of the train station in jubilation.

"I love you so much," Haider couldn't stop repeating.

"I love you too," I answered every time.

"Where do you want to stay for the night?" Haider then asked.

"I saw an ad earlier about a tent hostel somewhere," I said. "Sound interesting?"

"Let's look it up!"

We sat at the Starbucks again and looked up the tent hostel. Indeed, it was a gigantic tent with about 150 beds inside. The price was 10 euros per person, a bargain compared to at least 25 euros for any other hostel.

"Let's go!" Haider cheered.

We took the bus according to the directions and arrived in a quiet residential neighbourhood. Strange that this party place should be there, I thought. Several other girls also got off at the same stop as Haider and me.

"Going to the tent hostel?" one girl asked me.

"Yes! You too?" we replied.

"Yes, do you know which way it is?"

"No, let's find out together!"

We walked a few blocks where a growing number of young people with backpacks walked in the same direction. Then, there it was!

A banner was erected in the middle of the street with "Welcome to the Tent Hostel Munich" written on it. We immediately saw the main tent. It looked like a circus tent but was entirely white. Several other tents were installed surrounding it, one with *Open Bar* written on it.

We went to the Welcome booth. An old man was sitting at the window.

"Welcome guys," he said to us. "Here for the first time?"

"Yes!"

We paid for one night, and he gave us four wool blankets each, in a questionable brownish colour.

"It's going to be really cold at night," he explained. "If you're still cold with these, come back and get more, it's free. And don't worry, they are clean. We wash them after every use."

We smiled.

"I used to be a youngster like you guys," the old man confided. "I wanted to travel my whole life, but then I had a family and had to pay bills. So I opened this place for all youngsters like me to stay together. Seeing so many youth travelers here makes me so happy."

"Thanks man," Haider said. "We really appreciate this."

We went inside the tent and saw a sea of bunkbeds. There was a pool table and a ping-pong table in the middle and some couches. We picked a bunkbed near the edge and installed ourselves there.

"We're going to sleep together on the lower level anyway," I said. "Let's hang the extra blankets as curtains around our bed for some intimacy."

"Great idea!" Haider replied.

He went to get another four blankets. Soon we made a nest, with one blanket covering every side of the bed. How cozy it was inside! We spent some time chatting with the other folks, played a match at the pool table, sang some songs, and decided to retire early. We hadn't felt this intimate for what seemed like ages.

"I'm so glad we are here," Haider said. "I'm so glad I stayed. What an adventure this is!"

"I'm happy to have you here," I assented.

I rested my head on Haider's shoulder.

"It's like we have a new home together again!" I exclaimed.

"Indeed, how I wish to have a home with you always," Haider said. But he looked weary all of a sudden.

"Sweetie," he said, "I want you to understand something."

"What is it?"

"We might not have a home together for quite a while. I'm sorry I have to break it to you."

I nodded. I felt a familiar apprehension growing inside of me.

"I come from an Indian family, and in our culture, kids don't move out. Back then, even married kids lived with their parents. We're more liberal now. But it won't be easy for my parents to understand why I want to be with you and have a home with you. It will be especially hard to tell my father about you. My father's sister's daughter, my cousin, married a Hindu guy five years ago, and my father hasn't spoken to either her or even her mother, his own sister, since. It's going to be hard, real hard, for him to accept you."

I felt a sense of gravity. I expected trouble ahead, but I only realized then how hard it was going to be.

"But I know you, my sweetie," Haider continued. "You are a tough girl, you are smart, and you are understanding. I know you can bear it. Eventually, we will make it through. Remember this: we may not have a home in space, but we will have a home in time. One day, we will marry, live together, and have pretty little children, alright? Just be patient until that day comes."

I kissed Haider on the cheek. But I felt afraid. I held on to Haider tighter. Despite everything, I had fallen for him. My heart ached at the inevitable troubles that lay ahead.

"Liz, sweetie," Haider said, "don't be afraid. We'll make it through! We'll travel the world and live in all the tents in the world if you wish! And we will never have to be apart again. But for now, I don't want to delay you. You go travelling tomorrow, like a brave girl, alright? And tell me everything about it afterwards! Then one day, we can go visit all the places you went together, and you will lead and show me the way!"

I nodded and suppressed a sob in my throat. But he was right. *Yes, I will go on my own tomorrow!* I was ready to face the world.

19

August 1, 2011

After spending the night at the tent hostel, I bid farewell to Haider again at the Munich train station. As Haider's train departed, I sat alone, trying to piece together what I was to do next. I had long dreamt of visiting Austria, the Czech Republic, and even Poland. The pianist in me longed to visit the home countries of my favourite composers, Mozart, Chopin, and Liszt, to name a few. I had exactly ten days left in Europe. Where was I to spend them? I felt excitement welling up inside of me. I looked around me and saw a beautiful photograph of the Neuschwanstein Castle on the wall of the train station. *Yes, I'll visit it.* I thought to myself.

I took the train to the castle and, with a cohort of tourists, walked up the mountain to reach the castle. The pine forest surrounding me was straight out of a fairytale, especially with the horse-drawn carriages passing by full of passengers heading in the same direction. I felt like Beauty walking towards the Beast's castle. As I arrived at the foot of the castle, how small I felt, and how tall it looked! I wished Haider were there to make me feel like a princess. "Not this time, I can't come with you," he had said. "But you go and enjoy yourself." I sighed.

I entered the castle with a tour guide, and it was even more sumptuous on the inside. There was a chapel made out of marble and gold, ballrooms, and luxurious bedrooms with baldaquin beds. How lavish it must have been to live here! I later wandered on the footpath behind the castle to view it from a distance. As I walked along, I couldn't help but notice all of the happy families with kids travelling alongside me. I, who had grown up resenting children and looking down on large families with too many to handle, was suddenly envying their happiness. How idyllic and wholesome they look, I thought.

I arrived at Queen Mary's bridge behind the castle. It was a thin metal-framed bridge over a deep valley, and the view on it was incredible. I felt suspended in the liminal space between the heavens and the earth. A gentleman offered to take a picture of me with the castle in the background. I happily agreed. I looked at the photograph. Somehow, I looked lonely.

Later that day, I took the train to Salzburg in Austria to spend the evening. I almost got lost trying to find the hostel around midnight. When I finally arrived, I was completely exhausted and collapsed on the bed.

The next morning, I explored Salzburg's beautiful streets, eating apple strudel for breakfast. I bought some Mozart chocolate, a local delicacy consisting of pistachios, marzipan, and nougat covered in dark chocolate, for Haider and my piano teacher back in Montreal. I wandered into the Salzburg cathedral and sat on a wooden pew. I remembered Haider, I remembered Chris, I remembered my days in Köln, I remembered Haider praying for my happiness. How things had changed in one single summer! I silently understood that I'd grown like never before in the past few months. I was no longer the little girl who had arrived alone in Germany a few months ago, but who I was becoming, I had no idea. I was in a sort of transition state between phases of matter, to use yet another physics analogy. It was yet unclear what new phase I would take on. It was all up in the air at that point.

I saw little candles on the side of the cathedral that could be lit with a small donation to the church. I lit two candles side by side under Mother Mary's statue. *Mother Mary, please protect us in times of trouble*, I said silently to myself. I left the cathedral with a lighter heart.

As I walked out of the cathedral, I ran into a group of street musicians playing jazz. I was brought back to reality. I should enjoy my trip, I reminded myself. Haider can be with me in spirit. I found some comfort in this realization. I wandered through the tourist shops that littered the winding streets around the cathedral when I ran into Wendy, who had also finished her internship and was travelling alone. What a coincidence!

That afternoon, we visited the birthplace of Mozart, which was turned into a museum. We learned about the life and art of the composer and had a great time. Later in the evening, we went to a puppet show iconic of the city. The puppets were playing *The Sound of Music*. How Austrian of them. As I saw Maria falling in love with the Captain Georg von Trapp, I felt tears well up. I realized that I, too, wished to have a musical family with seven children. Yes, from the quirky physics nerd that I was, to this. What an ironic turn of events. Wendy and I spent the rest of the evening watching fireworks over the Salzach River.

The next day, Wendy went to Vienna, and I spent the morning alone climbing the hills to the Hohensalzburg fortress, a medieval relic. By the end of the climb, I felt exhausted. The castle was beautiful, but my heart wasn't there. I felt weary and out of sorts. I climbed down the castle and lay on the grass by the bank of the Salzach river. After a nap, every one of my muscles was hurting.

I walked to the nearest McDonald's, ordered a salad, and went online on my MacBook.

"Haider, are you there?" I messaged him on Skype.

He wasn't. He must be busy with his work at his internship, which hadn't yet ended. I felt a single tear run down my cheek.

"Haider, listen. I can't do this anymore," I typed again, oblivious to the fact that Haider wasn't around. "I feel sick. I think I got a cold. What should I do?" I just needed to tell him *something*, I needed to hear his voice and feel his presence somehow, as his spirit was waning in me.

I buried my head in my crossed arms on the cold plastic table. I felt tired. So tired. After what felt like an eternity, suddenly I heard Haider's message notification popping up on my laptop.

"Sorry bunny, I just finished work. Tell me, what's wrong?"

"I don't know Haider. I just feel sick."

"Something bad happened?"

"No."

"You exhausted yourself?"

"Perhaps."

"I thought you were enjoying your trip! I read your messages about the Mozart Museum and the puppet show. You sounded happy!"

"I was."

"Then what happened?"

"Haider, I don't know. I just don't know how to live without you anymore. I'm at loss. I'm afraid of the future and what it will bring. I don't feel at home unless I'm with you!"

"Oh my bunny, oh sweetie. It's not the time to worry about things like this! We will have a home in the future. For now, fly high and enjoy yourself!"

"I don't know, Haider. I feel like our time in Europe will be our last chance at being together. I'm sorry. I really can't live without you. I'm sick, I'm tired, I can't do this anymore."

"Then come home to me, if that's what you wish. I have a mattress here in Siddartha's room, we can share it. Let me nurse you back to health."

I was sobbing. I felt an unfathomable relief. Here I was, young and independent, with all of Europe to visit. Yet I just wanted to curl up on a tiny foam mattress with Haider for the rest of my life.

Home, I will be back home now. That's all that matters.

"Are you crying? Don't, sweetie. I'm not there yet to wipe your tears. Save them for when you'll be with me. I missed you too, my darling. I'm glad too, that you're coming back, that you're coming home. I can't wait to see you again."

I smiled through my tears. Yes, home was calling. I immediately went to the train station and booked last-minute train tickets to Duisburg, one after another. I didn't look at the price, I didn't care at all. All that mattered now was going home. I needed Haider. I needed him more than the air I breathed, cliché as it sounded.

I boarded the train an hour later, and, as the landscape fly past the windows, the late afternoon sun shone on me with a golden sheen. How beautiful the Earth was. When else would I have the freedom to just explore wherever I wanted to go? Warsaw, Paris, London, Prague, Budapest, Barcelona, Lisbon …. Yet all I cared about was coming back to Duisburg. Yes, shitty Duisburg. I missed it. I missed it so much. And, as I sat on the train, I saw in my mind's eye the rugged Duisburg Hauptbahnhof with its sinister red lettering on its grimy glass roof. Our little apartment, which was no longer ours. Volkstrasse, our street. Lidl the supermarket around the corner where we bought food for our daily meals. Our kitchen, where Haider taught me the basics of cooking, à la Indian. The tree outside our house, from which the birds would sing every morning before the sun was up. How glorious Duisburg had become to me. As I switched trains and transited in Munich then in Frankfurt, I only had Duisburg in mind.

I arrived in Duisburg at the strike of midnight, and, as I descended from the train, I ran straight to Haider who was waiting for me on the platform. I jumped into his embrace and I wept. I wept tears of happiness. Home sweet home here I have come!

20

August 4, 2011

The morning after I came back to Duisburg, I woke up with a huge cold. My nose was runny and I was having chills and fever. *First I was lovesick, now I am actually sick.*

"Poor thing," Haider said. "Stay in bed, I'll make you breakfast."

We had Nutella sandwiches and warm chai. I felt revived little by little.

"What do you want for lunch?" Haider asked me.

"Soup," I said immediately. "I'm so cold, I need something to warm me up."

"I have kohlrabi here in the kitchen, so I can make kohlrabi soup. Do you like it?"

"What is a kohlrabi?"

Haider showed me the odd-looking vegetable. It had a pale green bulbous stem, with dark green leaves growing out of it.

"You will like it I think," Haider said.

I nodded. I didn't have the energy to ask for anything else.

Haider made a vegetable soup with kohlrabi, onions, carrots, tomatoes, and various odds and ends that could be found in the sparsely stocked kitchen. He brought me a bowl that was still steaming.

"Careful, it's hot," he said. "Here's a spoon."

I tasted it. It was delicious and felt so nourishing. I had two bowls and by the end I was sweating a little.

"Will you make me kohlrabi soup every time I get sick?" I asked Haider.

"I will, and for when I'm not around, I will teach you how to make it yourself."

I nodded. I was so happy to be back in Duisburg. Later that day, Siddartha came back from work and greeted us.

"You guys look so happy together," he said. "Makes me miss my girl."

Siddartha loved a girl back in Nepal, Haider told me. He hadn't seen her in years. He would marry her when he returned to Nepal after graduating from college in England.

"I smoke when I miss her," Siddartha admitted. "Haider, don't be like me. Don't become a smoker, it's bad for you."

I spent the next few days in Siddartha's room, nursing myself back to health. Siddartha and Haider would come back after work, and we'd all share a meal together. They usually made South Asian food, sat on the floor, and ate with their hands while blasting Bollywood music. I joined them and felt at home in this atmosphere more than I could explain, even though it was so foreign, so far removed from what I was used to.

A couple days later, Haider and I spent our (actual) last Sunday together in Köln. As much as I wanted to stay, my plane ticket had already been booked and I had to prepare for the new semester. We revisited every place we'd been before. The cathedral. The chocolate museum. The banks of the Rhein. We were full of emotions by the end of the day when we got back to our Starbucks.

"Haider," I said with a heavy heart, "what a great time we had together this summer."

"Indeed we did," he answered. We were terse and matter-of-fact in order to avoid the emotional elephant in the room.

"I don't know what lies ahead. I don't know if I can do it."

"What are you afraid of?"

"You made your way into my life little by little and now I can't even find myself anymore. I don't know who I am anymore. I feel like half a person without you. Who will I be when I go back to Montreal?"

I knew I was never going to be the person I was before I met Haider ever again. I never thought I was the type to become *that girl*—in fact, I used to roll my eyes at that girl—but there I was. All those corny love stories and over the top romances in books I'd read and movies I'd seen suddenly made sense.

"Do you not want to continue our relationship beyond this summer? Are you afraid for our future?" Haider was calm yet tepid.

"I am afraid." More than he could ever imagine.

"Liz, I know I told you this already. It will not be easy. Long-distance relationships are tough. It will be very rocky. We will fight, we will hurt. You have to want to do this with your whole heart, or we won't make it."

I felt fear rising inside me. I wanted him more than ever, but I also didn't want the emotional rollercoaster.

"What shall I do then?" I asked, desperate.

"There are two options," Haider said solemnly. This was a conversation he knew he was going to have to have, but that he wanted to put off as long as possible. "Either we end the story here. You and I return to Canada as the strangers that we were before we met. You return to your old life and your old self, like nothing has changed." Haider paused. "Or, we return and continue to love each other through long distance and hardships and trials, with hopes that it will be worth it one day when we build our home together for good."

He looked at me. "Do you want to go back to your old life as if you've never known me?"

I looked down at my feet. I thought about my old life. About Chris. About the nihilistic physics department at McGill. No, I did not want it. I didn't want to do it. How could I pretend I hadn't been changed by Haider? I couldn't.

"Are we still together?" Haider asked. I felt the tension build with each second after he asked that pointed question.

Who was I kidding? I immediately teared up and hugged him tightly.

"There, there, I thought so."

Haider kissed me on the forehead. He looked relieved. So was I. We sat down on the couch and he held me.

"You've been telling me about these blogs on Tumblr that you follow," Haider said. "I've been thinking. Do you want us to create a blog together?"

"That would be so nice!" I replied. I immediately felt giddy with excitement about the prospect of connecting with him that way.

"You could put pictures of everything you find beautiful on it. It will be the template for the dream life of our future."

"And you should post your poetry!"

"Of course I will. I will never stop writing poetry to you!"

He was a published poet too. I felt so amazed that all of this immense talent would be consecrated to someone like me.

"What do you want to call the blog?" he asked.

"Something about love," I said, "but I don't know what."

"Make love not war?"

"That's so cliché. Also no, we will fight, there will be war. Let's call it 'Make love and war'."

"Yes!" Haider high fived me.

We created our blog and I posted two of my favourite pictures. One was of two kittens sitting on a windowsill looking at the stars. Another was of a young couple kissing on the top bunk of a bunkbed in a hippie-style room, with Tibetan prayer flags hanging alongside posters of bands from the '60s and tie-dye quilts draped across every surface imaginable.

"This is *so* us," Haider commented. "This has been our summer."

"I hope it lasts," I whispered to myself.

We spent my last day in Duisburg running errands: returning things I borrowed from Xin, withdrawing money from my German bank account, paying Max back the rent money I owed him with what money I had left, making sure I had everything I needed for my flight. I tried to use this business to distract myself, to remain calm and not be too upset, but my insides were screaming.

Haider made me risotto again that night and we ate in silence. I sat in his lap on one chair; we shared one plate and one fork. Like we always did. The sun set on Volkstrasse and in Siddartha's apartment we felt almost like we were in our own home. It dawned on me that he *was* my home. We held back tears and smiled at Siddartha trying to entertain us.

That night, we held each other tightly. Later on, Haider told me that he wanted to soak up as much as he could of our final moments together, so much so that when I was asleep, Haider stayed awake and looked at me breathing. Meanwhile, I wanted to evade these emotions by sleeping through them.

"Liz," he whispered into my ear, in earnest, "do you want to marry me?"

I groaned a "Yes" in my sleep. Somehow, I heard him. Haider repeatedly kissed my forehead and gently rocked himself to sleep as well.

Early the next morning, Haider woke up to make me breakfast. We ate in silence as I sobbed uncontrollably.

"Hey bunny," Haider tried to comfort me, "it's not the end. It's not; it's just the beginning of us."

I nodded. Soon we headed up to the Hauptbahnhof with all my luggage.

"Look at this Hauptbahnhof here," Haider said with fondness, motioning at the grotesque building, "one day we will be back here with all of our children and we will tell them. Mama and Baba met here for the first time ten years ago!"

I tried to smile but my spirits were failing me. We took the train to Dusseldorf airport.

"This is it, bunny," Haider said to me as we checked my lone suitcase onto the conveyor belt to nowhere. "Be brave my bunny."

I nodded, but I couldn't let go of his hand. We were now nearing the security checks.

"You have to be very brave," he repeated, like a general leading soldiers into battle. "Remember, it's only the beginning!"

I looked at Haider one last time. I took a deep breath and walked into the cordoned-off line leading to airport security. As the agent scanned my passport, I realized that one phase of my life was over, and that he had just checked me into the next. There was no going back.

Part II: Canada

21

August 10, 2011

The flight back to my parents' home felt like waking up slowly from a dream. I arrived in the Montreal-Pierre Elliott Trudeau Airport and was greeted by everything familiar, from Tim Horton's cafes to stores selling maple syrup. This is what I used to call home. And yet how far removed I felt from everything.

My parents picked me up at the airport and drove me home. They asked me several questions about my internship and I answered everything half-heartedly. I was mentally away. I was close to my parents as a child, but since my teenage years, we'd grown apart until our realities barely overlapped. My dreams, my aspirations, my concerns, my misgivings ... my parents had but a glimpse of them. My parents' dreams, aspirations, concerns, and misgivings were completely estranged from me in turn.

Nevertheless, we still lived under one roof up until my trip, so I moved back into my childhood bedroom. Nothing in the room had changed from the day I left on May 14. There was my twin bed, with my stuffed animals scattered around it, the old wicker chair, the too-small child-sized desk, and the white bookcase. Yet how changed I was. I set down my backpack and suitcase, and put Captain Ali on my bed next to the rest of my stuffed animals. I sat on my bed and sobbed.

Haider was still in Duisburg, his internship being five weeks longer than mine. How could I reach him? I called his phone around midnight Montreal time to tell him I had safely arrived. We talked a little, and then he had to go to work.

The next two weeks, we contacted each other mostly by phone, for Haider was still living with Siddartha and their house didn't have Wi-Fi. He'd call me or I'd call him and we'd talk for hours on end.

"I revisited the Tetraeder," Haider said, "and our padlock was still there."

It seemed so far away from my present reality.

"On my way back from Bottrop, I saw an elderly blind man walking slowly towards the platform. I asked him where he was heading and he said he was heading to Essen for his annual visit with his daughter. I suddenly realized the train to Essen was departing soon and he wouldn't make it. So I went to the train driver, told him the story of the old man and asked him to delay the train. He did, and I escorted the old man on the train. He looked so happy!"

What a man of character Haider was, I thought to myself. I'd have never had the guts to do something like that. Then another night, he told me about how he went out running: "At least eight stray cats were following me," he said. "I've become a cat whisperer apparently. I have a thing with animals and small children. They instinctively trust me. It must be my aura."

And on the final day when Haider was leaving for Dusseldorf Airport, he called me in the early morning.

"What a crazy night I had. I decided to leave in the evening to arrive in Dusseldorf early enough for my early flight. As I arrived at the Dusseldorf Hauptbahnhof, it was 3 a.m. A brown cab driver saw me and he started chatting with me. Turns out we're from the same province in India and he's also Muslim. He took me to the room where cab drivers wait for customers for the night. All the cab drivers greeted me with *Assalamu alaykum*, the greeting Muslims say to other Muslims meaning 'peace be upon you.' I felt so at home.

"In the morning I was at the departure hall and I saw an elderly man looking lost. I helped him find his way and when he told me he was Austrian, I got out my guitar and sang 'Edelweiss' to him as he was waiting in line. He cried happy tears. I'm now waiting to board the plane and I just met this Korean guy right here. His wife is Indian and he wished us all the best in our relationship. I have to go now, boarding time. All the best, sweetheart. Soon we will be in the same country again! Love you!"

Haider hung up. What a nutcase he was. But I loved it.

At the end of the month, my mother approached me with the phone bill.

"Did you just spend $180 in long-distance calls?" she asked me. I was not sure if her tone was accusatory, aghast, or just shocked.

My heart sank. I was not ready to open that can of worms with her just yet.

"I'm sorry," I answered timidly, kind of embarrassed. "I'll pay for it." I hoped she wouldn't ask anymore questions. I worried she'd judge me.

"It's alright, I'll pay for it, but what on earth happened to you? Who is that guy you're calling everyday?"

I was left with no choice but to explain to my mom that I'd been dating a guy I met in Germany. I had told her about him over the phone while in Germany, but only vaguely. She'd almost forgotten about it and seemed surprised that I was still with him. No, he's not German, but he's Indian. My mom had a funny look on her face.

"You guys are official?" she asked quizzically.

"Yes, except that he can't tell his father just yet."

My mom said nothing. I wondered whether she was silently judging us or worried about me. I didn't get an answer. Most girls wouldn't want their mothers to pry, and to some degree, neither did I, but I secretly wished she had shown a bit more interest. Her detached affect suddenly began to grate on me.

Meanwhile, Haider was finally back in his parents' Mississauga home. It was customary in his culture for children to live with their parents until they married, and sometimes even afterwards. With that added layer of secrecy in the mix, things were getting heavier.

"You can call me on Skype now to save money", Haider said, "but if my dad is around, then I'll have to mute the call, if not end it right away. I'm sorry sweetheart, but this is a process we have to go through."

Despite everything, we were calling each other during most of the day. School started again and I begrudgingly returned to campus. Of course, the first person I saw was Chris. We went to that cheap sandwich place we had always frequented the previous semester, up until my trip to Germany. On our way there, I asked him what he'd been up to during the summer, and he excitedly talked about all the new math he'd been working on. When we arrived at the sandwich place, he pushed three times on the door that said 'pull' before realizing it. I laughed out loud.

"How have you been?" he finally asked me.

I told him I was alright, that I had a new boyfriend.

"German?"

"Nope, Indian."

"You guys Facebook-official?"

"Yes."

"Good for you. Just don't come complaining to me when you guys break up."

Ouch. What a jerk. That hurt, that really hurt. I gave him the silent treatment, and we finished our sandwiches without either of us saying a word.

I later told Haider about it and he told me to forget it. "Like Karim, these guys are up to no good. Don't listen to their lies and threats." I tried to remain calm, but so many things were working against us. Our families, our vastly different cultures and backgrounds, the long-distance nature of our relationship. But that wasn't what kept me up at night. I would often wake up with a dreadful feeling about our future. It was driving me mad at times. Maybe we were just *too* different? Maybe we couldn't be right for each other?

What also drove me mad was that I still loved him. I was deeply in love with the essence of his being and craved him constantly, almost like I craved my favourite sweets. It came from a deep, visceral part of me that I didn't even know existed.

"Liz, what do you want?" Haider asked me.

"I don't know. I just get a dreadful feeling that we can't be together."

"What have I done wrong?" Haider was pleading.

"Nothing that I know of, maybe it's because I miss you too much."

"I've been having recurring dreams", Haider said. "Every time it is like this: we are together in a room, but suddenly a White guy comes in and hits me on my head and he brings you out of the room in his arms. It's so upsetting."

"That is so strange."

"Liz, you don't know how much I need you, how much I miss you, how much I want you. I'm not a violent person. But if someone out there hurts you even a bit, you know I will track him down and get revenge."

I went quiet.

"I have a black belt in karate, almost against my will," Haider explained. "My dad enrolled me in karate class when I was in high school. I didn't like fighting. I was the best of my class at learning every move, but every time it was time to fight, I'd only yield and never attack. To the point that my classmates started teasing me and calling me names. I still refused to fight. Then it was the time for the black belt examination and I had to win a fight. My opponent, the guy who was second best in the class, taunted me. I was really upset, so I decided to fight him. During that fight, in a few moves, I sent him to the hospital in an ambulance. After that, I quit karate for good. Still, nobody ever dared to make fun of me again. Liz, if someone ever murdered you or God forbid raped you, you know he's going to be dead. I'd probably kill him, then either kill myself or turn myself in to the police."

"And you will fight the White guy in your dreams?"

"I will, trust me, I will."

September flew by and things were getting rocky. I had a hard time with everything on Haider's side, from his style of dress, which I found too casual, to his slight Indian accent, to the way he talked and typed using so many informal abbreviations and silly emojis that went out of style when we were in middle school. I'd subconsciously associated that manner of typing with those random creepy messages I'd get out of nowhere from Pakistani guys on Facebook. He suddenly stood out as lacking class in every respect compared to my wealthier White friends. I browsed through his relatives' Facebook profiles, and seeing all their awkward, poorly taken photographs and their spelling and grammatical mistakes, I couldn't help but feel embarrassed, though I tried my best not to show it. Haider was clearly aware all the same.

"Liz, have you forgotten what is the meaning of us together?" He pleaded. "We make war, yes, but we make love, too! Remember how happy we were in Duisburg? We can have that again. Do you believe in us?"

Every time he'd remind me, I'd weep. I missed our Duisburg days, I truly did. Things were easy back then, but here, they were complicated. I missed him, despite everything.

Haider introduced me to one masterpiece of Indian cinema, the movie *Devdas*. I'd been marvelling about that tragic movie ever since. How I related to young Devdas and Paro being in love and being separated from each other! And how I loved the beautiful Madhuri Dixit in the role of Chandramukhi! As for me, I introduced Haider to the pinnacle of Broadway musicals: *Phantom of the Opera*. Haider instantly identified himself as Phantom, the hero with a dark past who fell in love with the beautiful Christine. But she loved someone else.

Finally, it was my birthday on September 22nd. I turned 20 and was no longer a teenager. Haider said, "Sweetheart, I have a surprise for you, I booked a bus ticket to Montreal to finally visit you! I'll be there in two weeks, for the Canadian thanksgiving weekend on October 7!"

I jumped excitedly a little, tears in my eyes.

"My beloved Haider," I exclaimed. "How sweet of you!"

"My mom finally agreed to let me go alone for once. I told my dad I'm visiting friends in Montreal and he agreed too. See, there's hope. Even though we're far apart, it is not forever, and we can still have time together."

"I hope my parents are okay with it."

"They will be. I'm good at winning parents over. Trust me."

I nodded. I was relieved.

"Cheer up, sweetie. We have something to look forward to! Every morning, count down the days until we meet!"

"I will," I promised him. "And I'm sorry if I give you a hard time sometimes. It's because I miss you too much."

"I had that dream again last night about the White guy taking you away from me. But instead of letting him, I fought him and drove him away. I feel confident, Liz. It's been a month that we've been apart, but we have not fallen apart. Nothing can stop us. They can take away our home in space, but nothing can take away our home in time!"

22

October 7, 2011

The Friday Haider was set to arrive, I spent the hours leading up to our reunion in anticipation. Haider was visiting, yes, but would we be like before, like in Germany? After my classes, I ran to the Central Bus Station through the corresponding exit from the Berri-UQAM subway station. I saw buses arriving one by one, people greeting each other with hugs and kisses. How I longed to see Haider! Finally, the bus from Toronto arrived. I rushed to the door and there he was, Haider, the first to come off the bus! Haider ran straight to me and held me tightly in his embrace.

"Bunny," Haider whispered, "I'm here, we're together again for a little while. Bunny, how I missed you!"

"I missed you too," I answered. I really did. "Come, let me take you home."

I took Haider to the metro station, and we waited for the subway to come, hand in hand. For the first time in my life, I was taking the subway with someone I loved, who loved me back. How wonderful a feeling it was, I realized. We took the green line and arrived at the terminus, Angrignon station, where I lived.

"We're getting off here," I said. "This is the subway I take everyday to go to school."

We walked outside the station.

"And this is the large boulevard I have to cross every-day to reach the subway station," I continued. "The cars go so fast, I wouldn't be surprised if I get killed here one day."

"Oh bunny, don't say that." Haider hugged me close.

"And now that we've crossed this boulevard, this is my street. And over there, the house with the single white light on the porch, and the outdoor staircase, that's my house. Welcome to my house, dear Haider."

We stopped in the middle of the street and contemplated the house I had called home for the past eight or nine years. It was a duplex where we lived on the ground floor and rented out the second floor. The facade was made out of dark red brick and the roof was flat. It was in no way extravagant, but it was welcoming.

"I moved around a lot as a child, both in China and in Canada," I said. "I even lived in Japan for a couple of months when I was little. Then, after we immigrated to Canada, my parents wanted a stable life so they started saving money. And then we bought this house. We've been living here for almost half of my life now. So much has happened between these walls. It is here that I really grew up. I'm so glad you're here!"

"I'm so glad to be here too, Liz," Haider replied. "I'm so glad that you've led me to your place, that you've trusted me enough to invite me into your home. I can't wait to have a home with you, a place to truly call our own!"

I took out my keys and we entered my house. My mom and my dad came out to greet Haider.

"Hello, my name is Haider," he introduced himself and shook hands with my parents. "You can call me Ali, if that is easier; that's my nickname. Here are some Indian sweets my mother made for you."

"Thank you, welcome, Ali," my mom greeted him.

She asked me in Chinese what Haider ate, and I said he ate everything, and she was relieved.

We had dinner together, my parents sitting on one side of the table and Haider and I sitting on the other side. My dad spoke some English and chatted casually with Haider. My mom was mostly quiet, since she spoke only French and Chinese. I felt a little awkward. My parents didn't seem to realize how real our relationship had gotten.

We retired to my room and I put on Rachmaninoff's second piano concerto for the ambiance. We slowly undressed each other and gently laid down in my bed cuddling.

"Oh my darling, how I missed this," Haider whispered in my ear. "How I ache for you!"

The music was growing and flowing like tidal waves. I felt Haider's hot skin against mine and smelled his raw scent. How I needed him too!

"One day," Haider said, "I will come knocking on your door to take you with me for good, and there will be no parting ways tomorrow. There will be no more fateful goodbyes."

The next few days, I took Haider around Montreal and showed him the McGill campus where I studied. I took him to my favourite restaurant, Lola Rosa, right near campus on Milton Street. Once we were together, it felt like nothing had changed, and the distance and time didn't matter at all. We climbed Mount Royal, the hill in the middle of our city. A beautiful stone platform was on top of the mount, with a prodigal view of the city. We sat on a stone bench and Haider turned towards me:

"I have something for you. It's a belated birthday gift, I suppose."

"You are so thoughtful," I couldn't help but whisper. "What is it?"

Haider handed me a silver chain with a pendant. The silver chain was rather thick and uneven. The pendant was made out of two hearts, one inside another.

"Take good care of it," Haider said. "This chain has a long history."

"What is it?"

"Let me start from the beginning. My grandmother, or my mother's mother, was a college graduate and was a famous tailor in our city. But back in the day, a woman with a college degree and, what's more, in her thirties, had a hard time getting married. Finally her family found my grandfather, who was the only one willing to marry her. My grandfather was a street sweeper. His father died before he was born, and back then, women were to mourn for their husbands for three months inside a white room, and if she's pregnant, she had to mourn until her child was born. His mother mourned his father, and by the time the mourning was over, it had exhausted her and she died during the birth of my grandfather. My grandfather grew up as an orphan."

The sun was shining on the glistening silver that Haider put in my hands.

"Not surprisingly, my grandmother despised my grandfather even though they got married. She took all her anger out on her first daughter, my mother. During the years after my mother was born, the family experienced many hardships and my grandmother thought my mother was to blame. Then, my mom's sister was born, and the family fortune reversed and they became very wealthy as my grandmother's tailoring business flourished, so my grandmother to this day praises only her younger daughter, my aunt, even though it was my mother who mostly took care of her."

I looked at my hands, and suddenly felt the gravity of the chain weighing them down.

"My mother grew up doing all the household chores, getting up at 4 a.m. to sweep the whole house and make breakfast, then going to school, coming home to make dinner, and then doing her homework alone until the early morning hours. My grandfather saw all of this and said nothing. But when my mother wept, he would hold her hand in silence. One day, my mom asked her father, 'My sister is always given so much jewelry; how I wish to have at least a single necklace!' My grandfather took it to heart and spent six months saving every penny he earned. Then he went to the market, and bought the cheapest silver chain he could find. This is the chain you're holding now in your hand. It is the only heirloom my family has of my grandfather now, besides my prayer mat."

My heart fluttered and the chain in my hand felt even heavier.

"My mother gave me this chain when I was young and told me never to part with it. But I've decided to give this chain to the girl I want to marry, so I told my mom I lost the chain. She was a little upset."

"Why would you do that to your mom?" I asked.

"This is not the whole story. See the pendant here? It has a history of its own. When I was a child, a family friend gave me a budgie. Sadly, it passed away soon. But I wanted birds so my mom went and bought a pair of love birds. We had many more love birds subsequently, but my favourite was the white female bird from the first pair. Love birds bond for life, and when one dies, the other dies within days. My white love bird died when I was ten, and I was really upset. I went to the dirt behind my building and dug a hole to bury her. When I was digging, I encountered something shiny. It is this pendant here that you hold. My love bird gave me a last gift. So I put the pendant on the chain and decided this was destined for the girl I will love with all my heart. It's meant to be."

I looked at Haider in complete wonder.

"Liz," he said gravely, "you deserve this gift. Let me put it around your neck. Never take it off even when you shower."

He put the chain over my head. I felt the coldness of the metal and shivered. How was I deserving of this gift? I couldn't help but wonder. And what a heavy weight it bore. I felt afraid. Afraid that it was too much for me.

"Come, now we must go shopping," Haider continued. "It's not going to be easy winning over my family. Here's the plan; let's buy gifts for my mother and my two elder sisters, and if they are on our side, my father would have a hard time going against our wishes."

"What do I have to do?" I asked anxiously.

"We need to buy these gifts."

And so Haider asked me to take him to some nice stores and I led him to the Eaton Centre. I felt my stomach clench into a knot. I was to buy gifts for pure strangers. I didn't feel comfortable with the idea. But Haider pushed me.

"We have to do it, bunny. It's for our future," Haider insisted.

We ended up buying a scarf for his mother, and a wallet for each sister. I spent over $50 for the three gifts. On our way home, I felt frustrated.

"Why must we do this?" I asked him when we were back in my room. "I only care about us. What does your family have to do with us? Why do I need to win them over?"

"Liz, you don't understand how my culture works," Haider answered. "White people only care about their own lives and once you're eighteen, you're free to marry or date whoever you want. But in our culture, it doesn't work this way. My family will always be my family, whether I'm fifteen or fifty. If you want me in your life, you have to accept my family and they have to accept you too."

I fell silent. The responsibility of bringing families together frightened me. Was I ready to be this serious with Haider? How serious were we?

"Liz", Haider said, "I want to marry you in the future. This is as real as it gets. Do you not feel the same?"

I was ambivalent for a moment. I wasn't sure if I could handle that intensity, that commitment. I had just turned twenty!

"Liz, think of one day when we will be living together, and having children. Do you even know what Indian and Chinese mixed race children look like? Do you not want to know?"

"I looked it up," I confessed. "Indian and Chinese mixed race children are called Chindians."

"Fantastic! Chindians! I can't wait to have an army of Chindians with you!"

I wept. It was too much.

"Please Liz," Haider pleaded, "if you want it, we have to do this and bear it together. When you find it becomes too hard, hold on to the necklace I gave you."

I nodded. The next morning Haider had to take the earliest bus to make it to his afternoon class. His fleeting visit was over. We were back in long-distance mode. I felt the apprehension grow.

"We've survived two months without seeing each other," Haider said. "We'll survive another two more. I will try my best to work out how we can spend the holidays together. For now, hold on to that hope."

"I will try," I answered.

I watched Haider climb onto the bus with his luggage. I waved at him as the bus departed. I stood alone at the bus station for a long time, digesting everything we had just gone through. It was a lot to handle.

23

The rest of October and November flew by. Every day, I went to classes and studied unhappily. And every evening, I'd call Haider on Skype and we'd talk, hoping for the day we would meet again. And it came. My parents gifted me with train tickets to Toronto for the holidays, departing on the 23rd of December and coming back on January 2nd. Haider arranged to get permission from his parents to 'go out with friends' during the holidays, with the condition of spending at least either Christmas Eve or New Year's Eve at home. We were ecstatic.

Haider picked me up at the VIA Rail station and we were over the moon to be together. We had booked a room at the cheapest youth hostel in town, Global Village Backpackers. We took the subway from the VIA Rail station and arrived at the little house painted in bright colours, looking cheerful and out of place in the middle of downtown Toronto, amidst grey concrete buildings and skyscrapers. It was as if we had a small piece of Europe to us again. We checked in and were offered cheap-looking condoms by the staff, which we declined. I had offered to pay for our stay to avoid trouble in Haider's family. Ten nights in total, it felt like an eternity after months of long distance.

The staff showed us to our room, and the stairs we took to go to the second floor were the most dilapidated stairs I'd ever seen in my life, the whole staircase having a roughly five-degree slant towards one side, where you were at risk of sliding off the steps altogether if it weren't for the railings. The paint on the walls was peeling everywhere. We walked down a long and cold hallway on the second floor and were shown a room with a metal-framed so-called double bed, barely larger than a twin hospital bed. The curtains were closed, it was dark and damp, and the room smelled of cigarette smoke.

"Enjoy your stay," the lady told us and left.

"Bunny." Haider looked at me. "I'm sorry. I'm sorry I cannot bring you home yet and this is the place where we have to meet. And I'm sorry for making you pay. Will you forgive me?"

"It's alright, don't you worry," I comforted him. "I survived sleeping on trains in Europe, I'll surely survive having a private room with you."

Haider was relieved and hugged me.

"You smell like curry," I couldn't help but laugh. It was obvious.

Haider laughed along.

"Nothing to do about it; my mom's cooking is too delicious."

We set our bags down on the worn-out wooden floor and opened the window to air out the stale room. We looked outside and saw a small alleyway facing a brick building, the windows of which glowed a warm yellow light. One small balcony was decorated with cheap tri-colour Christmas lights that looked surprisingly festive.

I sat down on the bed and it made a cracking sound. On one side of the bed was a floor lamp with a conical paper shade. I turned it on and a dim greenish yellow light diffused into the room. It wasn't much of a place, but it was still better than nothing. Haider sat down with me.

We spent the night in the room cuddling and caressing. It had been far too long since we could do that.

"Liz, it's been exactly half a year since that fateful day on June 23 on the beach in the Netherlands," Haider said. "And my feelings for you have only grown. You've turned out to be everything I wanted: sweet, caring, generous, and giving. I know you don't realize everything that you are, but I want you to know. Chin up, my lady, you're doing great!"

I rested my head on his shoulder and hugged him tight.

"Tomorrow, I arranged for you to meet my mother and my eldest sister for the first time. Be nice to them; my family means a lot to me. My mother's name is Fatema, and my eldest sister's name is Aminah. My other sister's name is Aliyah. My eldest sister is seven years older than me while my second sister is a year and a half older than me. When I was born, my eldest sister took care of me while my mom took care of Aliyah. I always call my eldest sister *Didi*, which means "older sister" in Hindi. You can call her Didi too."

"They know about me?"

"Yes they do. Didi asked me quite a few times about you. She will let me do anything as long as I am happy. You will get along with her. My mom is a bit more difficult. She'll say one thing but mean another. You will have to make a good impression on her."

The next morning, I dressed up, wearing a long black skirt and a grey sweater. I then put on my black trench coat and a red beret.

"Am I dressed up well enough?" I asked Haider.

"Yes you are, sweetheart. They aren't into fashion like you. They will probably be a little intimidated by your look if anything."

I wondered what I should expect upon meeting them. We took the bus to a Starbucks on the outskirts of Toronto near Mississauga. We sat inside and waited in silence. Suddenly Haider got a text message and stood up.

"They are here," he announced.

We walked outside towards the parking lot. A light snow was falling, covering everything in a translucent white. There was a navy blue van parked in the middle of the lot. Soon, Haider's mother emerged. She looked old and worn out. And then Didi emerged. She was severely overweight and looked not much younger than her mother. Both of them were wearing salwar kameez. I was taken aback, but they smiled at me, so I smiled back.

"Liz," Haider's mother said. "This is Liz right?"

"Yes ma'am."

I shook her hand and we headed into the coffeeshop.

"Haider told me you study physics," Didi said.

"I do."

"You must be so smart then." She smiled.

"What are your plans, in the future?" his mother interjected.

I had no idea, to be honest.

"I don't know yet. Maybe teach?" That was the best I could give her.

"Yes, being a teacher is good, a good job prospect," she concluded, but seemed unconvinced.

"You're in second year at university?" she asked.

"Technically I'd be in my third year because the Quebec undergraduate program is three years."

"And you're twenty?"

"Yes."

She seemed to have asked enough. We made small talk for another fifteen minutes or so, until she left with Didi, and Haider and I took the bus back to the hostel.

"Are they okay with me?" I asked.

There was a silence.

"I won't lie, sweetheart", he finally answered, "they are worried. Didi seemed to like you, but my mother, who already thinks you don't know what you want in life and are immature, didn't seem convinced."

We spent the rest of the trip back to the hostel in silence.

"I have told you that my parents required me to be home either for Christmas Eve or for New Year's Eve," Haider said. "You told me you wanted to kiss me at the stroke of midnight on the New Year, so I've reserved that day for you. Which means I have to go home tonight and leave you alone here. I really hate to do it, but I have no choice."

I felt some distress in my heart.

"I have to do it. I'm sorry." Haider sensed my uneasiness. "My family doesn't even celebrate Christmas. They would much rather be with me for the New Year. But you want to be with me for the New Year. So I compromised and said I'll be home for Christmas Eve at least. You have to give some and take some."

I nodded. There was nothing I could do.

"I know you're understanding enough for this. Watch a movie tonight, time will fly. Tomorrow morning I'm coming back on the first train! Be well, sweetie, you'll be alright."

Haider kissed me and left. I looked at the clock and it was seven in the evening. I lay down on the bed and stared at the ceiling. I felt my throat clench up. I felt helpless and powerless against everything Haider asked of me. That night, I wished I could elope with Haider. Anything to avoid the demands of this difficult family with whom I felt even more of a cultural divide than I did with Haider. That night felt like an eternity.

"I'm back!" Haider bursted into the room at 8 a.m. "You look like you've missed me as much as I missed you. I'm sorry, I'm so sorry. I'll try my best not to do this again. For the rest of the vacation I'm yours. I'm entirely yours, okay?"

Haider joined me under the covers, his hands and feet still icy from the cold outside. I held on to him as best as I could. It was not much, but it brought some comfort.

"We still have eight days ahead of us," Haider said after a while of just cuddling. "Let's go stock up on food, then decide what to do!"

We dressed up and went outside. It was snowing still, everything blanketed in white, and everywhere people were shoveling their cars out of snowbanks.

What a beautiful Christmas Day it was! Haider looked at me and grinned knowingly. He was thinking the same thing.

We went to the nearby dollar store and bought some canned soup and pasta. Then, we went to the grocery store next door for some fresh produce. We went back to the hostel kitchen.

"They do have utensils and pots for us to use," I remarked. "But do we trust their cleanliness?"

The pile of dishes looked questionable, and one bowl had some brown liquid at the bottom, despite a sign above the sink that read: Please clean your dishes and cutlery, and let good karma be your reward.

"No big deal, let's wash them then use them." Haider was cheerful.

Haider improvised a beef stew macaroni, and it turned out really delicious, as always.

"You're such a good cook," I said. "My bestie Arielle and I used to worry that we wouldn't find a guy because neither of us can cook. I got really lucky with you."

"Nah I'm the lucky one to have *you!*" Haider replied.

We took a walk after lunch. As we were walking, Haider burst out:

Sing once again with me,
Our strange duet …

"The Phantom of the Opera!" I exclaimed in recognition.

We sang the whole song together, with me as Christine and Haider as the Phantom. I felt an adrenaline rush creep up my spine. I had always dreamt of singing that song with someone. How special it felt to finally have someone to sing it with me! Yet, I also shivered at Haider's near obsession with the character of the Phantom.

"I can relate to him," he explained. "We both have a dark past."

"What do you mean?" I asked.

Haider was quiet and I didn't insist. We arrived at a small park and sat down on a bench. Haider looked me in the eyes and said, "Liz, my sweetheart, I think I'm ready to make love to you finally. Are you ready?"

I was part-willing and part-afraid.

"I know you didn't have a good experience with Chris," Haider continued, "I want to change that for you."

I nodded.

"Sure, let's do it," I finally said.

Haider kissed me and we stood up.

"Let's buy condoms!" Haider cheered.

"You sound like a kid going to buy candy!" I laughed.

At the pharmacy, Haider asked the cashier to give us an extra bag.

"I'm nervous that people will guess what we're carrying," he whispered in my ear.

On our way back, we kissed and laughed at every street corner. Back in the hostel, Haider slowly undressed me and I undressed him.

"I know my body is not beautiful like yours," Haider said with a strange solemnity, "but you seem to have learned to accept it. I'm grateful. Now it is entirely yours, please go ahead and explore its every nook and cranny; do everything you wish to do to me."

I went over his body with my hands, applying pressure, sensing him and feeling him. What an odd thing a human body is. I noticed his bony knees, his protruding second toes, his large hands and the flat back of his head. I held him tight and noticed his smell for the first time. He smelled like me, I thought. Then we embraced each other, caressed each other, and he slid a finger inside me.

"Heavens!" I cried out.

I could feel shooting stars around me.

"I'm sorry Chris could never make you feel this way," Haider whispered.

And so he put himself inside me, and it hurt a little, but it was blissful. It lasted a short while and when he was done, he said, "It's my first time, forgive me for being fast. It'll get better with time, I promise. But I'm happy I did it with you. I'm happy you're my first and hopefully my last as well."

I smiled back at him. Later on, I found a small pool of blood in my underwear. I was puzzled because I lost my virginity long ago with Chris. Then I remembered that the night I lost my virginity with Chris, I was so tense that he didn't go very deep inside me. Perhaps after all, I truly lost my virginity with Haider. I felt gratitude. Deep gratitude that things happened this way.

"I have a gift for you," I told Haider that night. "Something like an early birthday present since your birthday is January 10th."

"You're so sweet, what is it?"

"It's a *qilin* made out of jade"

I showed Haider a carved piece of green jade on a string.

"The qilin is a Chinese mythological animal, having the head of a dragon, the antlers of a deer, and the body of an ox but with scales. My grandmother gave it to me. She said that carrying it around you will protect you. May you always be protected by my qilin."

Haider teared up.

"Liz, oh Liz, my sweetheart you really do love me."

"I do, I really do."

We went to sleep that night in each other's arms as if we had always lived together.

24

December 27, 2012

Days and nights at the hostel merged together as Haider and I lay in the hostel bed. Whatever happened in the outside world, it didn't matter. We had each other and not a care in the world. I showed Haider some of my favourite movies, and he showed me some of his favourites.

"I saw this movie in high school and I really loved it," I said. "It's called *Baraka.*"

"Meaning 'blessing' in Arabic?" Haider asked.

"Yes! You know of the movie?"

"No."

"It shows many different countries and the diverse people that lived in them. It's really cool."

"Sure, let's watch it."

I showed Haider the documentary-like film. It had no speech, only music and nature sounds. Gorgeous imagery of Tibet, Japan, and Saudi Arabia passed in front of our eyes, and we witnessed aboriginal rituals, Auschwitz, the Killing Fields in Cambodia, Indian temples, and ruins of Ancient Egypt. It was a feast for the eyes.

"Did you like it?" I asked Haider.

"It's nicely done, the type of things White people like to see about the cultures of the world."

"Why do you say that?"

"It's just a feast for the eyes, focusing on everything exotic to the average White American. But does it even say anything?"

Well that was a way of seeing it that I'd never thought of.

"I'll show you something I really like: the Hulk movies," Haider said.

"Really?" I silently judged him for picking something so mainstream.

"You might laugh at me for the choice, but I bet you haven't even watched them."

He was right.

"Watch it and see the humanity of Hulk, I really relate to him."

We watched the Hulk movie from 2003, and Haider explained, "Hulk is just a normal guy but a huge power has been put on his shoulders. He bears a large responsibility towards the world, and it's not easy to control his superpower. But he chose to do good instead of evil. I find him inspiring."

Haider has a point, I thought to myself. But then I said, "Haider, why do you always see yourself in such dark characters like the Phantom or Hulk?"

"There is darkness in my past," he answered.

"You seem to insinuate that a lot. Can you tell me what is going on?"

"Alright, let's head out to Starbucks and talk."

He's opening up, I thought, and I was apprehensive. We headed out to the Starbucks on King Street. Haider got a tall coffee and he got me a medium London Fog. We sat down at a table and Haider began, "I belong to a tiny branch of Islam that exists only in our part of India. We're Shias, Ismaili Shias by blood, although it doesn't mean anything to me. If people ask me whether I'm Sunni or Shia, I say I'm Muslim and it doesn't matter. But our branch of Islam is a small sect of a million or so people that is led by a leader called the Dai. And things in this sect can get very ugly.

"My father's father was a high school principal in Mumbai. Back in the day, it was a very honourable position to hold. He was all about justice and fairness and, unlike other corrupt principals who accept pupils if their family sends them gifts, my grandfather never accepted bribes. And he spoke out about the corruption of the Dai's family, how they used their position to gain prestige and money from their poor working-class disciples. He changed his family name to Ali, to show his loyalty to the righteous Ali rather than to the Dai. And the Dai of course was upset with him.

"My grandfather was a righteous man. He lived simply, in a single room about eight square metres with his wife and eleven children, nine of whom survived beyond infancy. He valued dignity a lot and was very strict with his children. But his three eldest sons denounced him to the Dai, and the Dai captured him and punished him by making him crawl in a room full of people and lick the bottom of the Dai's shoes. My grandfather never recovered from this incident.

"My grandfather went home and went mad. He spent days on the couch sitting in his own waste saying rubbish. His own sons and wife sided against him, with the Dai. My mother, his niece, took him home and nursed him back to health. Then she sent him back to his home when he was well again. He died within four days of being returned home.

"Before dying, my grandfather had willed that my father, who was his fourth son and loyal to him, be married to my mother, who took care of him. Then my grandfather died, and the rest of his family sided with the Dai. My uncles all married women from families loyal to the Dai, and took all the wealth inherited from my grandfather. The law of inheritance goes that the eldest son inherits the father's title, the second son inherits his land, and the third son inherits his wealth. The rest of the sons inherited nothing. My father was the fourth son and inherited nothing.

"But my father was loyal to his father and earned enough money to study abroad in Kuwait. He studied sciences and became a supervisor of engineers for an oil company. He earned a lot of money in Kuwait compared to the Indian salary the rest of his family earned, so many people were really jealous of him.

"Moreover he decided to marry my mother against the wishes of the rest of his family. He came back from Kuwait and stated that his wedding would be in one month. There is a tradition in our family that the children in the family get married in the order of birth. His three elder brothers, my uncles, were married, but his elder sister, the fourth child, wasn't married yet. She was thus forced to find someone to marry in one month before my father, the fifth child, got married. She found someone, but her husband turned out to be abusive. She also blamed my father for her misfortune.

"Life for my parents became very difficult with so many members of our extended family against them. When my mother didn't have a son, my father's family taunted him so much that he would get upset and hit my mom. And my mom's own younger sister also sided with the rest of my father's family. When we had to flee Kuwait during the war and come back to India, both my father and my mother's side of the family treated my mother and father like servants. But that was not all. Both my father and mother's sides of the family used traditional Gujarati black magic on us."

"Black magic?" I finally interrupted. "You study sciences like me. You believe in that?"

"Liz, you don't understand." Haider was dead serious. "Let's go into our room at the hotel and talk about it."

We returned to our room at the hostel.

"Liz, my grandmother, the mother of my father, is a black magic witch. It's a trade that's passed down from mother to daughter in our part of the world. And all of my family has been using magic against us. And no, I have no idea how it works, but I can tell you that its consequences are very real. My parents and my sisters have unexpected ailments all the time. Nothing can heal them. Sometimes it's a skin rash, other times it is an infection. The most obvious sign is that my sisters are severely overweight. Nothing seems to help them lose weight. Once, Didi had a migraine for a week until we discovered that there were chicken bones and blood at the four corners of our house and lemons under our stairway. We removed them and the pain went away."

I was quiet. That sounded horrid.

"Once, after we had moved to Mississauga, my mother went back to India, and my father was still in Kuwait. My sisters and I were alone in the house for a couple months. The rest of the family chose this time to hurt us. They summoned my great grandmother's spirit to attack us. I was in the basement practicing guitar when the lights of the basement all turned on. I saw the switches flick on by themselves. Then I felt a presence run towards me. I heard footsteps! Fortunately I was steady enough such that the presence didn't faze me and flew away on its own. I was afraid, but mostly for the rest of my family. The black magic doesn't seem to affect me; it only affects the rest of my family. I'm really worried about the future of my family. And I'm worried that it'll end up affecting you."

Haider paused.

"Now you know. Please don't ever tell anyone about all I've told you. It's dangerous stuff. The fewer people know about this, the better. Magic is a curse. It is forbidden by the Prophet Muhammad. Only the wicked turn to it. And the best cure is not to believe in it."

I nodded. He was probably right on the last point.

"I feel old sometimes," Haider continued. "I feel like I have the responsibility of protecting my family and everyone that I encounter. It ages you."

I looked at Haider in the shadows of the room. The sun had set an hour ago. In that darkness, he looked dark and beast-like, like a shadow amidst the backdrop of the moonlight and street lamps filtering in through the window. I wondered about the Phantom of the Opera. About Hulk. About black magic. And I shivered, both from cold and from fear. Then Haider turned on the light, and his features were restored.

"Don't worry sweetheart. My family's trouble has nothing to do with you. You and I are safe. I promise."

The next morning, Haider got all of his friends from university to meet me. We had lunch at a pub and then went ice skating at the rink set up in front of City Hall.

"I've never skated before," Haider told me. "You'll have to teach me."

I laughed and his friend joined in the laughter. I stepped on the ice and held out my hands.

"Come I'll show you," I said, feeling like a true Canadian for once in my life.

Haider stepped on the ice and nearly lost his balance, narrowly escaping a fall.

"Come on, come on," I cheered. I skated at full speed while holding his hand, dragging him around the rink.

Haider held on to me for dear life as I flitted around. A couple of minutes later, he was catching his breath.

"Seems like I've survived!" he cried out.

Later he told me: "My sweetheart, you're such a gem. You trusted me more than I trusted myself on the ice rink, and you were right. It worked out. I'm amazed at you."

I smiled.

"Today's New Year's Eve," he continued. "Let me take you out to a restaurant and let me pay for this at least."

I was glad to accept. We walked a few streets and ended up at a small food joint.

"This is Chinese food," he said. "Do you like that?"

I wasn't impressed. I'd rather eat anything than Chinese food, which I had plenty to spare at home. And I didn't like the smell of the place. It was a plain, cheap food joint. I said nothing and we sat down.

"Liz, do you not like it here?" Haider finally asked me.

"Can I be honest with you?"

"Please be!"

"I'd rather we go somewhere else. I get enough Chinese food at home."

"Sure!"

We walked out.

"You thought that place wasn't good enough," Haider concluded dejectedly. "I should have known better."

He was spot on, but I didn't want to admit it. I wouldn't want to hurt his feelings, but the place was too modest for my taste, especially given the occasion. Call me superficial.

"No, it's alright," I protested.

"No, I want you to be comfortable, and I will do my best to suit you."

We wandered along Dundas Street.

"Pick any restaurant you like," Haider said. "It's New Year's Eve and you're in for a treat."

Finally I stopped in front of a small, chic Italian restaurant and was immediately attracted to the elevated European ambiance. I felt bad for my pretentious taste.

"Let's go," Haider said.

"I don't want you not to be able to afford it," I said.

"Don't worry about me, today is all about you!" Still, I did notice him checking the prices on the menu, despite his insistence that I could order whatever I wanted.

We were treated to one of the best meals I'd ever had, with fresh mozzarella and tomatoes with balsamic vinegar as the appetizer, authentic fettuccine alfredo as the main course, and tiramisu for dessert. Haider was finally convinced. We were ecstatic as we walked back to the hostel.

"There, there, this smile is a genuine smile on my sweetheart's face," Haider exclaimed. "I like it much better than the sour grimace you make when you aren't happy."

I went up to Haider and planted a kiss on his cheek. Despite our differences, perhaps there was a way to make things work for both of us, I thought to myself. I was glad. We passed by several cohorts of young girls wearing heels and miniskirts in the frigid sub-zero temperature. The atmosphere was so festive that night I barely noticed the cold. We returned to the hostel.

"Come, there's nobody in the men's shower room right now," Haider said. "Come and join me in the shower!"

"You're crazy!" I laughed.

"I'm dead serious. Everybody is downstairs drinking beer."

He was right. We both hopped inside a shower stall. The water was warm compared to the freezing breeze from the frosted window, which could not be properly shut. I stood on the slippery white tiles and looked up at the ceiling that had a sloppy coat of peeling white paint. Haider held me against him and took out his watch from the pocket of his shirt, which was hanging on the door. We counted down the seconds to midnight and kissed under the waterfall as we heard loud cheers downstairs.

"I love you sweetheart," Haider whispered. "Happy New Year."

"Happy New Year, I love you too," I whispered back.

We smiled and rinsed ourselves before running back to our room unnoticed.

25

January 2, 2012

On the train back to Montreal, the day after New Year's, I felt so alone, not knowing when I would have the chance to see Haider again. I got home and started posting on our Tumblr. Idyllic pictures of houses in the countryside surrounded by flowers and trees. Home-cooked gourmet food. People taking late-night trains to go home to meet their loved ones. Hugging in a car in the middle of nowhere. Anything to avoid facing the fact that I was going to be apart from Haider for another indeterminate stretch.

"Can't we just elope?" I pleaded with him over Skype.

"Sweetie, you're asking too much from me," Haider said. "Remember, I promised you a home together in time. But not now. It doesn't work this way."

I sighed. How I wish we were back in Germany again, in our little home on Volkstrasse. I missed hearing the birds sing in the morning. Drinking tea from the same bowl and sitting on the same chair. I missed it dearly.

Haider tried to distract me. "Let me show you where I grew up in Kuwait. Let me share my screen with you."

And through screen share, over Google Earth, I caught a glimpse of the oil factory where Haider's father Muhammad used to work. I saw the neighbourhood where he had lived. The Indian community primary school for boys and the coed school where he attended high school.

The beach and the towers by the Persian Gulf. How I wished to visit the Middle East with Haider one day.

"We'll travel to Kuwait and India and China on our honeymoon," Haider said.

"That would be nice. But now your mother seems to disapprove of me and your father doesn't even know I exist."

"Liz, how can I make you understand?" Haider looked sorrowful.

The winter semester had just started, but my heart wasn't there. Chris continued to maintain his 4.0 GPA while I felt like I was falling further and further behind.

"Liz, you need to get your degree," Haider urged me. "For our future together. Please do it for me. Or change majors, but do something."

I was very unmotivated, and couldn't survive a night without calling Haider. Thoughts of the day we would be together again for good consumed me, and I wasn't able to pay attention to much else. School assignments I used to find entertaining were nothing more than an unwelcome distraction from daydreaming about Haider. Everything except talking to Haider had become a chore, and I simply couldn't focus enough to keep up.

"I will do my best to comfort you, Liz," Haider said. "But you have to pull your own weight."

That night, I started hearing people yelling and screaming over the Skype call.

"What's going on?" I asked Haider.

"People fighting in my family. My father probably drank too much."

I heard his sister yelling in Gujarati and a lot of commotion.

"My dad is hitting my sister again. I gotta go take a look. I'll be right back, bunny."

I was taken aback by how casually he sounded. Was this a common occurrence?

Haider ended the call and left me hanging in suspense. Why were things so complicated in his world? Why so much trouble? So much drama? I felt fear and apprehension. Was this what I was getting myself into?

"I hate it when my father hits people," Haider said when he came back online about a half hour later, a half hour that felt like both a blink and an eternity. "Usually the father will hit everyone until the son is grown enough that he hits his father to make it stop. Then the son hits everyone. It's such a bad cycle. I will make sure not to hit anyone, I promise."

"So much drama in your family," I couldn't help but comment.

"But we really do love each other," he answered. "Whereas your family is entirely cold."

At least we don't hit each other in my family, I thought to myself. But Haider hit a sore spot. I couldn't for the life of me get along with my parents at all. And my mother more than once made snarky comments about Haider whereas she kept talking and gushing about Chris and his genius.

"Liz, my mother used to say, you can't get along with your wife if you don't first get along with your mother," Haider said. "This works for women too, Liz. I get along with my mother at least. Please get on the same page as your mother, instead of complaining to me about her."

I cried hard that night. I felt like a failure at something that should be so natural, so primal. I noticed that Haider had formed a very natural bond with his mother, yet I lacked those warm feelings toward my own. I was apathetic and numb. What was wrong with me? No wonder everyone was against me.

"Liz," Haider said another time, "we cannot be together physically, but we can still enjoy each other's company. Do you like playing online games? Do you want to join me on *World of Warcraft*?"

I gave it a try. Haider created a character for me and even created a new character for himself too so that we could level up together. Our life together became a game. I cared little about the actual game objectives and quests. We instead spent time fishing or cooking or mining in virtual reality. Sometimes there were genuine moments of warmth between us, experienced vicariously through our characters as proxies.

Chris laughed when I first told him I started to play *World of Warcraft*.

"Come on Liz, you can do better than this," Chris said. "*Starcraft* is a much better game."

Chris always knew how to rain on my parade. When I told Haider what Chris had said, he was furious.

"You keep saying Chris this and Chris that. Do you think Chris is somehow above me? What do you want me to do? Turn into Chris?"

While Chris was raining on my parade, by blurting out everything that Chris told me without thinking, I was, in turn, raining on Haider's parade, relaying Chris' opinions as if they were my own. But I genuinely saw Chris as the smartest person ever and therefore the authority on all things, so I subconsciously took on his opinions as my own, as categorical truths by virtue of his inherent superiority. I suspected Haider knew this by now.

I kept quiet but felt bad. Not being together with Haider was getting increasingly hard, because I felt I was losing grasp of what we had. It reached a point where my time with Haider felt like a past life. We now inhabited completely different worlds and had barely anything in common anymore. Haider talked to me about his favourite cars, technological gadgets, and alcohol, all things I couldn't care less about. He was preoccupied with the arduous task of finding a job after graduation. I was only in my second year, so I felt so far removed from his reality. At least Chris talked about things I knew about, like math and physics.

And the trouble was, since I had resolved to keep Chris at arm's length to avoid reawakening old feelings, Chris wasn't there to keep me interested in physics and math. I never realized just how much I'd relied on Chris to help me through our intense and demanding joint-honours program, and I felt increasingly frustrated with school. Without Chris' boundless and contagious enthusiasm to tide me over, I realized I no longer liked what I was doing, but didn't know any alternative. I spent nights staying up late talking to Haider and woke up the following mornings sleep-deprived and cranky. I was in a bad place.

"Liz." Haider finally put his foot down. "You'll have to let me sleep sometimes. My ideal schedule is getting up at 6 a.m. and going to bed at 10 or 11 p.m. You keep me up all night and it's going to negatively affect my work."

What could I say to that? I always justified my night owl schedule by saying that smart people stay up late. Going to bed early was for suckers. Chris used to stay up with me, as he also followed that schedule and its associated philosophy. I felt uneasy, hit with another reminder of how fundamentally different Haider and I were.

"Liz, pull yourself together," Haider pleaded. "Please, do it for me!"

I was steadily falling into depression. I wished I was in a different place. A different time. If I lived with Haider, perhaps we'd have worked it all out. In Germany, we lived as if we were on our honeymoon, constantly high off of the passion we shared and the novelty of the experience. We were young lovers blissfully exploring the world together unencumbered by long-term responsibilities and external commitments. Now, we were trying to transplant the other into the full worlds we had built for ourselves prior to meeting. As it was, it was not working.

"Liz," Haider said, "I need you to be patient. I cannot for the life of me just drop everything and move out to be with you just yet. I'm in my last year of undergrad. Once I start my Master's, maybe we can arrange something, but not now."

He was reasonable. Yes. It was clear he was the mature one. But I felt like my feelings were hurt. Why did he have to decide on everything? Why was it always me accommodating him? Why did it always feel like he was getting his way all the time? I looked at Haider that night over Skype, and I barely recognized who I saw. Do I love this man sitting on the other end of the line? What does love even mean?

I lay in bed awake that night. Did I love Haider? I was seriously starting to doubt myself. What was the difference between him and a random stranger in fact? I knew him, yes, or I thought I did. I knew he loved John Mayer, cooking, and muscle cars. But what did it mean to me? What did I care about what he liked? Did these things define him? Did I know him at all? How did this brown guy, corny, cheesy and cutesy as he was, get into my life? How on earth did I let that happen?

I felt like I was slowly dissociating from the girl who had fallen madly in love with this stranger on the opposite side of the world. I could barely recognize her anymore. She had become an alternate reality.

It was now April, and it had been three months since our New Year's shower kiss. It felt like a lifetime away.

The final exam period had just started, and trying to bring myself to study material that I barely had the energy to pay attention to when it was first taught made me realize that I was more behind in my classes than ever. Here I was, a stranger in my own home city, in my own home university. My life had been turned upside down since I met Haider.

I felt like I was straddling two worlds without fully belonging to either one. I was caught in a liminal space, both everywhere and nowhere. While I was right that meeting Haider had changed who I was irrevocably, I hadn't been given the chance to settle into my new identity. While it probably would have been a bad idea to drop everything and wholeheartedly embrace my new identity, I didn't know what else I could do. I had to pick a side of the threshold between my old life and my new one, but I couldn't. I resented him for it.

I took my finals and did more poorly than ever.

"Look at that! It seems like there's a trend in your overall GPA." Chris laughed. "See, it tends to dip by 0.5 every semester."

He was right and I was livid. How did it happen? There was only one answer in my mind: Haider did it to me.

"Liz," Haider said, "the finals are over; perhaps we can arrange a way to meet each other?"

"I'm not sure it's what I need right now." I was honest.

"Liz, what's going on?"

"I don't know."

There was a penetrating silence.

"You seem unwell, Liz," Haider said. "What can I do to help?"

I had no answer. All I could give him was a vacant stare.

Instantaneously, I frantically started packing things, all the things Haider gave me. The black shirt he left in my closet so he could wear it when he was with me. That cute hand-sewn T-shirt his mother had made for me. Captain Ali, the puppy from the Dusseldorf carnival. The silver heirloom necklace he gave me for my birthday. I looked at the pile of all these things, and I started to cry. The amalgam, the weight of it all had suddenly caught up with me.

No, I mustn't cry. I must part with them. They must be returned. Returned to the one who gave them to me and gave me so much trouble. Then, I could live like he never existed. I could go back to my old life unburdened by the weight of it all.

"What are you doing?" Haider asked, worried. I had gotten so engrossed in my packing trance that I had forgotten he was still on the line.

"I'm leaving."

"For where?"

"I'm coming to Toronto to return everything you ever gave me."

"What? Sweetheart, what?"

"I need my space to be mine! I need quiet! I need calm! You've made a mess of my life, and I need you out of it!"

"Liz, you're crazy!" Haider was frantic.

"You, you just made your way into my life and turned it upside down. I've had enough of it!"

"What are you going to do?"

"I'm returning everything you ever gave to me, I booked the bus ticket, I'm leaving in an hour and arriving at 3 a.m."

"Liz, what on earth is going on with you?" Haider was crying. "You can't do that. Downtown Toronto is not safe at that hour of the night!"

"I gotta. I need to get you out of my life so I can get back with Chris!"

"Liz, you've lost your mind."

Perhaps I had. I was losing it.

"Liz, come to Toronto, I'll call you on your phone when you're on the bus. It's okay sweetheart. I know it's hard to be with me. We can talk it through. I promise, it will be okay."

By then he was pleading.

I hung up and walked out of my house with nothing but a $5 bill I'd stuffed in my pocket and the bag I had packed of all his stuff. I took the subway to the bus station. As I sat on the bus, hot tears started flowing down on my cheeks. Soon I was sobbing uncontrollably. What on earth was I doing?

26

May 12, 2012

The bus started moving. Haider called on my phone. I ignored him. I couldn't deal with him. A slew of text notifications started blowing up my phone:

> *"Liz, please answer the phone!"*
> *"Please sweetheart!"*
> *"I'm coming to pick you up at the bus station at 3am."*
> *"Please, we can talk it through."*

He called again. I felt my insides break down. He called a third time. I picked up.

"Sweetie, I'm here, you're going to be okay!" Haider pleaded over the phone.

I quietly sobbed.

"I'm here, don't worry. I'm going to pick you up at the bus stop and we'll go to a coffee shop and we'll talk it through."

I sobbed loudly.

"I know it's hard, I entirely understand. I spoke to my mom and Didi. They will find a way for you to come to our house tomorrow morning. Maybe it'll do you good to stay at our house for a couple days."

I was floored by Haider's thoughtfulness.

"Are you alright?" he asked.

"I'm sorry," I stammered.

"You should be," Haider was serious. "But don't worry about it for now. Let's focus on making things better."

"I'm sorry," I repeated, sobbing.

"It's okay, sweetie," Haider reassured me. "I have to end the call now, gotta take the last bus from my house to the bus station to pick you up. I'll be there when you arrive. Be well, sweetie."

I sat in the bus silently, in the dark. What a mess I had just made. There was nothing to do now but wait. Just wait. Wait like that time I took the train from Salzburg back to Duisburg. Life seemed to be a long bus ride or train ride. I was always waiting to be home.

I arrived at ten to three at the bus stop. Everybody hobbled off the bus half asleep like an army of zombies. Haider was by the door of the station, waiting. He had large dark circles under his eyes.

"Liz, here you are," he uttered. We did not kiss or hug this time. I felt the cold of the night around me.

"Let's go to a coffee shop to spend the night," he continued. "There's a Starbucks at the children's hospital a few streets from here. Let's go there."

We walked in the dead of the night through deserted city streets, passing only a couple of homeless people dotting the side of the road. We arrived at the hospital building, entering a large hall with a Starbucks nestled in a corner.

"What do you want to order?" Haider asked.

"It's okay. I'll pay myself."

"No, you're still my guest."

I sighed and was hit with some serious remorse. Haider ordered a large coffee and I got a small hot chocolate. We sat down at a bench on the side of the hall near the Starbucks. There was no one except the half-asleep Starbucks barista.

"So, tell me. What's going on?" Haider asked, wanting to get to the bottom of this.

"I feel like the whole world is against me." I was barely articulate and suddenly burst into tears.

"There, there." Haider finally put his arm around my shoulder. "It's okay, I'm here, we can talk it through."

I nodded.

"So what's been bothering you? Can we list these things?" he asked.

"I don't know where to begin." I felt lost and disoriented. Was it because of the time of night, lack of sleep, or just a state of mind? I was unsure.

"You had trouble at school. Is that one thing?"

He was right. The tip of the iceberg, but definitely part of it.

"Tell me what the trouble is?"

I burst.

"I absolutely despise what I'm studying. I was a pianist, but my music career didn't work out, so I picked something completely random. I did it to impress people."

"Did you really? I thought you liked physics at some point in your life?"

"Well I hate it now. And I hate Chris, and I hate my parents, and everyone!"

"Slow down. Breathe in and out. Let's tackle one thing at the time."

I nodded, suppressing a sob.

"There are several options for you," Haider continued. "Let me tell you about my two sisters. Didi is a musician like you. She is a very talented singer and her dream is to work in Bollywood. She won a first prize at a Canadian Bollywood singing contest a year ago. But it's a hard career, you can imagine. And so she realistically earned a degree first in India in IT, and then a computer engineering degree in Canada. Now she works at an IT company, contributing her salary to our family, while still working on her dream of singing. She recently got a deal to record two songs from *Devdas*. My mother plays it on repeat in the house. See, this is a way to deal with things.

"Or how about my other sister Aliyah. She was never good at sciences no matter what we tried. My parents still forced her to study sciences at university, but after failing for three years, she decided to give up. Now, she's working on her passion, painting, at a local community college here in Toronto. If you feel like you really can't carry on in your program, consider speaking to Aliyah, maybe she can hook you up with some art classes, if not for a career, at least it'll be a good change from your environment.

"As for myself, I've had a tough time during my third year. My program at U of T, Engineering Sciences, is by far the hardest engineering program all across Canada. And I was doubting myself a lot during that year. I almost thought I wouldn't make it. But Didi talked me through it. And I've decided to finish my degree after all. I understand, the science and engineering programs are tough on everyone, especially on women. It's really hard to survive. So if you do end up finishing your degree, you are a champion."

I was tearing up again. He was so kind.

"Liz, whatever you choose to do in your life, I want to support you through it. I will finish my Engineering degree and get a high paying job so that even if you choose to be a stay-at-home mom, you will never have to worry about having enough money. I don't want you to have financial pressure of any sort in the future. Feel free to chase your dream, whether it be music or something else. Alright?"

Haider's words got my wheels turning. The fog inside my brain was slowly clearing. He made too much sense for me to disregard what he was saying. I was starting to see again what I'd seen in him.

"And what else did you say?" Haider continued. "You want to get back with Chris?"

I nodded, but I was starting to feel really silly.

"I understand that you hoped you had more time to process your breakup with him. That you never had a chance to have closure. Is that it? You felt bad about suddenly cutting contact with him?"

"That's part of it."

"Well, I want you to get a proper closure. I think you deserve it, and he deserves it too. How about when you go back to Montreal, you invite him for dinner? Then talk to him over everything you want to talk about. Say sorry to him if you feel sorry."

I nodded.

"See, we can talk this out. You didn't have to run here and return to me all of my things. There are rational ways of dealing with things."

By then, I was feeling really silly for letting that warped headspace get the best of me.

"But that's not all, is it? You keep comparing me to the genius of Chris. Do you regret having picked me?"

I was quiet.

"Well, this point, I can't do much about it. I'm not a math genius like him. Never will be. Nor will I be a music genius like you. I'll probably never be as good in any field as you in music, or Chris in math. You will have to accept this. But am I worthless? I am not. I have morals. I have values. And I love you and will give my life to you. Is that not enough?"

There was nothing I could say.

"I know my family's bothering you. That is a thorny problem indeed. It's hard, I understand. I find it hard too. And this is where you will really have to bear with me and be patient. But know that my mother and Didi are at least on my side. All they want is my happiness. So if they are convinced that you bring me happiness, then they will advocate for us. Today, you'll come live in my house for a few days. This is our chance to convince them that we're good for each other. I know you will win them over. I believe in us, sweetie. Do you?"

I looked at Haider with new eyes. Somewhere deep inside me, I felt like I'd finally stopped resisting him.

"Liz, it's getting brighter outside. Let's head out and have breakfast, shall we?"

We walked out onto the streets as the city was waking up from its desolate slumber. I was reminded of that morning when we walked to the Tetraeder in Bottrop. I felt the same longing, looking up at the violet sky.

"This is my favourite Tim Horton's in town," Haider said, pointing at a store of the coffee chain. "I'm hungry. Are you?"

I was. The place was still empty. It was barely 6 a.m.

"Two breakfast sandwiches please, with eggs, cheese, and sausage," Haider ordered.

Soon we were served and we sat at a table, side by side on cushioned grey benches. I took a bite of my sandwich and felt the bitter taste of tears interspersed with the egg. I had started sobbing uncontrollably.

"Honey, what's wrong?" Haider whispered. "Are you still unhappy? Say out loud what's bothering you."

"I'm sorry," I uttered, "I'm so sorry about everything I did tonight. I feel bad about it."

Haider sighed.

"It's okay," he answered. "Everyone makes mistakes. The important thing is, we learn from them."

"I'll do my best." I was sincere.

"You'll have to be nice when we arrive at my house though," Haider said. "So this is the plan: My mother and sisters know what's up with you, but my father doesn't. We will tell him that you're a friend I met in Germany and you are stranded in Toronto because you missed your bus to Montreal. So of course we will invite you to stay in our house. In the presence of anyone from my family, we're not supposed to be affectionate at all. Understood?"

I nodded.

"My mom will want to talk to you. Just be straightforward with her. Tell her the honest truth. I trust that she will understand. As for my father, he will be nice superficially. But don't be fooled. He generally hates Chinese people. He thinks they are stingy. He thinks that all Chinese women are gold diggers. It will be hard to change that prejudice. I doubt he'll ever come around, but if the rest of my family approves of you, he will barely have a say."

"I hope so."

"Let me call mom to let her know we'll be arriving soon."

Haider called his mom in Gujarati, and I leaned against him. He finished the call and gave me a kiss.

"I've missed you a lot too, sweetie," he said in my ear.

We hugged and kissed and headed to the GO bus station to take a commuter bus to Mississauga. We waited and the bus came. We were alone during the whole ride. I looked at Haider as we sat on the bus. The early morning sun's rays were shining on his face. And at that moment, I felt a deep longing to stay with him for life. He was for real, yes, I finally understood that he was for real with me and there was no joke in anything he said. He really loved me.

"What are you thinking?" Haider asked as I was looking at him.

"Nothing," I fumbled. But at that moment, I was really terrified of losing him. Terribly afraid of having to part with him ever again.

27

May 13, 2012

As we got off the bus, we arrived in a typical suburban neighbourhood, where the houses all looked the same. We walked deep into the residential area, where roads were mostly dead-ends and cul-de-sacs. We passed by a children's playground where two young girls in hijab were sitting on swings and arrived in front of a semi-detached house. How plain it looked, I thought, though it housed a family with such a storied past.

"Welcome to my house," Haider said.

Haider opened the door, and we were greeted by his father, mother, and two sisters.

"Welcome!" Haider's father said. His face looked very genuine to me.

"Come in. We were just having breakfast," his mother said.

I took off my shoes at the door and walked in. The entire house was painted in pale green and the floors were cheap vinyl tiles. A sign faced the entrance: In this house, we trust God. On the living room wall was a large tapestry picturing Mecca. I felt like I was in India, a few decades back in time.

"Please sit down at the table," Didi said, with an air of formality reminiscent of a time gone by. "We will serve you tea and naan."

She was wearing a flowy salwar kameez like the last time I saw her. She looked slightly haggard, like she could have passed for Haider's mother. But I only saw benevolence in her eyes.

I sat at the table, and they offered me tea in a saucer and a plate of their flatbread.

"This is authentic Brown style," Haider chuckled.

I tasted the tea, and it was heavenly. Smooth and strong.

"It's not too strong, is it?" his mother asked. "We put a large handful of tea leaves, then boil everything with milk. That's not how Chinese people drink tea, is it?"

"It's not. But I really like the Indian way."

She smiled. I copied Haider and broke a piece of the naan with my hands, dipping it into the tea. I almost felt like we were back in our Duisburg home.

"You study physics?" Haider's father asked. "Smart girl!"

He smiled and I smiled back. Where was the hostility Haider had warned me about? I wondered. I wanted to believe that his family was truly sincere.

"You must be tired from spending the night outside," Haider's mother said. "Do you want to lay down and take a nap?"

I nodded. She took me upstairs and showed me her bedroom. The bed was gigantic, in wrought iron. She pushed the covers to one side.

"Here, lay down here," she told me.

I felt incredulous. I was a stranger, was I to sleep in the master bedroom in Haider's parents' bed? I was amazed at their generosity. I lay down and shut my eyes. The mother left the door ajar as she exited the room.

Could it be that they were genuinely kind to me? I wondered. Perhaps this family really cared about me, I thought. Perhaps there was hope for Haider and me?

The door opened and a man walked in. In the semi darkness of closed curtains, I thought Haider had come in. Then a deep voice asked, "Are you cold? Do you want me to close the window?"

It was Haider's father.

"Pa," I wanted to say, "you are so kind, and your son is kind just like you. I love him."

But I bit my tongue.

"Yes it's a bit cold. Thanks for closing the window," I uttered.

He closed the window, smiled at me, and left the room. I was in disbelief. Could this kindly man really be against Haider and me? Did he really despise us as Haider had insinuated?

I must have fallen asleep, for I was woken up by Haider's mother and Didi coming into the room.

"Haider told us you didn't pack clothing when you came here," the mother said. "I work at Sears in the retail department, so after work, I bought some clothing for you. We're not sure of your size so check what fits and keep it."

I was taken aback. How thoughtful of them! My mind flashed to the time when I went back to China and my aunt and my grandma insisted on buying me a full suitcase of clothing. I looked at Didi and Haider's mother. Hospitality was the same around the world, I thought. They felt like family to me.

"You can try out the clothes in the walk-in closet over there," Didi said.

I opened the bags and examined the booty. It was cheap clothing, mostly in neon colours. I laughed. These were exactly the kind of clothes my extended family in China would buy me against my will. How did I explain that I didn't wear things like that? But I couldn't explain it. The least I could do was be grateful for their generosity.

The pants didn't fit, to my relief. I kept a yellow t-shirt, a white blouse, and some underwear. I lied that the neon pink shirt didn't fit either. And I kept the socks.

"I'm so grateful for everything you have done to help me," I told Haider's mother when she came back.

"Do you love my son?" she asked, looking me dead in the eye.

My stomach was in a knot. I wasn't ready to answer this question to her, I barely knew what love meant anymore.

"Yes," I answered. There was nothing else to say.

"Then you are family to us. Call me Ma from now on." She hugged me. In her arms, I felt so much relief.

"Come, let's talk in the living room before Pa comes home," she said.

I followed her downstairs. We sat on the couches, each covered with a white sheet to protect them from dust. There was a tall glass cabinet with all the children's trophies and achievements displayed in the corner facing me.

"A woman's life is not easy," she began, "I was a very outgoing girl when I was younger. I studied in university and got a degree in English literature. I loved Shakespeare. When I graduated, I found a job as a secretary. I would see dozens of people everyday, and I felt very useful. But my husband found a better paying job in Kuwait and we had to move there. So I became a stay-at-home mom. It was a really tough change. I had the whole sky to myself in India, but in Kuwait, I was confined to a house with a window big like this."

She gestured a size about two feet by one foot. Small indeed.

"But what else could I do? I had no choice but to accept my reality. So I did my best to happily raise my three children. And then, when the children grew up, we had to move to Canada. In Kuwait, foreigners like ourselves, and even children of foreigners, can't ever get citizenship. There is practically no chance for a foreigner to ever study in a Kuwaiti university. Didi studied in India for a while, but we decided to move the whole family to Canada for our children's future."

She sighed.

"And so, I got a job as a saleswoman at the local Sears. I work long hours, my knees and my back hurt when I get home. It's a tough and physical job. But what can I do? My husband moved here too, and I found a job for him at Sears as well. He downgraded from being supervisor of engineers to a salesclerk. He's always complaining, and I have to comfort him too on top of working myself to the bone.

"Liz, life is tough. People will come into your life, some nice, some not, but you have to fight for yourself, or else no one will. You have to know what you want, and you have to stand up for it. You cannot rely on the kindness of strangers. I know Haider loves you a lot and will do anything for you, now, that is. But you have to be prepared to survive on your own."

I nodded.

"And be careful when someone else gives you advice," she carried on. "See that TV on the wall in front of us? If someone ever sits facing you and gives you advice, be sure that they don't know what's best for you. Why? Because what they see is not what you see. You see the TV in front of you and they see the couch in front of them. However, if they sit besides you, like I'm sitting here right now, then they have the same perspective as you. Then they are in a position to help you. Remember this when other people try to help you."

I pondered the meaning of what she had said.

"But don't you worry now. We all want your well-being, here in this house. You will feel better soon. You will be in better spirits when you go back home. Come give Ma a hug."

She hugged me tight, and I felt tears welling up in my eyes. She was like the mother I never had, giving me warmth and life advice I sorely needed.

That night, Ma cooked biryani chicken with rice in the pressure cooker. The food was served on two large metal plates, one slightly smaller for Haider and me, and another one larger for the rest of the family. We sat on the couches to eat, and the plates were placed on the living room coffee table.

"Do you remember how to eat with your hands? I taught you before." Haider winked.

I tried my best, and ended up making quite a mess. They laughed, and gave me a spoon. The food was really delicious, and equally spicy.

After the meal, we watched a TV show together. It was one of those vintage TV shows with terrible production value that did not age well, about Indian mythology. It was the last episode, about Krishna's final victory over evil. I watched the English subtitles and couldn't help but laugh at how poorly the special effects were made. It reminded me of those terribly long and boring Peking Opera TV shows my grandma loved to watch. It also reminded me of my White friends' hip obsession with Hindu mythology, the latest flavour of the week. Was this show terribly avant-garde, or terribly backward? I could not decide.

My stomach decided to act up in mid-evening, the dinner being too spicy for me to handle. Didi and Ma rushed to the kitchen and made me a glass of basil seeds soaked in milk.

"Drink this, Liz," Didi said. "We usually drink this during Ramadan if we decide to eat spicy food. It creates a lining in the stomach which prevents the spices from hurting you."

"Your family is so kind," I said to Haider, and he smiled at me.

Didi and Ma insisted on hearing me play some music, after hearing Haider tell them about my talent, so we went downstairs to the basement. Didi had a small keyboard, which she used as a harmonium to accompany her singing. She switched the settings to piano, and I sang a song in English, accompanying myself on the keyboard.

"You're very talented," Pa said, patting my head.

"My father seems to warm up to you," Haider whispered in my ear. I was glad.

We went upstairs and Ma offered me one of her new nightgowns for me to sleep in. I pulled it over my head. It was so large I almost got lost in it. I felt like I was floating in a bedsheet. Ma and Didi laughed at me. Ma then made me stand in front of her. She looked at me and made me turn around.

"She's pretty, isn't she," she whispered to herself. "So fair ...." I wasn't sure whether to feel relieved after a positive judgment, mildly offended for being looked at like merchandise, or disgusted by the blatant colourism exhibited, although, being Chinese, I was used to it. I laughed it off. Every Asian mother did this, I reminded myself.

Later that night, Didi was folding clothes right out of the dryer. I offered to help and she gladly accepted. We were like two sisters folding the family's clothes, ranging from Ma's shirts to Pa's underwear. Didi and I chatted about music and a potential collaboration between us. I marvelled at how much I felt at home in this house.

The usual sleeping arrangements in the family was the large bed for the parents, Haider in his single bed in his room, and the sisters sharing a large bed in their room. That night, it was decided that Ma and Didi slept in the master bedroom. An air mattress was added on the floor in the same room for me. Pa slept in Haider's room, and Aliyah and Haider slept on the same bed in the sisters' room.

Everyone bid everyone else good night, and each lay down in their own spot. Doors remained open throughout the night. Soon everyone was snoring. I laid awake in my bed, listening to the chorus of snores, and felt both culture shock and at home, all at once.

28

May 14, 2012

Some commotion woke me up early the next morning. The sky was a deep blue. Didi accompanied Ma to the washroom, and then they returned to the master bedroom where I was sleeping. Ma covered herself with a white shawl, laid a small carpet on the floor, and started praying. I looked at her, half asleep. What dedication it took to get up so early to pray, I thought to myself. Would I be able to do it if I had been born into their family, their world? I wished I was taught how to pray as a young girl. I thought it was beautiful, the serenity, the devotion.

I drifted back to sleep and got up later that morning. I spent the day hanging out with Didi and Haider, just chatting about life. A while later, Ma came and said we were going to McDonald's for a late lunch. We drove through Mississauga, passing through residential areas with rows upon rows of semi-detached houses, with more and more tall apartment buildings appearing as we neared city centre. Sitting in their van, seeing them in their traditional dress, hearing them chat amongst themselves in rapid-fire Gujarati with Bollywood songs playing in the background, I had the eerie feeling that I wasn't in Mississauga, but in a different part of the world.

I was jarred out of my Gujarati travels when we reached the McDonald's, with its distinctively American theme.

I tried to order the healthiest item I could find, and settled on a grilled chicken burger. In contrast, Ma, Didi, and Haider went all out and ordered what seemed like every fried item on the menu. We sat at a table, and I couldn't help but feel like the odd one out in so many ways. Didi and Ma were still talking in Gujarati and I had no idea what they were chatting about. At the next table was a Chinese family speaking in Mandarin. I briefly considered whether I'd feel more at home if I moved to their table, even though I didn't know them at all.

When we got home, Ma decided to introduce me to Reiki.

"It's an ancient Japanese technique," she explained. "The concept is that there is cosmic energy everywhere, and you manipulate this energy to flow through you, for healing purposes."

"Haider had told me a little about it," I answered.

"Haider is a level two practitioner. At level one, you can only use Reiki to heal yourself. At level two, you can heal someone else also. I'm a Reiki Master, or level three. I can use Reiki in long-distance healing and I can teach others how to use Reiki. I studied Reiki back in India and taught all my children myself. I want to introduce you to level one Reiki. For this, we need to do an attunement. Reiki flows through the seven chakras of a person. Are you familiar with the chakra system?"

I nodded. I knew about the seven chakras and their attributes, and positions in the body associated with them. I had hung out with a bunch of hipsters in CEGEP who were all into that New Age stuff, and I had kind of jumped on the bandwagon.

"I will use Reiki to open all your chakras," she continued. "Then you will have to spend about an hour every-day using Reiki on yourself for thirty days. Then you will be considered a level one Reiki practitioner. Do you want to try it?"

"Sure, thanks Ma." I was ready to try anything to heal myself from the destructive tendencies that led me down the thought spiral that had brought me here in the first place.

She went downstairs to get her things. Then she came back with an incense stick and incense holder, shaped like an Om symbol. She lit the incense and spread the fumes around the room.

"I'm going to invoke the cosmic energy," Ma explained. "I'm going to thank my teachers, gurus and God, and protect myself from harmful energy."

Ma sat on the bed, closed her eyes, joined her hands in a prayer position, and stayed still for about two minutes. Then, when she was ready, she made me sit in a chair in the middle of the room.

"You just sit relaxed and let the Reiki flow through you and do its work. It shouldn't hurt or feel bad in any way."

I nodded.

Ma pressed her hands on my head, then on my shoulder. I felt some tingling in my neck. I felt something cold flowing through me. I wondered if this meant the Reiki was working. I sat patiently as Ma worked on me for almost an hour.

After the attunement, Ma collapsed on a chair, and Didi came back into the room. Later on Didi said, "Ma said you were the hardest person to attune that she has ever met. She said you had a lot of pent-up energy, especially in the crown chakra and the throat chakra. She said you will feel better soon, as you complete your attunement."

Ma lent me a small booklet on the different positions to use for the rest of my month-long practice. I looked at it doubtfully. Would it work?

"I will also send long-distance Reiki to your family," Ma said. "Your family shall be in better spirits after this." I tried to believe her.

The next day, Haider took me to Toronto for the day. We headed to a park on the shores of Lake Ontario that had a great view of the Toronto skyline. We shared a box of poutine, a Québécois dish consisting of french fries and cheese curds smothered in gravy, for a picnic lunch.

A Chinese peddler approached me, trying to win me over.

"Congrats on …" she began in Chinese, and stopped in the middle of her sentence. She saw Haider with me and looked confused for a second.

"On what?" I asked.

"Congrats on getting a foreign boyfriend," she finally finished the sentence.

I laughed and cringed. She would have known what to say if I were dating a prized White guy, but dating a Brown guy must have confused her. I pondered on how I felt about dating a Brown guy myself.

Haider and I lay on the grass after lunch, watching the clouds go by in silence.

"Do you like my family?" he finally asked me.

"They are very nice," I answered. "Really, I wasn't expecting so much from them."

"They are good at making a first impression, I guess, but things aren't always as rosy as you saw."

"What do you mean?"

"My parents' marriage is pretty much doomed. My extended family is partially to blame, saying terrible things to my father about my mother. And so my father would beat my mother and everyone else out of anger. I feel bad for my father. He's a coward. He used to practise boxing and even made it to a provincial championship in

India back in the day. But once, when we were in Kuwait, someone insulted my mother. He could have gotten up and said something but he didn't. He was afraid. By then, my mother, who had probably had enough of him, had started an affair with a really shady guy. She doesn't know that we kids know about this. She used to take us to the park and leave us there with the nanny. Then, she'd go hide in the bushes with that guy. We know this because our nanny told us. Our nanny wanted us to resent our mother so that she could split the couple. She was interested in my father because he was wealthy, working high up in the oil industry in Kuwait.

"My mom went to court for a divorce, and things got really ugly. It was such a shameful thing, in Kuwait and in India alike. My father pleaded with my mother to stay with us. But my mom wanted to leave. She even tried to take us away with that guy that she was with. That guy was up to no good. He molested Aliyah when she was little. Well, in the end, my father got a court order such that the guy was banned from ever entering Kuwait again. And my parents stayed together. But I don't think they ever recovered from that time. The marriage is dead. There is little love between my parents. On good days, my mom reads romance novels. On bad days, she gets drunk and complains."

I sighed.

"Every family has its own troubles," Haider said. "You know. You should be kind to your parents. They seem like good people. They just don't understand you. Give them a chance."

I wondered how that was ever going to happen.

"It's almost a year since we were together, on that beach in the Netherlands," Haider said. "I'm happy we've made it so far. I hope we do better than our parents."

We took a selfie of us lying on the grass, the grandpa chain on my neck and the grandma qilin on his neck. I felt thankful at that moment. Even hopeful, dare I say.

That night, Ma insisted we go out for dinner.

"It's a fusion restaurant, the type popular in India," Haider explained. "It's basically Chinese food made by Indians."

I laughed.

"Will we be eating this when we live together?" I said.

"That would be delicious!" Haider replied.

Ma dressed up in a pink sari, and looked beautiful despite her age. Didi and Aliyah both put on makeup. It felt like a fancy occasion. I felt underdressed in my plain yellow crewneck T-shirt and jeans.

"The sari is the garment that is the most suited to the female body," Haider whispered to me. "You'd look so beautiful in one."

How I wished to wear a sari one day, I thought, perhaps at our wedding …. I imagined myself in a glittering red sari, red being the traditional wedding colour both in Chinese and Indian cultures. Would that day ever come to be?

At the restaurant, we had fried rice, fried noodles, and some meat dishes. It didn't quite look or taste like Chinese food to me, and was way too spicy. But I liked it in spite of that.

Later in the evening, Ma had to go shop for some things. Pa, Didi, and Aliyah all went out with her. Haider and I locked ourselves in the master bedroom. We lay on the large bed and cuddled.

"This bed was bought in Kuwait," Haider said. "We shipped it here in a large container via boat. But it was so large that it couldn't be brought into the house. We had to ask a local ironsmith to cut it into pieces and we had to reinstall it back together. It is such a nice bed, larger than they would make it here in Canada."

"It is nice indeed."

"If my parents found out we were sleeping together here, we'd be dead, and that's an understatement."

I laughed but felt apprehensive.

"I missed you. I really did," Haider said. "I hope you will feel better when you return to Montreal. I hope things improve for us."

We held each other tight, and as we lay in each other's arms, time seemed to stop. We were snapped out of that when we heard the front door open. We both jumped up and quickly tidied up the sheets. The rest of the evening was spent chatting with Didi and Aliyah about a whole host of things. By the end of my night, I had begun to feel bonded with this family, in spite of what I knew about them.

I had booked the bus ticket back to Montreal for the next evening. Haider and I spent much of the day together with his parents and sisters, and we almost felt like we were one family. Haider showed me around his room. His bed, his desk from where he would Skype me. The window facing the children's playground. The highway beyond the noise barrier wall. The single ornament in the room, a cloth tapestry with four verses of the Quran hanging on the wall from a single protruding nail.

"*Qul huwa Allahu ahad. Allahu samad. Lam yalid wa lam yulad, Wa lam yakun lahu kufuwan ahad,*" Haider read.

"What does it mean?"

"Say: Allah, He is One. Allah, the Eternal Refuge. He neither begets nor is begotten, Nor is there to Him any equivalent."

Ma called and Haider went downstairs. I stood alone in this room, which I had seen countless times over Skype but never in person. I felt the weight of the years Haider spent here. And I felt a deep sadness. Somewhere, somehow, I felt that I would never put my feet in this room ever again. I shuddered at the feeling and tried to shake it out of me.

At seven o'clock in the evening, Haider and I headed out to Toronto.

"You're welcome to visit us anytime," Pa and Ma said to me as they each bid me goodbye.

I was almost tearing up. I had barely closed the door behind me but I already wished to be back, I wished to be back as one family. But I kept quiet.

On the bus from Mississauga to Toronto, it started raining outside. The rainwater splattered and smeared over the bus windows. I looked outside and saw a man on a motorcycle, blurry from streaks of the rain like watercolour painting. I pictured myself in India years from now, a woman on a bus searching for the one she calls home. Suddenly an identical-looking motorcyclist passed by the bus and disappeared in the fog and rain. What if that motorcyclist was the one she was searching for, and they passed each other without ever knowing they did?

"Haider ..." I trailed off.

"What is it, bunny?"

"Promise me one thing. Promise me that if one day, you realize that we aren't right for each other, then you will break up with me. I don't think I would ever have the heart to break up with you."

Haider nodded but was quiet. We hugged each other in the semi-darkness.

We got to the bus station, shivering. May evenings were still chilly sometimes, but this one was particularly bitter cold. Haider lent me his navy hoodie and we were teasing each other that we looked like hobos again. The bus arrived, and people formed a line to board.

"Can I keep your hoodie, Haider?"

"My mom will ask where it went."

"Say you lost it?"

"Sure. Be well, bunny." Haider looked emotional.

I kissed him goodbye, a lingering peck on the lips, and waited until the last possible moment to board the bus. I was worried that once I had left this all behind, the clarity I had gratefully found would be left behind with it. As the bus left, my eyes lingered on him standing on the sidewalk, staring at me in the distance. I wondered if he felt the same way. I did not know how long he stayed there after I left.

29

May 18, 2012

I duly practised Reiki when I got home from Haider's house. Were things better? It was hard to tell. I had one more year of undergrad left, and I didn't know how to carry on like this. Haider, however, graduated as an engineer and obtained his iron ring, which every graduating engineer receives in Canada. I congratulated him. We were happy, but our future was as uncertain as ever.

"What will you do after graduating?" I asked him.

"My friends all got jobs, but I don't feel like it."

"What about grad school?"

"I applied but didn't get the supervisor of my first choice."

As someone who used to joke about collecting PhD's, I felt the necessity to push Haider into graduate education. I insisted that he should consider getting a Master's at least. At least *try* to keep up with my PhD collection.

"Sure, I think I can do it," Haider said.

I was glad.

"But sometimes, I feel like I'd rather be a high school teacher. I want to inspire young people to learn," he continued.

I felt uneasy. Being a schoolteacher was a noble job, but I didn't see myself dating a schoolteacher when I'd go on to earn a PhD. Was I being elitist? I said nothing.

In truth, I was having many doubts about living a life with Haider. How could we possibly get along when we came from such different places? I was starting to resent everything Haider did. Haider and I visited each other multiple times over the summer, coming on the earliest bus in the morning and returning on the midnight bus in the evening. We didn't have to worry as much about accommodation nor disturbing the parents. Was I happy when I saw him? I was. But so many things got in the way between us. I didn't like how Haider dressed, being too casual and lacking class. I didn't like what he ate at home either, which was unhealthy in my opinion. I didn't like the way he washed dishes, using too much soap which was bad for the environment. Since I had reached a point where I felt comfortable telling Haider everything, I did not shy away from telling him the many ways in which he grated on me. Often it resulted in Haider feeling like he was walking on eggshells around me. It made everyone miserable.

One day Haider told me: "Liz, you have to learn not to make my life any more difficult than it already is. You have to be on my side because I am on your side. My parents have been giving me so much trouble. Especially Ma. The minute you left our house in May, she started bitching about you. Saying how ungrateful and spoiled you were. How you dared coming to my house to return everything I gave you. She was furious and adamant about us breaking up."

"I'm sorry, Haider."

"I know you're sorry and I want us to hold on together. But it is becoming increasingly hard. The least you can do is stop picking on me all the time."

I nodded. Was I becoming my mother? I shuddered at the thought. My mother spent her days complaining about my dad, and my nice dad never said anything back. I had vowed to myself not to end up with a doormat like my dad. But it suddenly dawned on me that if my partner wasn't a doormat, then they'd leave if I treated them the way my mother treated my father.

But could Haider and I survive together? I just didn't see it. I was a thinker, interested in philosophy, science, classical art, and everything intellectual. Haider shunned philosophy as best as he could. He was a feeler, a lover, into pop culture more than anything else. I wasn't trying to be a snob, but I ended up like one every time I talked to him.

Meanwhile, I had made a new friend during the previous semester. One early spring day, I was studying at my usual Second Cup coffee shop near McGill, and noticed a strangely familiar-looking guy with tanned skin and a ponytail sitting at a table by himself. He had a tattoo of a grey wolf on his arm, a chain of mala beads around his neck, and a pierced eyebrow. He seemed to have noticed me too and kept looking over. Finally, he came over to my table.

"I think I saw you in Electricity and Magnetism," he said with a smirk. "Hi, I'm Raul."

Of course, I'd seen him in class.

"I'm Liz. Nice to meet you," I replied with a smile.

Raul was a year ahead of me in the Honours Physics program. He was Peruvian, having immigrated to Canada with his family when he was seven, just like me. He seemed a little interested in me, so I told him I had a boyfriend.

"No worries," he said, "I'm not looking at the moment anyway. I'm more interested in living in a van while rock climbing for a living or hitchhiking solo to Alaska."

I laughed. He exuded strong bad boy vibes. We might get along, I thought.

Soon, we found out we were both musicians, although the music we played was like night and day. Raul played Latin guitar and the cajon, a Peruvian percussion instrument shaped like a box that you sit on to play. We decided to form a band together and started jamming on a weekly basis along with other mutual friends from our physics program. His sense of rhythm was wicked and baffled me every time. He was in turn in awe at what my fingers could do on the piano. There was more than just a little bit of chemistry when we played together, it was undeniable.

Raul was quite a charming storyteller, too, though I never knew whether I could entirely believe the wild accounts he told me of his life. He told me he grew up on the outskirts of Lima in poverty, often having to steal bread from local bakeries to satisfy his hunger. When, in first grade, he didn't apply himself at school, his mother beat him up, and he decided to leave. He spent three months living by himself on the streets, at age seven, dodging local gangs and surviving on his own. He finally went back home, having had enough adventures. After moving to Canada, he worked from the age of fourteen to earn his stay in his parents' home. He'd thrive at literally any job you could give him, be it a canned foods factory worker, an ice cream scooper, or a bar musician. When his relationship with his family deteriorated, he moved out on his own at sixteen and occasionally had to sleep in the subway or in his car. Still, he aced his way through school and settled on studying physics at McGill, though he secretly wished to quit everything, live a nomadic life on the road, and work as either a tattoo artist, a masseur, or a rock climbing coach, extreme sports being his other passion besides physics.

I could also see, however, that his Latin American and working class background made him feel like an outcast in the department at times. He'd joke about how he looked like his Inca ancestors. "The Incas were cool, you know why? They used gold to make their weapons because they hadn't discovered iron," he'd say. "But then the Spanish came and destroyed them." I understood him the way only racialized people understand each other.

He'd then tell me, however, that he was not the poorest, but the richest of my friends.

"How come?" I'd ask him, incredulously.

"I've earned a living since I was fourteen," he'd answer. "How many of your friends have bought their own car, secondhand or not? The furniture in their own room? How many can survive on their own income?" He had a point. I couldn't help but marvel at his independence, resourcefulness, and adventurousness, and compare Haider to him. Haider lived with his parents well into his twenties; his mom did his laundry and cooked his meals. Why couldn't Haider embody Raul's rugged, masculine individualism that made him so appealing to me?

During the summer, I also reconnected with Jonathan, a Jewish guy I had befriended the semester prior to going to Germany. Jonathan was also in Honours Physics, and often joined Raul and me at our jamming sessions as the second pianist. He mostly played jazz, but started wanting to learn classical piano when he heard me play. So, I introduced him to my piano professor, Garen. It turned out that Garen was invited to teach at a summer classical music festival in Spain that year and decided to take Jonathan and me with him, along with some of his other students.

I spent the first three weeks of July, first in Burgos for the music festival, then in Andalusia with Jonathan, where the mother of one of his friends had a house by the sea. Jonathan was perhaps my most handsome male friend and, being something of a rich kid, had the best taste in art, food, music, culture, and entertainment I'd ever encountered. He had a girlfriend of course, a girl from Paris. Haider was happy that I went with Jonathan: "No guy in his right mind would bother hitting on you when they see you with Jonathan," he joked.

When we arrived in Andalusia, Jonathan's friend's mom, Valery, greeted us and invited us into her home in a small village that consisted of all-white houses nestled on a cliff. She looked at us, a young man and a young woman travelling together, with that classic wink wink nudge nudge. She made sure to hint for the whole night that it would be a great opportunity for a hookup. Jonathan and I laughed. But I nevertheless thought to myself, it would have been a dream come true in my younger years to travel with such a perfect guy. Why wasn't I taking advantage of the opportunity? What had changed? And more importantly, how did Haider stack up to Jonathan? Was I ready to commit to Haider, knowing that so many great guys were out there?

When I came back to Canada, Haider told me his mother had gone to see an Indian astrologer.

"She was desperate for answers about us, and this was her way of seeking them," he explained.

"Do you also believe in astrology, besides black magic?" I couldn't help but ask.

"I don't really believe in astrology, no, but this man we saw knew many things about my life that weren't so obvious."

"Like what?"

"He spoke to my mom and Didi first, but they didn't mention anything about me. Then when I came into the room, he immediately said: 'You're dating someone not from your culture.' I said that's correct. Then he said: 'She's a musician.' He was correct too. 'And trouble with her is the reason why you are seeing me,' he said. He was totally right."

"He's shrewd," I said.

"He is. He told me that there was nothing he could tell me that I didn't know, and that I should only trust my instinct. He told me he saw that in the future we'd be married together. I will be an engineer and you will be a musician. And later in life, we will be wealthy by investing in real estate."

I laughed at the real estate part. How utterly mundane and unromantic. Why would I care about knowing my future if living a normal life was all there was to know? But then, what kind of life did I want? I did not know. What I did know was that I had always felt like I was never destined to live a normal, mundane life.

"It would be quite extraordinary if we did make it together," Haider reminded me.

By this point, I had realized that that was also true.

"I'm glad we went to the astrologer," he continued. "My mother is now reassured that we can have a future together."

I was glad too. But while it settled questions for his mother, it raised questions for me. Could I live plainly with Haider as a dutiful suburban wife for the rest of my life? Was that who I was? Was I ready to settle down? What kind of life did I want to live? Was I missing out on adventures with guys like Raul or Jonathan?

"Like Raul or Jonathan?" Haider was indignant. "What do they have that I don't?"

I bit my tongue. I probably shouldn't have been so blunt.

"Liz, life isn't all roses and butterflies, or gallivanting all over Europe," Haider said, visibly alarmed. "Yes, Germany was fun, and if you want more of that, go ahead and go travel with your Raul or Jonathan. But no matter who you're with, it won't always be this way. You have to be ready to live a whole life, and every step of it won't be easy."

I was unwilling to face reality.

"You're living in a glass jar suspended in a fairy tale world," Haider scolded me. "When will you just smash it and snap out of it?"

Haider sent me the link to watch *Rocky*, one of his favourite movies. Of course I knew nothing about movies, let alone old ones, but I watched all five Rocky movies. Haider related to Rocky's morning runs while training to become a boxing champion. But I saw myself in the role of Adrian, who lovingly supported Rocky throughout his life. Adrian was all brain while Rocky was all brawn. Could I become the Adrian to Haider's Rocky?

"Liz. I'll put it plainly," Haider said, "I'm no champion and have no desire to be. I just want to live my life and love the people close to me. And I want you to live happily. That's all I'm asking for."

One afternoon, as I sat alone in the kitchen drinking tea, I pictured myself living in a foreign country, patiently waiting for Haider to come home with our daughter when she finished school. I pictured myself caring for the baby boy while they walked in. And Haider would pick both children up and kiss me. And we'd eat dinner together.

I wiped away tears. That is the sweet idyllic life I wanted to have. But how would I achieve it?

I'd started picturing my first name with his last name: Elizabeth Ali. Was it nice-sounding?

I'd been letting my hair grow since I returned from Germany. My hair was surprisingly growing out curly. It had always been straight my whole life. What was happening to me? Was I turning Indian? As my hair grew longer, I tied it in a low bun. Like a married Chinese woman. In the hopes of being a good wife one day. A hope I held on to for dear life. But was it *my* hope, or was it the hope I felt I was supposed to have?

I lay down at night, and my own smell suddenly seemed familiar in a strange way. It resembled Haider's smell. It was as if laying together had blended our smells into a pleasant whole.

I remembered as a child fearing death to the point of not being able to sleep at night and having to knock on the door to my parents' room. I remembered the late-night panic attacks at the thought of an eternal void, what my atheist parents had taught me that death meant. But I realized that I no longer feared death. If Haider passed away, I only wished to be happily buried next to him. To lay for eternity with him was a peaceful, welcomed thought. Sati, the practice of widowed women burning themselves alive on their husband's funeral pyre, suddenly felt like a noble choice if willingly committed by the women.

I sighed. In truth, laying in eternity with Haider was easy. But I had to figure out how to live with him.

30

Before the start of the semester, Haider came over once more to stay at my house. That morning when he arrived, I suggested we go out for bubble tea.

"What's bubble tea?" he asked.

"It's a Chinese thing. It's basically a cold drink, juice or milkshake, in which there are tapioca bubbles at the bottom. They are super fun and chewy."

I took him to L2 in Chinatown, probably the best bubble tea place in town.

"So many flavours!" Haider exclaimed. "What do you recommend?"

"I love all the sweet ones, so lychee, watermelon, honeydew, coconut, and so on. I think you'll like the taro one. It's less sweet but really interesting."

I got a coconut one and Haider got taro.

"These bubbles are so much fun," Haider said. "I'm afraid I'll swallow one whole though."

"Happens to the best of us!" I quipped.

That afternoon, we came home and my parents had just come back from Ikea. We'd been renovating the house. Basically, my dad was rebuilding the whole second floor, after the former tenants had ruined everything. We were installing a staircase and transforming a duplex into a two storey townhouse. My parents also bought some furniture for downstairs. They might as well redo the whole house while they were at it. I got a new armoire for my room, which lay on the ground, unassembled. I stood wondering what to do with it.

"Liz, let me build it for you," Haider offered.

My parents were glad to have one less chore, and I was thanking my lucky stars that I had someone so dedicated to help me. The whole afternoon, Haider and I chatted while he built my cabinet step by step. I watched him closely as he worked. I was amazed by his patience and thoroughness. Every little detail was taken into account. I sighed at how thoughtless I'd been with him, while he had only been thoughtful and kind with me. I felt ashamed of myself.

The cabinet built, we had dinner, and Haider offered my father a bottle of Jack Daniels and mixed it with apple juice. My father looked touched by the gesture.

Later that night, we took a shower together. Before the shower, Haider used the bathroom, and I was surprised he was sitting down to use it.

"I've heard guys say standing up to pee is the hallmark of manhood," I couldn't help but comment.

"Then these guys don't know what it means to be a man. We Muslims are taught to use the bathroom sitting down to avoid making a mess that our mothers or wives will have to clean later."

I pondered how considerate that simple gesture was.

Haider turned on the shower and we stood inside the bathtub together. I watched Haider wash his hair. He stood tall, shampooing his head. I looked at his broad shoulders and thick chest. A thinner waist and generous hips. His skin, silky brown and shining. His hair, jet black and curly. Stretch marks and all, this sight had become a familiar one. Yet how different it was from the male standard of beauty in North America. I watched Haider, and was reminded of pictures I'd seen from travel blogs. Haider reminded me of those bronze statues of the Buddha from Thailand and Laos. His generous frame had a king-like stature. Like an ancient Buddhist prince of Indian kingdoms of antiquity, or a Mughal emperor. His body bore the traces of faraway places around the world. He carried with him the heart of the desert and the hospitality of another world. I felt humbled. I felt small and ordinary. Was I worthy of love from this majestic, kingly being?

As we lay in bed that night, I marvelled at how I had ended up with this noble, yet kind and humble person. Perhaps he had finally touched me to the core.

The next day, I took Haider to visit some of the places from my childhood. I took him to the gates of my high school, and brought him to NDG, the neighbourhood where I grew up. We ended up in a Starbucks in Westmount, right next to the building where I used to live, and where my adopted Italian grandma still lived. We sat down for coffee, which meant tea for me.

"Tell me a story," I asked Haider.

He looked down into his cup and thought about it.

"Do you know how the drink of immortality, *amrita*, is made?" he finally asked.

"How?" I was intrigued

"The whole ocean was churned like milk. Two large mountains were used as rods, and the king of serpents was used as a rope. Gods and demons pulled back and forth on the serpent rod and the ocean started to curd. Fourteen treasures were obtained from the churning of the ocean, including the *amrita*, the drink of immortality. Another one was a lethal poison that could poison the whole universe. The Gods were concerned and approached Lord Shiva for help. He swallowed the poison and his consort Parvati grabbed his throat to prevent him from ingesting it and being harmed from it. As a result, Shiva's throat turned blue."

"Hindu mythology is fascinating."

"It is. The churning of ocean is told in the Mahabharata, the longest epic in the world. The Mahabharata tells the story of the Pandavas, five brothers and sons of King Pandu, and the Dhartarashtras, the one hundred sons of blind King Dhritarashtra. The Pandavas were actually fathered by Gods, whereas the Dhartarashtras were of demonic parentage. The five Pandavas brothers had a common wife Draupati. The Dhartarashtras humiliated the Pandavas and their common wife, and the Pandavas were driven into the wilderness for thirteen years. After the thirteen years had passed, the Pandavas and the Dhartarashtras fought an eighteen-day battle. The Pandavas won, but at the great cost of killing some of their own relatives."

My eyes were bright as I listened intently to Haider.

"My mom insisted that I learn Hindu mythology as a child," Haider explained. "Because even though I'm Muslim, I should know the tradition of my own country. As for me, I decided I also wanted to learn more about Islam as well, so I took an introductory course on Islam at university. Do you want to hear the story of the Prophet Muhammad?"

I was delighted to.

"The prophet came from a lineage that could be traced back to Adam, Noah, and Abraham. But he grew up as an orphan. His father died before he was born, and his mother died only a few years after his birth. He was raised by his grandfather, who also passed away when he was young. He grew up and became a merchant. He was hired by a lady called Khadija, a widow who was fifteen years older than him, but she liked him, so they married. They had several children, including his most famous daughter, Fatima, but they had no sons. The prophet had a habit of going into the hills in the desert for a spiritual retreat. During one such retreat in the holy month of Ramadan, he received his first revelation from angel Gabriel.

"He was terrified, ran home, and called Khadija to cover him with a blanket. He was afraid that he was possessed. But Khadija reassured him that he was not deviant. He learned to accept the revelation and more came over the next twenty-three years. This is how the Quran came to be. It is believed to be the word of God Himself. It was revealed word by word to the prophet, and he memorized everything. Only later on, people wrote it down on paper.

"Many people in his community were afraid of what Muhammad was up to. They were upset that he preached about One God and was opposed to their polytheism, thereby threatening their way of life. The prophet only exhorted people to do good, but he was shunned, beaten, starved, and he narrowly escaped murder. He had to move to a different city, Medina, to escape the threat of his own tribe. But his followers fought for him, and he regained his home city, Mecca.

"After his wife Khadija died, he did marry many other wives. But they were almost all widows and he married them for alliance purposes, or to give them a better standing in society than as widows. The prophet was truly dedicated to his women and honoured them way before the days of feminism.

"By the time Muhammad passed away, he was reigning over most Arab lands. His successors built a large empire. The Sunnis believe that his successors were rightly chosen and were his companions Abu Bakr, Umar, Uthman, and then Ali. But we Shia believe that his immediate successor should have been Ali, who was the husband of Muhammad's daughter Fatima, and who grew up in Muhammad's household. We believe that only Ali inherited many of Muhammad's qualities. It is an age-old debate that no one has the answer to."

I looked at Haider. This was the first time I was given a full account of the origin of Islam. How foreign and intriguing it was. How little did I know about things of this world, I thought to myself.

"You know," Haider said, "a lot of Hindus in India blame us Muslims for breaking the country in two, into Pakistan and India. They say that we can't live peacefully with them. But it's not true, there are still many Muslims in India even now, and we can coexist. It was the British who, after their colonization of India, used the divide and rule tactics to prevent a rebellion from the natives, and it was them who sowed the seeds of discord among us. I believe that people of all religions can live together and that all religions have the same divine source."

Haider's eyes were bright.

"Gandhi believed that Indians formed one single nation. He fought against caste, for the common humanity of us all. My family came from the same village as Gandhi did. Our family name was originally 'Gandhi', even after my family converted to Islam several generations ago. Only two generations ago, my grandfather changed it to Ali. Half the village still had the same surname. Many of my relatives marched together with Gandhiji during his famous salt march against the British."

Was my prince a relative of Gandhi on top of everything? I couldn't believe it.

That night, as we wandered in town, I noticed every brown person on the bus and in the subway. And in every one of them, I saw Haider. Though Haider protested—"Come on. They are just some random migrant workers from Calcutta"—in them I saw the struggle of their nation. I saw the nobility of their history. And I saw their resilience.

And then it dawned on me that Haider must see the same in every Chinese person he encountered. Beggars, street sweepers, waitresses, and all. I felt taken aback. What if the whole world shared a common humanity? What if there was no difference between me and the homeless person down the street? I felt my world expand, expand to include whole nations as my brethren. I felt the weight of having whole nations as my kin. I felt immense compassion and sorrow towards the world.

The next day, I had arranged to meet my Armenian piano professor Garen, who was almost a father figure to me. I brought Haider with me, and we had coffee downstairs in the building at Concordia University where he taught.

"So he's the famous Haider you've been telling me about," Garen said as he greeted us.

I nodded. Garen thoroughly asked Haider about his life plans, about his studies, about his personal convictions. Finally he said, "We Eastern people are warm people. Haider is like myself. And I know this can be so attractive compared to cold folks here in North America and Western Europe. But you have to be careful because our values are different. I have a friend, a lady who got married to a Pakistani man, who complained to me that every time they went somewhere, her Pakistani husband drove, and his mother sat beside him. The wife and children always took the back seat. You get the idea, wives are not typically priorities in Eastern cultures."

He was right.

"But I have talked to Haider and he is a good guy. I have nothing bad to say about him. I wish you both good luck."

I was glad. That evening, we went to McDonald's and I ordered a happy meal. Haider teased me, but I was enjoying a good moment with him and it brought happy memories from my childhood, making me forget all about having to be healthy and other bullshit. As I ate, I felt relieved and sad at once. I was glad to be having a good moment with Haider, but I had a feeling that it wouldn't last.

As we headed home, I remembered what my friends Clara, Arielle, and even Wendy in Germany had told me. They all saw only good in Haider.

"Keep him, for heaven's sake, you've found a keeper!"

"I wish I could find a boyfriend like him!"

"He's so kind to you. Be kind to him back!"

I sighed. He was a keeper. Yes, they were right. And he'd been starting to change my whole perspective on life. But keeping him was not as easy as they made it sound.

31

September 2, 2012

That night, we squeezed to fit in my single bed like we usually did when he visited about once a month or so. Around 2 a.m., I suddenly awoke in terror. Was it a bad dream? I didn't know, but I felt mortally afraid. I jostled Haider awake in a fit of panic and, with a mix of incredulity and anguish, he asked me what was up. I freaked out and asked him not to touch me.

"Get as far as you can; it's a panic attack," I cried out.

Haider got up and stood next to the door, still trying to process what was happening.

I sat on the bed and, as I took some deep breaths, I slowly calmed down.

"You can come back now," I said.

"I can sleep outside if you wish," he offered.

"No, no, it's okay."

"You sure?"

"Yes."

Haider came back and we both lay down, side by side, staring at the ceiling. We both felt uneasy for the rest of the night.

We got up the next day and had breakfast together in the kitchen. The sun was shining through the window, creating a blinding glare.

"You have not overcome your doubts about me," Haider said gravely.

I looked down at my feet. I didn't know what to say.

"Liz, I can't hold on much longer if this continues. We have to be on the same page."

I nodded. I felt a vague sense of horror growing inside me.

In the afternoon, we prepared for the party we planned that day. We tidied up the room and bought some chips and snacks. We set out some chairs and I even wiped down my piano, for it was a jamming party. We were busy and we were happier.

Soon, friends started rolling in. Jonathan came first, and soon, we were on the piano improvising on four hands. Then, Raul arrived with Thomas, a Québécois guy from the Honours Physics program who was also in our band. Haider and I helped them unpack Raul's car. They brought an acoustic guitar each, and Thomas also brought an additional electric guitar, amp, fancy pedals, and all the bells and whistles. Raul also brought his cajon, that wooden box out of which unfathomable rhythm can be produced by those who know how. My living room was being crammed with more and more instruments.

Then Katie came, a friend of Raul's, a singer. And then John, Raul's best friend, a laid-back Black guy with an afro, and a drummer showed up. We sat together in the cramped living room.

"Raul, start a beat," I called out.

It was one of those funky Latin American samba beats. I soon joined in on the higher registry of the keyboard. Jonathan started a rhythm in the lower registry of the piano. Katie started humming. Thomas went full on with his pedals. We jammed for a good twenty minutes on this tune. Haider stood around watching intently.

"Haider, why don't you get a guitar and join us?" I asked. "And John, do you want to do some beats?"

Haider borrowed Raul's guitar.

"I'm happy to listen, but I don't have a drum set with me," John said.

"Try my cajon!" Raul suggested.

"It's not a drum set," John mumbled.

Raul jokingly shot him a death stare, as if to say *what do you mean, it's not a drum set?* We all laughed.

"I'm bad at it but I'll try," John said humbly, but immediately started finding his groove on the cajon.

I was caught off guard. It was a beat I'd never heard before. Suddenly Haider joined in with a jazzy jam. It sounded really nice and everyone joined in. I was impressed.

We decided to order pizza for dinner. As we waited, we started another song.

"*Pizza man,*" Katie sang, and we all laughed,

"Pizza man,

Won't you come knocking on our door?"

Everyone joined in on the Pizza Man chorus, and we carried on until the doorbell rang.

"Here comes the Pizza Man!" I exclaimed as I answered the door. We all rushed to the dining room and devoured the large pepperoni pizza and soft drinks. The night was settling in, and we were all chatting around the kitchen table about school, travelling, music, and the student life. Then, our guests left one by one. I said goodbye to each of them, until only Haider and I remained, sitting in the kitchen. My parents had gone out to see a movie that night and weren't home.

"That was fun!" I exclaimed.

"I'm glad you enjoyed it," Haider replied, but he looked uneasy.

We sat in silence as a tension grew between us.

Finally, Haider broke it.

"So these are the people you compare me to?" Haider asked sardonically.

Oh no. I didn't want to get into it.

"You say I'm not as cool as them?"

Why did he have to bring this up now? Of course, he had read my mind as usual, and I felt ashamed for even thinking this way, but on the other hand, was I really the problem, or was he?

I stammered, "Well … depends on which way you look at it."

"First of all, I get along with them, don't I? Even with that Raul guy, who I know has a crush on you. I say nothing and I let you guys be!"

"Come on," I pleaded, trying to talk him down. I didn't like where this was going.

"In which way are they superior to me, exactly?" Haider demanded.

I was quiet. It wasn't that they were superior to him, but I just … wished he was more like them? I didn't know what to say.

"They play music? I also play music."

He was right. But that wasn't it.

"Well, they live independently from their parents, they can travel on their own and everything," I finally said.

"So I have baggage, is that it? You'd rather I don't have a family?"

That wasn't it either. I actually enjoyed staying with his family. I could deal with them. That wasn't the problem. But what was?

Haider was furious.

"Well …" I trailed off. I couldn't put my finger on what about him seemed so … out of place. No matter how much he hung around me, it still felt to me like he didn't belong in my circle. Like he was the odd one out, and everyone knew about it, and nobody spoke of it.

"Yes, I have a family, and I love them, and I know that they love me. I want you to understand them, and I want them to love you too. That's why we have to compromise. But you don't seem to realize how much I'm doing for you."

He was not wrong. I couldn't argue with him.

Haider looked at me sternly. "You said you wanted to have a place in Toronto with me so we can be together. I finally got permission from my parents to move out. I will do so next week. I did this all for you. And you wanted to see me more often. Well, we've been visiting each other every other week over this summer. Do you know how hard it is to negotiate with my parents for these things?"

I sighed. I wished I didn't have to deal with all this.

"Liz, I want you to have the best possible life with me, and I try to accommodate your every need. I don't even ask you to do the same, because I love you and all I want is to make you happy. I'd be glad if you even just noticed what I've been doing instead of comparing me to these folks you call *friends*. Will they do all of that for you?"

Where was he going with this? What was he trying to prove? I felt exposed, on trial. How dare he accuse my friends of not being willing to be there for me, like he was? He barely knew them!

"I went travelling with Jonathan over the summer, we stayed at a fancy villa!" I was defensive and, at this point, frankly mad. I wanted to get back at him for hitting a nerve. "And Raul says he'll take me with him on a road trip!"

"Sweetheart," Haider looked exasperated, "you want us to live this bohemian life, you want to travel, you want to see the world. It's so easy for you to say this. Let me remind you: you still live at home with your parents and they still pay for everything, including tuition and travel expenses! Yet you're completely ungrateful and keep bitching about your family. Do you know how privileged you are?"

I was taken aback. He had a point, but I wasn't willing to consider what he was saying.

"You want me to be like *you*," Haider carried on, "to be ungrateful towards my family, and leave them and stop being responsible. You want me to leave them to their lot while I gallivant around the world with you. You want me to leave my aging parents to languish in their mediocre jobs while I earn money for myself? You want me to stop supporting my sisters in their endeavours, while they sacrificed their whole lives to support me and care for me?"

Haider was fuming. He looked at me as if he barely even recognized me anymore, like I was a pure stranger, a stranger who had wronged him.

"Liz, *Elizabeth*, you have to break out of this glass jar you live in. You need to see reality as it is. It isn't all rainbows and butterflies. Get a grip! Do better at school. Get your degree, like I got my degree, then we can talk. Look, I can have standards, too. Stop daydreaming about living all over the world like some hippie vagabond. Yes, I want a future with you, to have our own house and live with our Chindian babies. But unlike you, I'm actually working towards it. What do you have to say for yourself?"

I was quiet. I didn't want to address it. Doing so would mean that I actually had to get my act together—to take life seriously enough to play my part in our relationship, to be deserving of him.

"You remind me of my mother," Haider said, "and not in a good way. My mom always creates drama for attention. When I was growing up, she kept saying she was going to die young. You know what it's like to grow up feeling like you'll be an orphan at some point? It's horrid.

So we cajoled our mother, we reassured her, and we gave her attention. And we did our best to help her out. It took us years to realize that she was only doing it for attention. You are behaving the same way, threatening to break up with me for every little thing and acting uncertain about me over nothing. And I've had enough of this bullshit!"

I was tearing up. This wasn't fair! I was trying too, but it was never enough for him. He was accusing me of struggling like this on purpose, for attention.

I sniffled and repressed a sob.

"You know what," Haider balked, "talking to you is useless! I'm heading back to Toronto. Call me when you get a grip!"

Haider took his jacket and his backpack in one fell swoop and stormed out of the house in a whirlwind.

I sat on my bed, frozen in the darkness. This had just become really serious. I was afraid. I was genuinely just trying to figure my life out. What did I want? I wanted that opportunity to just explore myself—who I was and where I fit into the world—before committing to anything for the rest of my life. I wanted some time to figure things out for myself. And these guys Haider felt I was comparing him to were in the same life stage as me, doing just that. I felt hurt that he assumed the worst of me, like I thought he was inferior. I wiped my tears and ran out. I sprinted towards the subway station and saw Haider's silhouette disappearing in the distance.

I called out, "Haider! Please, hold on!"

He carried on walking as if he hadn't heard me.

"Haider, please, I beg you!"

He stopped and turned around slowly.

"What now?" he uttered.

"I'm sorry," I pleaded, hesitating. "You're right about a lot of things. I'm sorry I don't appreciate you enough."

"Is that all?"

"No. Haider. I get that you're doing all of this for us, and I should be grateful. I *should* be. But I'm not feeling it. Ever since the beginning, it was you who picked me, then you who tried to make us happen because you wanted it. Everything you did on your terms. You insisted on making me get along with your family. For your sake."

Haider looked at me with some concern.

I continued, "Remember when you said that dating me was the only thing you ever did for yourself? Well, you surely did it for yourself. Not for me. You aren't trying to please me, only yourself. Have you ever considered that through it all, *you* were actually being selfish?"

It was my turn to be fed up and stick it to him.

Haider had stopped and was clearly pondering what I had just said.

He wanted the conventional life, the white picket fence, but was that what I wanted? Maybe in his part of the world, children were raised to prepare for marriage and husbands were expected to provide, while wives were expected to settle down and care for the family. Haider was full-swing in Eastern settling-down mode, but I was in Western the-world-is-my-oyster mode. And here I was, thinking I was the immigrant who couldn't fully assimilate!

I wasn't ready to be. I couldn't see myself yet as a housewife with the army of kids he wanted so badly. I wanted all of this too, theoretically, but in practice, I still had a long way to go to get there. I still had so much to experience, so much to figure out before I settled down for good in a boring suburban home. He was only two years older than me, but these two years felt like a lifetime's worth of difference at this point. It was the difference between backpacking Europe on a shoestring budget partying every night and working a 9-to-5 job with a pension plan.

"Do you even care about what kind of life I want?" I asked.

"Liz, what do you *actually* want?" Haider asked, perplexed. "One minute you're fantasizing about raising children with me and the next you're lamenting about missed opportunities. Make up your mind!"

"I ... I don't know." I whimpered. "I want to be with *you*, but not *this* way. The long distance, the awkward accommodations, me having to tiptoe around your family, all the pressure to choose a career where I could earn a living ... when I'm not even sure what I want to do for the rest of my life!"

"Then how would you suppose we go about it?" Haider implored.

"I don't know, I really don't ...." Tears were streaming down my face. I was as lost as he was. I loved him, but I couldn't face what it would take to be with him.

"Liz, forgive me. Yes, I have been selfish with you, you're right. I want you for myself. Yes, I really do want you all for myself. Is that so bad? I don't know what I'd do without you. Please forgive me for wanting you so bad, Liz. I don't know if I could live without you. I don't know how else I'd live!" He was grovelling by now, and I couldn't help but feel a flood of admiration for how vulnerable he had gotten with me, and a pang of pity towards how precarious his situation had become.

When I looked into Haider's eyes, I saw only sincerity and earnestness behind the tears that were welling up. I had to relent and hug him tightly. I couldn't bear to see him this distraught. After all I put him through, he still loved me wholeheartedly.

"It's okay," I whispered into his ear, stroking a stray lock of hair that I tucked behind his ear. The only worse thing I could fathom than not living out my wanderlust fantasies was losing him. "In truth I don't know how I can live without you either."

Haider held on to me, his face buried into my chest, and he cried. And I cried with him. We held onto each other for a long time.

"I forgive you, Haider," I said. "Please forgive me too."

"I do."

"Let's go home then. Let's spend one last night together before your bus leaves tomorrow morning."

We walked home hand in hand. By the time we were back in my room, it was past midnight. We undressed each other, and cuddled together, naked, under the blankets. As I lay awake next to him, I pondered if perhaps we would still hold on to each other till the end.

"Pray for us, for our future," Haider said in the darkness.

"I will."

32

September passed and we managed to see each other every two weeks or so. When we were together, things were generally smooth. But when we weren't together, things were really starting to fall apart.

Haider kept pushing me to get my act together. Focus on school, figure out a career path, and make a decision about whether or not I was ready to commit to him. But I couldn't help it. I didn't like what I was studying, I didn't like where I was living, and I didn't know what was best for me. I kept wanting to quit school and travel.

"That's silly and dangerous," Haider warned. "And where would you go?"

I had no idea. I just wanted out of my life.

"Liz, you're being immature."

Haider had finally said it, the elephant in the room. "There is no magic cure to any of this. You gotta work for the future you want."

What did he mean, the future I want? I didn't know what future I wanted! That was the problem! How could he be so dense not to understand that!

I was angry. Haider felt like a third parent. I needed to figure things out by myself. I didn't need someone back-seat driving, always telling me what to do. I was feeling more miserable by the day. I barely did any assignments or went to class, relying on copying friends' assignments and class notes.

"Haider," I said, "I need to figure out my life. The world is big and I feel stuck here in a small corner of it with no way out. I don't know what I want and I want to find it."

"How are you going to do that?"

"I don't know."

"Maybe my mom is right, you really don't know what you want in your life."

I fought back tears.

"Haider, you mean everything to me, and I want to come home to you, but for now I need time out," I finally said.

"What do you mean?"

"I want a break from us."

"A what?"

"Some time alone."

"Liz, please don't do this to me. I don't like this Western trend bullshit where people take time off from each other. Why can't you figure out your life while being by my side?"

I didn't know what to say.

"Fine, have it," he said.

He ended the Skype call. A minute later, our relationship status on Facebook was removed.

I lay in my room, suddenly terrified. What on earth should I do now?

I pictured myself years later, decades older. Somewhere in Siberia. I was laying on a low bed made out of coyote fur. It was cold outside, but I was warm in my blanket. Only, I had no recollection of how I got there.

"You finally woke up," an old man said to me.

"Who are you?" I asked him.

"It doesn't matter," he said.

Day after day, he made me warm kohlrabi soup and nursed me back to health. I could finally sit up for a little bit.

"You look familiar," I said.

"Of course I do."

"And I've had this kohlrabi soup before."

"You surely did."

I was searching and searching in my mind, but everything felt like a fog. I only had recollection of being in this tiny wooden house with this kind stranger.

"Have I met you before?" I asked him.

"A long time ago."

"Then what happened to us?"

The old man was quiet.

"It doesn't matter," he finally said. "You are here. I'll keep you safe."

"Thank you," I said.

"No, don't you ever thank me. Serving you is my pleasure."

"Haider … is that you?"

A single tear rolled down his wrinkled cheek.

"Liz, my sweetheart, my bunny," he whispered, his voice cracking, "how I missed you …."

I cried, sitting alone in my room in my parent's house. I wept and wept. Was this story my future?

The next morning, Haider called me on Skype again.

"Feeling better?" he asked.

"I had a miserable night."

"Me too."

We both sighed.

"Bunny, what are we going to do with each other?" Haider looked exhausted and worn out.

We spent the next few days with our relationship status up and down. I was doing worse than ever in class. I didn't even attend one of the midterms. I'd just cram for the final and ace it, I decided.

"Liz, that's ridiculous," Haider said when I told him. "You're ruining your life like this."

I spent my days wandering around campus and the nearby downtown, and everywhere I went, I couldn't run away from the question that was pressing me: did I love Haider enough to stay with him? I lay awake at night thinking about it. I spent all the classes I did attend wondering about it. And during the classes I didn't attend, I sat paralyzed with fear and indecision. There was no escape.

I listened to the songs Haider had sent me. One about love and life, the other about ending and separation. I listened to one, then to the other, and I religiously kept track of which one I listened to the most. If God forbid I listened to the song about ending and separation once more than the other, I fell into a panic and rushed to listen to the latter. I was afraid of saying goodbye, and of ending Skype calls with Haider. Sometimes I would refuse to hang up, sleeping with my laptop by my side with Haider's snoring audible from the other end. I needed reassurance. I needed to know that I wasn't going to end up alone.

"Liz, what are you going to do with me? What do you want to do with me?" Haider asked.

I didn't know. I was scared. I was torn. Did I love him, or did I just hate being alone?

At night, I had recurring dreams. I kept seeing Haider with my father. And they kept talking in my home dialect. The language from the small city of Liuzhou where my parents came from. The language that no one spoke outside that city, or even inside that city anymore. The language that we still spoke at home like a living fossil. Haider spoke it fluently in my dreams. What did it mean? It could only mean one thing: Haider was getting dangerously close to me.

"Liz, we've passed the point of no return," Haider said. "At this point, we can either fight each other to our demise or help each other out and survive."

He was right. There was no going back. And I'd never been more afraid of losing him.

"Liz, stop leaving me hanging. Do you want to be with me or not? Make up your mind!"

"I'm lost, Haider, lost, and I just want to go home."

"And where is that home?"

"I don't know."

"Liz, you're making me lose my mind! I can't bear this anymore. I can't believe it's been over a year that we're together and you still haven't made up your mind about me."

"I'm sorry."

"That's not going to cut it. You're a mess and you're turning me into a mess."

Haider was furious.

"God, Liz, you should be glad you aren't right here with me. Because I would have slapped you. Yes, I would have hurt you. Something I never thought I could ever do to anyone, let alone you."

Haider was crying.

"I'm losing it. Liz, I can't endure this anymore. You're turning me into someone I hate."

"Haider, what can I do?"

"I don't know Liz, I don't know. I'm going to pray." Haider ended the call.

I sat on the floor in my room. I remember, as a child, making up a religion of my own. I had my own rituals and prayer routines. I used to face the north because I thought nobody lived at the north pole and that would be a good and fair common point to face for everyone. I turned towards the north and kneeled down.

No, it didn't feel right. It wasn't who I was anymore. Those childish days were over. I needed something stronger, something mightier than me. And so I slanted towards the northeast. The direction of Mecca. And I felt a force inside me rise. A strength beyond my soul. I felt the collective power of every Muslim in the whole world who ever prostrated in the same direction. I felt kinship with every one of them. And I felt the magnetic pull of Mecca, which forced me to my knees. I kneeled, and I wept.

"God, lead us," I whispered, "show us the way out!"

And I fell to the ground, prostrating on all fours. I felt the ache of my back and the harshness of the scratchy carpeted floor. And I felt the weight of my entire life rest upon me.

I wept. "God, please forgive me. I don't know how to pray. I'm just a simple girl in a wide world. And I'm lost, Allah, I'm lost. Please guide me. Please guide us. Please help us!"

I finally collapsed onto the floor, and I curled myself into a ball. I held my knees tight, and I lay down rocking myself back and forth in the fetal position.

And I felt as if I was back in our room in Duisburg. Our home on Volkstrasse street. It was a summer day. The sun was shining outside. Birds were singing. Everything was as it was: our one mattress, one chair and one table we shared. The pictures and maps and poetry on the walls. Home, I was finally home.

I looked down at the floor, and then I saw a deformed mass on the floor. Loose brown skin and fat. And blood, a lot of blood. Then I saw the mass had the shape of a man. My heart was beating. Was it who I thought it was?

"Haider," I called out.

The mass didn't move.

"Haider, please don't give up on me!"

I crawled up to the shape on the floor.

"Haider, please tell me you're still breathing!"

I heard a rough sound. Was it breathing? And a heartbeat, did I hear?

"Haider, we're home, we are safe! We've made it!"

I lay down by his side and held him gently. And then suddenly the breathing and the heartbeat stopped.

"Haider, please don't leave me! Don't leave me alone to my fate! Haider!"

The sunlight started to dim. And the walls started melting. The birdsongs were turning into shrieks. And the floor started sinking.

I found myself shaking on the floor in my parents' house, still rocking myself back and forth.

"God help us," I kept whispering that night. And I slept on the floor of my room, unable to make it into bed.

33

October 12, 2012

Haider moved out of his family home for good, and Canadian Thanksgiving was coming up. I decided to spend it with Haider at his new place. Perhaps, perhaps with a place to call our own, we could work out a way to live together, I thought. I was hopeful.

Haider picked me up Friday afternoon at the bus stop, and this time, instead of heading to Mississauga or to the hostel, we took the bus to Finch Avenue, walked a few blocks, and arrived at a small three-storey building in a residential area.

"Welcome to our new home," Haider beckoned.

Haider opened the front door with his keys, and we walked up two flights of stairs to the second floor. He then opened another door, and we found ourselves in a kitchen.

"Here's my room on the left," he said. "In the back lives Felicia, a Black girl who's away for Thanksgiving, and Peter, a White guy who's finishing his Bachelor's at the University of Toronto."

The place was clean and bright. My spirits were high. Haider opened his door and I was faced with a large room, with windows along almost one whole wall. There was a bed in one corner, a desk in another corner, and cabinets against the wall opposite the windows.

"This is really nice," I remarked.

"I'm glad you like it," he replied. "I spent two whole weekends with my father building this room you see here. We put two tables together to form the desk. We built the new bed from Ikea. And you see against the wall, that's two cabinets. We placed them a distance apart and installed a rod between them so I could hang my clothes. There is no closet in this room so we had to make do. We put a roof over the space between the cabinets to avoid dust, and we installed a curtain in front to hide the clothing from sight."

"Haider, I didn't expect this …. "I was taken aback."

"Why not?"

"I was expecting but a simple space to live in, while waiting for us to move in together for good, but you've actually put so much thought into it. You didn't need to do all of this."

"Why not? I want to live well wherever I go. And I wanted to bring you to a nice place, not some dirty hostel room."

"That's really thoughtful of you," I said. I marvelled at how much Haider did for me despite everything we'd been fighting about. I felt grateful, and undeserving of it.

"But I have something for you," I said. "Here's a drawing I did in pencil. This is the picture we took at the Duisburg Hauptbahnhof while heading to the Tetraeder for the second time. I reproduced it from sight. I drew it the other night when I missed you and you went to sleep early."

"That's really well done." Haider was visibly touched. "Bunny, you're so sweet."

He kissed me gently on the lips.

"It's a pity I can't hang it here," he said, "because my father still comes here every so often. But I will keep it as a treasure and it will be on the wall of the home we ultimately share."

I wished he could hang it here, but decided to keep quiet and try to be understanding.

"Liz, I can't wait to have a home with you," Haider said.

Was it still possible to dream?

"We'll have to have an Islamic wedding," he said, "to please my parents. You don't mind, right?"

"Of course not."

"And you'll wear a sari. How I wish to see you wearing a sari."

I sighed. Could we still hope to see that day?

"We'll raise a household of Chindians and we will celebrate every holiday, be it Christmas, or Eid, or Ramadan, or Diwali. It will be beautiful!"

I hugged Haider tight. I was trying to hold onto every ounce of comfort I could find through him.

"What do you want to eat tonight?" Haider finally asked.

"Indian food. I miss your mom's cooking."

Haider laughed.

"Actually I have some leftover dal soup my mom brought here. You want to have that with rice?"

"That'd be fantastic!" I was giddy.

"It's really good. It's my favourite food. But in India it's actually poor people's food because dal, or lentils, are cheap."

"Once a hobo, always a hobo," I said, and we both laughed. Then, I almost choked up. I missed the Tetraeder. I missed living together. I missed our Volkstrasse days.

"Come, bunny, it's ready." Haider emerged from the kitchen with a bowl of steaming golden soup.

We sat in one chair and ate from one bowl and one spoon. We were almost like we were back in Germany.

"Do you think we'll manage to hold on together?" I asked.

"I don't know, sweetie, I really don't know." Haider sighed. "But we can let go and let God. And we can hope. Hope is what keeps us alive."

The next day, we went grocery shopping. It felt good playing house.

"Peter will be back tonight," Haider said. "Let's make something delicious to share with him. He said he'll cover dessert and is making us a surprise."

"That's so sweet!" I exclaimed.

"We're probably not enough people to make a whole turkey, but we can roast a chicken, right?"

"Do you know how?"

"Of course, bunny, who do you think I am?" Haider laughed, 'When my father first moved to Kuwait, he was living there alone and ate bread dipped in water because he could cook nothing else. In every letter my mom wrote to him, she sent him a recipe. She vowed that all her children, male or female, would learn to cook properly."

Haider bought a whole chicken, onions, vegetables, and apples for the stuffing. We also got some baby potatoes to go on the side.

We came home and got busy in the kitchen. As Haider seasoned the chicken, we put on some music. "Lucky" began playing.

"Remember that night before going to the Tetraeder for the first time," Haider reminisced. "I showed you this song and you looked like you were too good to sing this cheesy song with anyone?"

I laughed.

"Let's sing it together," he offered.

And we did. I knew every word from listening to the song every time I missed him. We sang

I'm lucky I'm in love with my best friend,
Lucky to have been where I have been ...

I was starting to tear up. At that moment, I felt lucky. I truly felt more than lucky to still be by Haider's side.

"Hey bunny, don't cry," Haider said. "I'm done with the chicken, let me sing to you, *Tum se hi* on my guitar."

I felt transported far away, to Germany, to India, to Kuwait, to the whole world. How powerful a song can be. When Haider was finished, I said, "Let me sing you something."

"What is it?"

"*Silsila yeh chaahat ka na maine bujhne diya*," I began.

"Bunny!" Haider was stupefied.

I carried on until the first chorus.

"Bunny, how did you learn this? It's from *Devdas!*"

"I listened to Didi's recording a million times. I love *Devdas*, and relate so much to both Paro and Chandramukhi."

"I hope life treats you better than it treated either of them."

There was a solemn silence. Then suddenly we heard the doorknob turn.

"Hey Haider, I'm back!" Peter cried out.

"Peter! This is my girlfriend, Liz!"

"Hi Liz!" he said.

"Hey!" I answered him.

"My, you guys made roast chicken and potatoes!" Peter observed.

"We did. What are you making us for dessert?" Haider asked.

"Pumpkin rolls! We're having a really fancy Thanksgiving, well as fancy as student budgets go!"

We all laughed. We watched Peter mix the flour and get out a can of pumpkin purée. He made a thin layer of pumpkin dough, baked it, and rolled it up with frosting. We chatted while he was busy in the kitchen.

"I come from Windsor," Peter said, "and I study biology at U of T."

"Cool, I'm from Montreal and study math and physics at McGill," I answered.

"That's intense! Do you intend to do research afterwards? Sounds like a really cool field."

"Thanks, and yes, I'm considering research."

"My elder brother studies physics actually. He's doing his PhD in the States. If ever you need career advice, you can speak to him," Peter offered.

I was glad. Perhaps there is a way out career-wise for me?

The evening eased in, and Haider, Peter, and I sat around the kitchen table for the Thanksgiving meal.

"I'm really thankful for another year passed in peace," Haider said before the meal. "I'm thankful for my family, and I'm thankful for having Liz in my life."

"And I'm thankful for Haider," I added.

"You guys are really cute," Peter said after we started eating. "And what a nice match, Indian and Chinese. Your kids are going to be the smartest people in the world."

Haider and I laughed.

"You come from India but lived in Kuwait, right?" Peter asked Haider. "And Liz is Chinese and from Montreal. And you guys met in Germany."

"And we got together in the Netherlands!" Haider added.

"Man, that's so cool," Peter said. "Your relationship spans the whole world. And you study engineering and math and physics. What a power couple you guys are. I'm jealous."

He was right, I thought. We finished off the chicken and the potatoes and had some delicious pumpkin rolls. What a nice night, what a relief, I thought to myself.

The door opened and Felicia came back.

"Happy Thanksgiving!" she called out to everyone.

We served her dinner and introduced ourselves to each other. It was a cheerful night indeed. That night, we chatted till late in the evening, and everyone retired to their rooms tired and overfed.

"Haider," I said when we were back in his room, "thank you. Thank you for this beautiful night and for giving me hope. I'm grateful, I'm so grateful to still be with you."

"I'm grateful too, bunny."

I gave Haider a massage, for he had neck and back pain. Then, we lay down on the bed, cuddling. I daydreamed about us being a power couple, about creating a community of like-minded people who cared about the world, about helping people everywhere in need, about standing up for justice, for peace, and for tolerance, about speaking up against injustice, about making the world a better place. Haider was snoring beside me.

"How you've changed me, Haider," I whispered half to myself. "How you've taught me to grow and become a new person."

34

By the time I was back in Montreal, our relationship troubles were happening again. I was thoroughly unhappy with my life and was taking it out on Haider.

"What do you want?" Haider asked. "What more do you want from me?"

"I don't know. I'm lost."

"Sweetie, this is the last call. If you don't pull yourself together, I can't endure this anymore."

"Hold on to me, please!"

"I'm trying!"

I sighed. I'd been wandering around town, avoiding home, avoiding my parents, avoiding responsibilities.

"Liz, it's going to be okay. Just a few weeks and it will be winter break; we will see each other again," Haider said.

But instead of feeling reassured, I was worried. Too much had happened. If I were to meet Haider again, would it still be the same?

I went jamming with Jonathan one day and he drove me home at night. In his car, I broke down in tears.

"What should I do with Haider?" I asked Jonathan.

"How do you feel about him?" he answered.

"I don't know."

"Do you feel like he truly understands you?"

Jonathan's words stayed with me the whole night. Did Haider really understand where I was coming from? For the first time, I doubted. I doubted whether he was what I truly needed at that point.

I spoke to Arielle another day.

"How should I deal with him?" I asked her.

"Let it be, for heaven's sake," she answered. "He's the best guy you'll ever be able to find. Don't ruin it."

I sighed. Was he the best person for me? I did not know.

I felt nearly spent. I was losing it. Losing my appetite and losing weight. I remember Haider's motto, Live from the heart, one foot below the brain. But how did I live from my heart? What did my heart want exactly? I had no answers.

"Haider," I asked, "what does love mean?"

"Sweetie, it is different for everyone. You'll have to figure it out for yourself."

I thought about Haider's family. Despite everything, did Ma love Pa? Did Pa love Ma? How could I know? They ended up not divorcing, but there was no warmth between them anymore. Was what was left still love? Was there anything left? And then, did Ma love Haider? She certainly seemed to want what she felt was best for him. But she was also giving him trouble by opposing our relationship. Was this out of love? And what about Pa and Haider? They seemed to despise each other, but could it be that Pa was secretly proud of Haider?

And I wondered about my family. Did my parents love each other? They used to, for sure. But at this point, they were just living, or coexisting together in the same space. Each did their own thing and they fought over petty things all the time. Was tolerating each other love? And then, did my mother love me? She surely said so, but did she understand me? Could there be love without understanding? I had many questions and no answers.

"Haider," I asked him again, "what does love mean to you?"

"To me, love means sacrificing yourself for the well-being of someone else."

How much was I willing to sacrifice for Haider? Was I willing to sacrifice my freedom? I thought about my love of travelling. With so many places to visit on this Earth, was I ready to wait for Haider to come with me? I thought about all my guy friends. Was I ready to commit to Haider and miss out on the opportunity to see what else was out there? What if I wanted to drop everything and move to Alaska the next day? What if I was to change my career and study something else? What if I wanted to go back into classical music? What if I wanted to go on a spiritual retreat in Nepal? Would Haider support me or hinder me?

I sighed. I felt so ambivalent. Was my love for Haider not enough? Did I love him at all? I was lost. If I wasn't even sure what love was to begin with, how could I know if I loved him?

The final exam period came and I had taken two graduate level courses as required by my honours program. Things were getting really tough and I wasn't ready. The exams for the grad courses happened first, and for quantum theory, it was a twenty-four-hour take home exam.

I met up with Raul after receiving the exam papers, and we decided to tackle the exam together in one of the quieter lounges he found in the Geography department. We pulled an all-nighter and did as best as we could.

"I'm so over this," Raul said, past 3 a.m.

"Me too. I'm just aiming for a pass at this point," I answered.

"You know what?" Raul said, "I want to take a road trip during the winter break. Drive up to Northern Quebec. Park my car in the middle of the wilderness and watch the snow fall outside. Go ice climbing or skiing. Do you want to come with me?"

I thought about Haider. He surely wanted to see me during the break. But could I turn down an offer for some fun and adventure? I craved it badly. I needed to get away and reassess things.

"Sure, I'll come with you," I answered, and almost immediately started regretting it and panicking inside. What now, what would Haider say to this?

We handed in the exam the next day and when I got home, I said nothing to Haider. I tried to prepare for my next three finals that were scheduled in a row the next Monday, Tuesday, and Wednesday. Finally, on Sunday night, I couldn't take it anymore and called Haider.

"Haider, I have something to tell you," I said over Skype.

"What is it, bunny?"

"Raul is going on a road trip during the winter break and offered to take me along with him. I said yes. I'm sorry I ..."

"What, Liz, what?"

"I'm sorry I said yes before asking you about it."

"Liz, oh God Liz, you didn't."

"I'm so sorry."

"Liz, end the call, I'll be back in a few minutes."

I sat on the floor of my room. It was almost midnight. I sensed the eerie quiet before a large storm and felt apprehensive. I looked at the ceiling and back on the ground. What will Haider do now? I thought. I felt my heart pounding and I was starting to lose it.

"Liz, I'm back," Haider typed suddenly.

"Call me?"

"No, I'd rather not."

Something was seriously wrong.

"Liz, listen to me carefully," Haider typed. "It's been a year and a half since we've been together. You know how much I did for you. I loved you deeply. And I still love you. You were everything I wanted."

He paused.

"But you've crossed the line today. You've been ambivalent about me for far too long, and I tolerated it. I thought you'd come around if I gave you enough time. But clearly, you wanted someone else. You've chosen another guy over me. Another guy who, I've been telling you, has feelings for you."

My heart sank in my chest.

"I don't know what to say. My mother is right. You are too immature. You don't know what you want in life and, instead of figuring it out, you just create drama. Could we come together in the future? I don't know. But for today, it's goodbye. Goodbye Liz. This is it. We're done with each other. I wish you the best of luck."

He went offline. I sat on the floor, completely dumbfounded. No, it wasn't happening. I didn't believe it. It couldn't be. It could not end like this. No. It could not! It was too fast. It was too early. It was too easy. No! I was in denial.

I looked at my laptop and reread everything he wrote to me.

"Goodbye Liz. This is it. We're done with each other. I wish you the best of luck." I read it again.

No. No this could not be. No, please! And that was when the dam broke, and the tears started pouring out, flooding my entire face, dripping in giant blobs onto the floor. I gently kneeled onto the floor.

"Heart," I said, looking down at my chest, "heart, is this what you wanted?"

I sobbed and sobbed.

"Heart, are you happy now?" I asked. "Did you get what you wanted?"

I was trembling all over.

"Heart, we've only got each other now. It's over. It's just you and me. Can we make peace? Can you lead me to a way out?"

I collapsed into a prostration towards Mecca.

"God," I cried out, "Allah! Save me!"

But in the dead of night, I heard only my own heart-beat. No one was going to save me tonight. *No one.* I was starting to feel numbness in my hands and feet. *No, this cannot be. This cannot be right. I must be trapped in the wrong universe!*

I wandered out of my room, in a trance-like state. I opened the front door and, wearing only a thin sweater, barely felt the sub-zero cold rush in. The world still looked the same, I thought. How could this be? How could it be that we were no more? Why hadn't the sky collapsed yet?

I wanted to yell. But I didn't find it inside me to break the surreal snow-covered silence. I stepped outside, bare-foot, and started running on the icy sidewalk. Where I was headed, I didn't know. I wanted to escape, escape my real-ity. Run to save my life. But soon, I started feeling stabbing pain in my feet. I arrived at the end of the block. No one was around. Where could I go? There was no way out.

I ran back to my house, back into my room. My feet were bleeding slightly. I got a bandage out to cover the small cut. But my heart was bleeding profusely and I could do nothing about it.

I went online and found Arielle, still awake.

"He broke up with me, Arielle," I typed, frantically. "He broke up with me!"

"No way!"

"What do I do now?"

289

"How are you feeling?"

"Suicidal."

"My dear, you need to go to the hospital."

"Take me there."

"I can't. I have a final tomorrow and I'm still cramming for it."

"Me too. I have a final tomorrow."

"You should go to the nearest hospital for your safety. My dear friend, I'm worried about you."

I laid my laptop down. There was nothing to do.

"Are you still around? Did you go to the hospital?" I saw Arielle's incoming messages flicker as notifications on the screen.

I shut down my laptop. I shut down my phone. And I lay motionless on the ground. I let the stillness sink in. I looked up at my ceiling, dotted with colourful paper stars I made in fourth grade. I looked at my flowy white curtains. I looked at the Tibetan mantra written above my door. I looked at the cabinet Haider had built for me, still standing in the corner with all of my clothes inside. I looked at the angel he once gave me to protect me from self harm. I looked at Captain Ali the bull terrier, with his gentle smile sitting on my bed.

I closed my eyes. And I gently bid goodbye to everything around me.

35

The next morning, my parents found me collapsed on the floor in the same position. They asked me what happened and I told them. They called me a coward for wanting to skip my final. And they pushed me to head out regardless of circumstances.

I headed out like a zombie. I sat in the examination room for the whole three hours, my mind a total blank. I returned the examination papers unmarked except by tears. The next day went exactly the same way. On the third day, I'd had enough. I skipped my final and went to Student Services to drop the course for medical reasons.

I got home after the devastating end of the semester and lay on the floor, weeping. Everything I knew was over, everything I stood for was gone.

Raul texted me and I told him what happened. He cancelled the road trip and spent the holidays with me. On New Year's Eve, we wandered on the Mont Royal hiking trails. Under the giant cross on top of the hill, he kissed me. I felt like trash, total trash. How low had I fallen! How could it be that I was so naive that I never saw this coming? Haider had warned me several times about Raul's intentions, and I always dismissed him as being overly possessive or jealous. Now I saw the truth. Haider was right. I felt sick to my stomach.

I sat at home in January, broken, a shell of my former self. Raul was gone after I told him I wasn't ready for another relationship. Arielle gave me the cold shoulder after blaming the breakup entirely on me when I told her the details. And I'd lost touch with most of my other friends in the months of turmoil with Haider. I was alone. Yes, quite alone.

I sat at home and binge watched Bollywood movie after Bollywood movie. I saw *Dilwale Dulhania Le Jayenge*, about two Indian expats who fell in love on a trip in Europe. I saw *Mughal-e-azam*, the love story of Jahangir, the son of the great Indian king Akbar. And I watched *Devdas* over and over, drenched in tears.

I related both to Paro and Chandramukhi. Paro, who cannot not marry the man she loves because his family rejected her. And Chandramukhi, a prostitute who loves a man who doesn't love her.

I sang with Paro:

> *The scar that you gave me, this scar has made my face blossom.*
> *I will keep this as a memento, on my head, always decorated.*

How I wished this weren't so true. Every time I saw a woman wearing a sari, I wanted to hide my face and weep. Every time I saw an Indian couple, I wanted to rage and cry. My life was a life no more. It was but memories and ashes.

I wanted out of my life. I wanted to travel and go far, far away. And I started planning trips. Where did I want to go? India, Morocco, Kuwait, Saudi Arabia, Turkey? Or Germany, France, the UK, Spain, Czech Republic? What could I possibly do?

By the end of January, I'd completely stopped attending classes. And by February, I had officially dropped out of school. I was wandering in the streets, looking for something I could never find. I tried looking for jobs to finance my travels. I knocked on supermarket doors, tried restaurants and convenience stores. I had zero work experience. And I was so out of it. Who was I kidding? I wasn't going anywhere!

I stood in front of the mirror one night, and I didn't recognize the face I saw. My cheeks were pale, my eyes were sullen. And there was a single strand of white hair, standing out against a sea of thick black locks, breaking the symmetry of my part line.

Who was I at this point? What was left of me? I did not know. I did not want to know. I put together a playlist of every song Haider introduced me to and called the list Kohlrabi Soup. But instead of nursing me back to health, it drove me deeper into despair. I had nothing to hold on to, and so I drifted further and further.

I went to the bookstore, having nothing better to do, and ran into the spirituality section. One book was laying ajar on top of a shelf. I picked it up. It was the *Bhagavad Gita*, the Song of the Lord, a famous extract of the Mahabharata. I read it in one go, swallowing the advice of Krishna for the young prince Arjuna. It did not cure my thirst. And so I looked at the book placed directly under it. It was The Interior Castle, a book by Teresa de Avila, a thirteenth-century Catholic saint.

I bought it and went home to read it. I read about Teresa talking about her relationship with God and kept on reading. One line stood out to me. She wrote that a community was mandatory for anyone on a spiritual path. And so, the next day, I went to the McGill Chaplaincy looking for community.

I got an appointment with the McGill chaplain, an Anglican priest. Outside his office, a brown man was sitting there having coffee. I walked into the chaplain's office and told him I was looking for a spiritual path. He duly recommended several religious centres, from churches to mosques to Buddhist temples. I noted down his recommendations and walked out.

I was on the street when someone called me from behind. I turned around. It was the brown man who sat outside the chaplain's office.

"I heard you say you're interested in sufism," he said.

"Indeed I am."

"I can take you to a Sufi centre here in Montreal."

I thanked him. He introduced himself. His name was Ahmad, from Bangladesh. He was a PhD student at McGill in computer science. He asked me why I was interested in sufism. I said I loved a Muslim man once.

The next day, Ahmad gave me a copy of the Quran and took me to the McGill *musalla*, a small room in the student society building, used as a makeshift prayer room. I removed my shoes at the entrance and opened the door. It was a small space, with brick walls painted white and a green carpet with an intricate floral pattern. There was a white curtain dividing the room into roughly two thirds outside and one third inside. I saw men praying in the outside section of the room. I felt like I had just set foot in Pakistan.

"The section behind the curtain is for women," Ahmad said. "You can sit there if you want."

I sat down on the carpet. A man started calling the call to prayer.

"Allahu akbar, Allahu akbar!" I heard.

Akbar was the name of the great Indian king. His name meant "The Greatest." *Allahu Albar* meant "Allah is the Greatest." *God is the Greatest!* And I started sobbing uncontrollably.

A girl wearing a hijab in the musalla just finished praying and saw me crying. She came to my side.

"Are you okay?" she asked gently.

"I just heard the call to prayer for the first time," I said, tears flowing down my cheeks.

"It happens." She smiled. "It will be okay. Don't you worry. God is guiding you."

I nodded. That night when I went home, I faced Mecca, and I prayed.

"Oh Allah," I called out, "Allah guide me. Show me the way."

Suddenly I felt a presence in front of me, in mid air. I saw a silhouette floating among thick clouds, right there in my room. I heard sounds of thunder. I leaned back, afraid.

"Come to me," I heard a voice call out above the thunder.

Was God calling me to Him? I prostrated onto the ground and shuddered in fear.

"Oh Allah!" I cried out, "I will heed your call. I will come to you!"

Two weeks later, Ahmad took me to the Sufi gathering. We took the bus towards the northwest of the city and, while on the bus, passed by a mosque. I wondered if I was still in the Montreal I grew up in or if I'd changed continents.

We got off in a residential area and saw brown hijab-wearing youth hanging out at the street corner. We approached a nondescript bungalow, and, through the open windows, I heard chanting in Arabic. Ahmad opened the unlocked side door and invited me in. It was a small wooden house, and a family lived on the ground floor. We left our shoes on the shoe rack at the entrance and we went downstairs. The basement was covered in carpet, and the walls were covered in framed Arabic calligraphy.

"This is a *zawiya*," Ahmad said. "It's the North African term for a small place of study or worship. This place was founded by Sheikh Youssef, whom I will introduce you to. His name is Yousself ben Brahim; the term 'sheikh' is an honorific because he is a religious scholar."

I sat on the women's side once again, behind a lace curtain. I found myself amongst women and girls of all ages, all wearing hijab. A woman in her thirties introduced herself to me as Maryam. She was the cousin of Sheikh Youssef and lived upstairs, on the ground floor of the bungalow. She sat by my side the whole evening. I witnessed an evening of singing and worship, ending with a speech by Sheikh Youssef, half in Arabic and half in French. I wondered where the rabbit hole I'd fallen into was leading me.

After the worship, everyone shared a potluck and I was introduced to food from all around the world. The women introduced themselves to each other. There was the elderly Heba from Tunisia, Khadija from Morocco, young Asma from Palestine, and others whom I didn't remember. In each of their eyes, I saw sincerity, I saw pain, I saw joy, I saw kindness. They strangely felt familiar to me, as if I'd met them before.

Ahmad introduced me to Sheikh Youssef at the end. Sheikh Youssef asked me if I wanted to convert to Islam.

"I will convert the day it rains," I told the sheikh. I needed a sign from God, and I knew the rain was one of them.

Three weeks passed and there was not a single drop of rain. I came to the zawiya every Sunday night for the weekly *mawlid*, the celebration of the birth of Prophet Muhammad. And each week, I looked outside and it was dry.

On the night that marked one month since I'd been introduced to the zawiya, the people there had started to feel like family to me. Old Heba would talk to me like her own daughters, and Maryam treated me like a sister. The mawlid was an intense one, and people were crying. Suddenly a roll of thunder was heard outside. Soon, it was pouring.

After the mawlid, Sheikh Youssef approached me.

"Are you ready?" he asked.

I nodded.

And so, both Youssef and I sat in the middle of the room, me on the women's side and him on the men's side. He gave me a strap for me to hold one end and him to hold the other end. He made me pronounce the *Shahada*, the declaration of which would make me a Muslim.

"*Ashhadu an la ilaha illa-llah, wa ashhadu anna Muhammadan rasul Allah*. I testify that there is no god but God and I testify that Muhammad is the messenger of God," Youssef said, and I repeated it.

Around me, men and women cheered, each on their side. Maryam stood up and started ululating. Many were sobbing. I sat in the middle of the commotion, pondering where fate was leading me.

36

June 7, 2013

I had embraced Islam, and within a week, learned how to pray by reading a small booklet for children that Maryam had given me. It was summer and Ramadan had just started. I tried fasting, and that was when my parents got really worried.

"You have to eat. You can't go a whole day without eating," my mom pleaded.

"Your stomach will hurt. We have hereditary stomach problems in our family," my dad added.

Despite their pleas, I was resolute. I heard my mom cry in her room late at night. I wondered what I was doing wrong.

I went to mosques for *taraweeh*, the nightly prayers offered during Ramadan. Every night, women flooded in around 10 p.m., in various styles of dress, from trendy Western clothing, skinny jeans, skintight T-shirts, and all, to full Islamic dress with only eyes uncovered, and everything in between. Everyone then took out their beautifully extravagant prayer clothes, either a one-piece long gown with built-in fabric to wrap around the head, or a long hijab draping down to the waist, where it met a long skirt to the ankles. These were all made in exquisite fabrics that were colourful, shimmery, and flowy. I looked at them in awe. Would I ever be an elegant muslimah like them?

Upon arriving late to the mosque one night, an old man opened the door for me.

"Where is your hijab?" he yelled at me.

From that day on, I started wearing the hijab. When Garen saw me, he looked sad.

"You're like my own little girl," he said. "I'm sorry about Haider. Some things shouldn't be experienced so young. I know you're hurt, but what you are doing isn't right. You're leaning into his culture, but it will never be yours. The hijab is not part of your heritage."

I was furious at him and decided to stop my music lessons.

I saw Arielle finally, and she got mad at me.

"What are you doing now?" she asked. "Are you turning into a fundamentalist? I see some of your new friends posting some crazy offensive stuff on Twitter against Israel, calling terrorists heroes! Does this mean you are anti-Israel now, too? You know, I'm Jewish. I feel concerned."

I felt ashamed of what I had gotten so heavily into so quickly, to the point where I felt I had to lie to Arielle about where I was going to be able to get out and pray on time. I sighed.

"Heart?" I asked again, "is this what you want?"

After Ramadan, I was wandering the streets again. I had dropped out of school. I felt aimless. *I should find some work*, I thought. I job-hunted in various neighbourhoods and finally arrived at a supermarket not too far from my house. I asked the cashier if they were hiring, and she said yes. I gave her a copy of my CV and left. The next day, the store called me, telling me to see the manager.

"We have an opening in the deli meat section. Do you have experience slicing meat?" the manager asked me.

"No."

"We'll show you how then."

Just like that, I was hired, and the next morning, they showed me around. I was given a uniform, a thick beige long-sleeved cotton smock, black pants, and a small pillbox hat with the store's logo. I was shown how to operate the meat slicer and how to clean it. I was shown how to use the oven to roast chicken, how to keep track of our inventory and refill the stock we sold, how to pack ready-made meals, and how to clean up everything.

I started working full time, forty hours a week. Every morning, I'd arrive in hijab, then remove it to change into the uniform and spend the rest of my day selling pork. It was getting ridiculous. I learned the name of every meat, roast, ham, salami, pepperoni, you name it, I'd sliced it. I even learned the right thickness for each, catering to each client's individual preferences. I carried eight whole chickens at a time in a box. I washed loads of dishes from the ready-made meals we sold, sometimes in ice-cold water. I slithered my hand deep into the drain when it got clogged to remove the week-old greasy food remnants that were to blame. I mopped the floor every day with three different detergents, and, during my few breaks from selling forbidden meats, prayed on the dirty cafeteria floor.

"What on earth are you doing with your life?" Ahmad implored. "Go back to school. Working at that place is useless!"

But I was stubborn and stuck with it. My coworkers teased me about being a pianist and being Muslim. I burnt my hands in the oven twice and nearly sliced my finger off along with the ham once. I slept in and came in late almost everyday. I was very nearly spent. Three months had passed when the manager finally approached me.

"Liz, it looks to me like this job isn't right for you."

I was on the verge of tears. Of course it wasn't right for me. I knew I wasn't exactly cut out for manual labour.

"I'm going to do you a favour," she said. "I'm going to fire you. You're an intellectual. It's written all over your face. You can't handle this kind of work. Don't worry. I will write you a good reference if you ever need it. Now go back to your studies!"

I went back home, lost and tired. I was near rock bottom. What on earth was going to happen next? What was I doing with myself? I'd stopped going to the zawiya.I'd almost stopped talking with my parents. I'd lost touch with most of my friends.

I decided to hit the McGill libraries. I just wanted to figure things out, figure life out. I tried reading about Gandhi. I borrowed books on the history of India. I read about Islam. I read about world history and politics. I read about the British colonization of India. I read about the partition between India and Pakistan. I read about Muhammad Ali Jinnah and Swami Vivekananda. I read about the Ismailis and other Shia denominations. I wanted to understand the world. I wanted to know how to live. I wanted to know who I was. My mind was being crammed with facts, but I was more lost than ever.

My friend Elanna invited me to a party at her house for the Jewish New Year. At the party, a little old lady approached me and started talking.

"I got married when I was eighteen," she said in a tiny, crackling old lady voice. "I lived with my husband for exactly sixty years. He passed away two years ago. I'm eighty now. I've been so lonely ever since. I don't want to live anymore. I want to be reunited with my husband."

I held her hand the whole night. We clung onto each other, unable to face the horrors of this world. She was old enough to be my grandmother, but I felt an instant bond with her. I got her.

Having exhausted what I felt were all my options, I enrolled back in school. I might as well finish my degree. By January, I was studying physics again, now in the regular major program instead of the Joint Honours because of my failed courses. I went to classes daily and did my best to focus. But inside, I was starting to lose it.

Sheikh Youssef held weekly classes about the life of Prophet Muhammad at McGill, and I attended most weeks. What I was looking for, I didn't know. One week, I went and started feeling really unwell. I started crying, first softly, then loudly. Sheikh Youssef asked the lady next to me to escort me outside. She asked me what happened. I said I didn't know, but I was having a panic attack. Sheikh Youssef later asked me what was going on. I said I was unwell.

The next morning, I woke up feeling completely gross. I was nearly depleted. There was no way I could make it to my classes.

"Ahmad," I texted him, "I can't do this anymore. Take me to a clinic."

"I can meet you at the Roddick Gates at McGill at 1 p.m.," he replied. "I'll take you to the psychiatric clinic here on campus."

I did my best to get up and take the subway to school. Ahmad was there waiting for me.

"What's wrong, Liz?" he asked me.

I didn't answer. On our way to the clinic, we passed by Jonathan. He said hi to me and I ignored him. At the clinic, Ahmad spoke to the secretary.

"My friend Elizabeth here is unwell. She needs an emergency appointment today."

"Please sit here and wait for us to call you," she answered.

Ahmad gestured for me to sit down. I stood still. Music was playing in the waiting room. It was Chopin. The first piano concerto by Chopin. I'd played it when I was fifteen. It was bringing back memories from another era, and I couldn't take it anymore.

"Can someone shut off the music?" I yelled. "Please, I can't do this anymore!"

Several people in the waiting room scrambled to get the radio turned off.

"Thank you." Ahmad covered for me. "She's really stressed lately and is not feeling well today."

They nodded, understanding. An hour later, a female doctor in her forties called my name. I wouldn't move. Ahmad pushed me forward. The doctor gestured for Ahmad to come with me into her office. Ahmad and I sat down inside her office, and she closed the door.

"So, what brings you here?" the doctor asked me.

I was mute. I couldn't find it in me to speak.

"Can't she speak?" she asked Ahmad.

"She's under a lot of stress I think," Ahmad answered.

The doctor asked Ahmad what was wrong, and Ahmad told her he wasn't sure, but that I wasn't in a good state.

"Sometimes, the smartest people are like the sharpest instruments," Ahmad said. "They can perform incredibly when well, but they are also very fragile and easy to break down."

The doctor nodded.

"Elizabeth, I gather that you are not well," she said. "I want you to be taken care of. Please come back next week. I won't be around because I will be on vacation, but I got an appointment for you with another doctor. Please, do come."

She dismissed me and Ahmad. We walked out of the clinic.

"Liz, take care of yourself and rest well tonight," Ahmad said. "You'll be fine tomorrow morning. Don't worry."

I started tearing up.

"You'll be fine," he reassured me.

I nodded and headed home. When I got home, tiredness got the best of me and I went to bed early.

37

The next morning, I woke up and something was very wrong. My parents were already out, but I heard footsteps everywhere in the house. There were men in my house! Seven men dressed up in black looking for me. I panicked a little. What on earth was happening? I was losing my mind. Clearly that was it.

I locked the door of my room and sat on my bed. What should I do now? I had to brush my teeth. I had to eat breakfast. I had to get out of the house. How could I do it? I opened my drawer and found a pair of scissors. That was it. As a makeshift weapon, it was good enough. I held my scissors high with one hand and opened my door half an inch.

"Who's there?" I yelled.

No one spoke, but I heard some wind howling outside. I cautiously stepped out of my room into the hallway and hid behind every corner that I turned. The men in black were out; I was in luck. I walked into the bathroom and forced myself to brush my teeth, trying to avoid looking into the mirror in front of me. Quick, before something happens! From the corner of my eye I caught a glimpse of my reflection in the mirror. Yellow reptilian scales have started growing on my shoulder! I panicked and ran back into my room. I was definitely losing my mind. What now?

I threw on a winter jacket on top of a random sweater and jeans and headed towards the subway station, scissors in my pocket, glancing behind me every few steps in case the men decided to return. They've lost trace of me, I told myself and found some calm when I got to school. I didn't go to class, it was useless. I spent the day at my regular Second Cup close to McGill. When I had to use the bathroom, I made sure to have my scissors ready when I opened the door, in case a murderer was inside. I came home on the last train, at midnight and scrambled back into my room immediately.

I spent the next few days outside, hanging out at various cafes, avoiding my house as much as I could. I told Ahmad what was going on.

"If you feel like you're going to be a danger to yourself or someone else," he said, "go to the emergency room."

"I'm fine," I insisted.

I spent my days at Second Cup reading about mental illnesses. This looks dreadfully like schizophrenia, I thought to myself. But I was incredulous.

"Tell your parents about this," Ahmad texted me. "They might be able to help you."

Hell no, I thought, *they would blame it all on me.* But I didn't dare eat food at my house anymore, afraid that it was poisoned, so I stocked up on food I bought myself to ensure it wasn't tampered with. Soon enough I was even afraid of spending nights at home.

A few days later, I took the subway home around midnight, and as I walked towards my house, I was seized with so much fear that I felt like I was going to kill everything moving inside the house. I might stab my parents by mistake, I thought. I was overcome with horror and decided to head back into town. I took the last subway back to the Second Cup near McGill.

I sat at the coffee shop, amongst a handful of homeless people. I was tired. I was sore. And I was afraid for my life. *What on earth do I do now?* I thought. I had nowhere to go.

My phone rang. I looked at it. My parents were calling. I let it ring without picking up. It rang again, a couple minutes later. I ignored it again. A text came in:

"Where are you? -dad"

My eyes were watery. I was losing it. I turned off the phone, stood up, and started walking towards campus. That night, everything felt extraordinary. I saw a parking sign on the street, or was it a stone statue indicating the way? I wandered into campus, and every footstep I saw in the snow had a special meaning known only to me. I was in a fairytale! Here, the wolf went left. The hunter went right. And the goblins went into the Rutherford building, or was it a nuclear facility?

I started running. Quick! I must catch the train. The train to Hogwarts! To the school of Magic! I sat down near the Anatomy Building, or was it a train station? I waited. And a train made out of glass came. I stood inside it, and soon the train was moving, or was I running with it? Either way, it carried me up the hill towards Pine Avenue.

I stood still on Pine Avenue, on top of the soccer field, above campus. There was a sniper with his gun pointed towards me! Or was it a lamp post? No, it was definitely a sniper. And soon many more joined him! I panicked and ran westward as far as I could along Pine Avenue

A fox jumped across the street, or was it a plastic bag blown by the wind? How could I tell? I was running and I had no idea where I was heading. Out of breath, abruptly, I stopped. There was a small forest to my left, enclosed by a metal fence. I looked at it cautiously. *This is a sign. This is the entrance to a secret path, into another world.* I clumsily climbed the fence and jumped to the other side. My sweater got caught on one of the iron fence's many spikes. I quickly removed my sweater and left it there.

I walked on and stumbled upon a road. Here I was, in wonderland! The place I had dreamt of, as a child, where all classical musicians, artists, and poets gathered for parties. I heard piano playing all around me. Where was the concert hall where Chopin and Liszt were playing? I looked and looked but could not find it. I looked at every house along the street. Should I knock on their door? *No, silly, people live in them and are sleeping*, I thought. But what if the house hosted the concert inside? I hemmed and hawed, straddling the line between lucidity and fantasy.

No, I will walk towards the apartment building where Garen lived. But wait, that was eight years ago. He moved. Well, Ahmad lives in that same building, he could surely find Garen? I was sold. I walked all the way back east to Parc Avenue, avoiding every person on the street, and I rang the doorbell.

"Liz!" Ahmad came running downstairs in his pajamas, a plain blue Bengali tunic with loose matching pants. "What on earth are you doing here?"

"Lead me to Garen's apartment. I want to become a pianist again!" I said.

"Who is Garen? And what on earth are you doing here at 4 a.m.?"

I pondered what he was saying. Did he not know Garen?

"Liz, you've lost your mind, I'm going to call an ambulance for you."

"No!" I yelled, "No! No! No!" I was screaming.

Ahmad put his hands over my mouth.

"For heaven's sake, people are sleeping, hush!" he whispered. "Come inside and calm down."

Ahmad took me into his room, in his flat that he shared with another student.

"Liz, I'm going to call a cab for you to go home," Ahmad said, "but before that, you're going to write an email to your parents telling them exactly what happened."

"I'm broken, I'm lost, I can't do this!" I was crying.

"I will help you."

Ahmad dictated a note I sent to my parents, adding at the end a link to an article about schizophrenia. He then duly called a cab to take me home. He spoke with me on the phone the whole time to calm me down. When I arrived home, my mom was crying on the doorstep.

"Liz, we've been so worried!" she sobbed. "You're sick! Come home, come rest."

I came in and locked myself in my room for the next three days. I was scared out of my mind and completely drained. My tears had gone dry. I sat on my bed, wondering what had become of me.

"Heart," I cried out, "heart, help me out!"

The McGill Mental Health Clinic called, reminding me of my appointment. I went, accompanied by my dad, who had to walk fifty metres behind me because I feared him. A young psychiatrist saw me and gave me some antipsychotic drugs.

"Try these and come back in a week," she said.

I came home and took the meds. I felt dizzy and nauseous for the rest of the week. And they weren't working. I was more terrified than ever, fearing looking anyone in the eye. My mom pleaded with me to eat some food she cooked. I refused every time, eating only stale bread in my room and drinking tap water.

"Liz," my mom cried. "Oh what has happened to our daughter!"

I sat in my room in silence. How much lower could I fall? I pondered. Was this rock bottom yet? Each time I thought I'd hit rock bottom, I'd fall further still.

The following week, my dad took me again to the psychiatrist. When I entered the office, I immediately turned the chair to face the wall.

"Why are you doing that?" she asked.

"So I don't look you in the eye," I answered.

"What will happen if you look me in the eye?"

"It will kill me."

"I think the meds are not working," she concluded. "Any other symptoms?"

"My mom is trying to poison me, and seven men in black are still looking for me."

"I'm afraid I will have to send you to the emergency room."

"No. I will not go."

"If you don't go willingly, I will make you go." There was a sternness in her voice.

I panicked.

"Please don't make me go, please!" I was crying and frantic.

"You have to, my dear. It will be for your own good," she urged.

She gave me an hour to go back home and pack my things, and ordered a cab to pick me up.

On my way home, I cried and cried.

"You will be taken care of," my dad tried to reassure me. "It's better this way."

"There is no other way," my mom said when we got home. "You will be okay!"

"I don't want to go to the emergency psych ward! I'm not crazy! I swear I'm not crazy!" I cried out. I was lucid! Lucid about the fact that I was going crazy! Oh wait …

My mom was crying with me.

"Liz, let's go. The cab is here," she said.

I gathered my Quran and a toothbrush and headed out. My mom and I got in the cab and she gave the driver directions. I kept sobbing in the backseat.

"Oh Allah," I whispered, "Oh Allah help me! This is as low as it can get. What more do you want from me?"

The cab dropped us off at the emergency room of the Royal Victoria Hospital. We walked inside and my mom registered at the front desk by the door. They told us to wait until my name was called. I stood aloof and lost in the hallway. About twenty people sat in the waiting room, bored out of their minds. Half of them were looking at me, wondering what had overcome this crazy girl.

I kept looking at the tiled floor, and little by little, the tiles started waving around and dancing, like one of those old *Dance Dance Revolution* arcade games. They'd light up one by one and I had to step on the bright ones. I pranced around, trying to keep afloat in a sea of tiles.

"Elizabeth!" I faintly heard my name called in the distance.

"Liz," my mom said to me, "they are calling you to go to their office."

She gently pushed me towards the office at the end of the hallway.

"Elizabeth," a nurse asked me, "what's wrong?"

I was mute. I tried to move my hand and it didn't move at all.

"Liz, tell us so we can help you," she asked again.

Suddenly my thumb was out of my control, it was moving and moving like a little mouse having a seizure! I panicked. I shrieked a deafening shriek.

"I'm afraid we will have to use the hard way," she muttered.

A hospital bed was wheeled towards me. I saw restraints on it, the kind they used to tie people up. I shrieked again, and again, and again, as if pushed into death throes. A team of nurses came and started tying me up on the bed. I screamed again, and suddenly, I felt my heart wake up! *Everything makes sense now!*

The nurses wheeled me deep inside the belly of the hospital, away from my crying mother. *No! This is not the end! This is just the beginning!* Memories flooded my mind. I saw Duisburg, I saw the Netherlands beach, I saw our Volkstrasse home, and I saw our life together, I saw us falling apart, I saw my wandering alone. I saw how, in my eyes, Haider went from being that corny, cheesy, love-struck stranger, to the hardworking, overachieving winner at everything he touches, to the self-sacrificing, life-giving paragon of love. Never again could I judge a book by its cover. *I have looked into someone else's eyes. I have tasted true love. I have tasted life. I have grown. I have lived. My heart has been opened to the world like never before. Everything that happened was meant to happen. God willed it! And I'm seeing everything with new eyes!*

The nurses wheeled me into a darker room and started removing my clothes, one article at a time. *It's going to be okay*, I told myself. *As long as my mother doesn't see me like this.* I was slowly being stripped of everything. *I have nothing to hide. I am beautiful. I am strong. And I am kind. I will survive and thrive! I have not loved in vain!*

"Poor girl," a senior nurse muttered, compassion in her eyes, "I wish we didn't have to do this to her."

I'm alright, I answered inside. *Don't you worry about me. This is just the beginning of my life, and I'm ready for my future. Life finally makes sense now. And it is beautiful. What a beautiful world we live in!* I felt gratitude, immense gratitude. *My heart has been filled with love to the brim. It is time I give back to the world now. Haider wanted to be remembered for how much he loved me, and I will honour him! I will honour his wish! I will study, I will work hard, I will give everything my best from now on, I will change the world! I have learned how to bow down and how to stand up at the same time. Never again will I be lost and broken.* The nurses dressed me in a blue hospital gown that was open in the back.

Encountering him has freed me to be everything I could ever dream to be. It has taught me that I was loved, that I mattered, always and no matter what! And I have in turn fallen in love with the whole world! I will live, I will thrive! It's just the beginning of my life! And I have so much to give to this world! Alhamdulillah! Praise be to God! Love triumphs! I repeated to myself, as they began injecting me with tranquilizers. *Love triumphs!* I felt an immense cold rush in my veins and the world started drifting apart.

Dear Haider,

*Don't worry about me. Sometimes you have to fall
to pieces to put yourself back together in a way that
makes sense. I eventually got well, and with the right
medications and therapy, I've been doing better and
better over the years. I ultimately finished my Bachelor's
degree with Joint Honours, completed a Master's
program, and I am on my way to getting a PhD in
biophysics. I even found love again, as well as meaning
in life. But all of this, it is because of you. You showed
me what life was all about. You showed me how to live
from the heart. And you awakened my heart. You did
not save my life, but you saved my soul. I forever thank
God and my lucky stars for having met you. Whether
we cross paths again or not in this lifetime, I wish
you all the best. And I will always pray for you.
May God save your soul, too.*

Amen.

ACKNOWLEDGMENTS

I would like to first thank my wonderful publisher, Robin Philpot, and my editor at Baraka Books, Blossom Thom. This book would not be in your hands if it weren't for Robin's and Blossom's belief in me from the start and hard work to bring this novel to fruition.

My bestie Alexandra Markus Hutz deserves a big shoutout as well. I had written a first draft of my novel by 2016, but was not satisfied. Unsure of what to do with it, I let it sit in a figurative drawer in my computer for five years. When I brought it up with Alexandra in 2021, however, she offered to sit down with me and edit the book together line by line. For a full four months during the pandemic, we met on Zoom every Sunday to go over two or three chapters at a time. Through her sharp edits, insightful questions, and brilliant ideas, my novel was transformed from rough draft to polished work.

I'd like to thank the very first readers of my novel, my mother's friends, Sophie Lu and Weiqing Lu, whose faith in my book from the beginning gave me the confidence to move forward with it. Thanks to my dear friends Layla Jasic, Briah Cahana, and Maral Farrokh for reading my manuscript as well and providing invaluable feedback. Thanks to Zainab Abalkhail and Daniel Varon for reading the very first version of the first chapter I wrote. Your early encouragement and insistence that it was a story worth telling motivated me to continue writing. Thanks as well to my close friend of many years, Bernard Blander, and writers Yiwei Xue and Dimitri Nasrallah, for help and advice throughout the publication process.

I must also thank my psychiatrist, Karim Tabbane, and therapist, Pascale D'Astous, for keeping me (somewhat) sane all these years as I write. Thanks to my close friends, Alex Cowan, Giovanni Vizcardo, and Ervin Luka Sešek, for your ongoing support. Thanks to my PhD supervisor, Walter Reisner, for your mentorship and guidance on my career path, most notably your flexibility with me through these years. And finally, the biggest thanks to my mom and dad for always being there, rooting for my success through good times and bad.

ABOUT THE AUTHOR

Lili Zeng holds a PhD in biophysics from McGill University. She has several peer-reviewed papers under her name and has given a dozen scientific and public outreach talks. Also a classically trained pianist, she has won numerous music competitions and soloed with prestigious chamber and symphony orchestras. She was born in Guangzhou, China, and moved to Montreal, Canada, with her parents as a child. *Dear Haider* is Lili's first novel.

Printed by Imprimerie Gauvin
Gatineau, Québec